transferences

transferences

a novel by James Twiggs

The University of Arkansas Press
Fayetteville 1987

DESIGNER: Chiquita Babb
TYPEFACE: Linotron 202 Sabon
TYPESETTER: G & S Typesetters, Inc.
PRINTER: Thomson-Shore, Inc.
BINDER: John H. Dekker & Sons, Inc.
The paper used in this publication meets the minimum requirements of the American National Standard for Permanence of Paper for Printed Library Materials Z39.48-1984. ∞™

The lines of poetry on the dedication page are from "Poem Called Poem" by James Whitehead. Reprinted from the chapbook *Actual Size* (The Trilobite Press), copyright © 1985 by James Whitehead, by permission of the author.

The lines from "Ash Wednesday" on pages 36 and 185 are reprinted from *Collected Poems 1909–1962* by T. S. Eliot. Copyright 1936 by Harcourt Brace Jovanovich, Inc.; copyright © 1963, 1964 by T. S. Eliot. Reprinted by permission of Harcourt Brace Jovanovich, Inc., and Faber and Faber Ltd.

LIBRARY OF CONGRESS CATALOGING-IN-PUBLICATION DATA
Twiggs, James, 1933–
  Transferences.
    I. Title
PS3570. W48T7 1987   813'.54   87-5081
ISBN 0-939626-89-2
ISBN 0-938626-90-6 (pbk.)

For Eileen—
Best therapist, dearest friend

"I will give you kisses again next time
In a safe place . . ."

Is it not an extremely noteworthy fact that we succeed in transforming every neurosis, whatever its content, into a condition of pathological love?

—Freud

The one I presume to know is the one I love.

—Lacan

Look at the way you're looking at me. I can't wait for you, I'm bowled over, I'm totally knocked out, you dazzle me, you jewel, my jewel, I can't ever sleep again, no, listen, it's the truth, I won't walk, I'll descend, I'll diminish, into total paralysis, my life is in your hands, that's what you're banishing me to, a state of catatonia, do you know the state of catatonia? do you? do you? the state of . . . where the reigning prince is the prince of emptiness, the prince of desolation. I love you.

—Harold Pinter, *Betrayal*

part one

1

Oct 31

Wanda—

You said I couldn't write to you, but obviously I can.

What you did to me was unprofessional, unconscionable, and unforgivable. Please die and arrange for your obituary notice to be sent to me.

I have been out of the hospital and out of therapy for about two months. I tried it with the new therapist, but it didn't work. I hate everything, especially you and me. Please die. If you will I will. The idea that you're alive and not with me is unendurable. I hate all you God damned people for setting me up that way. Please die. I would have written sooner except—I guess you'd say—for the same reason I never raised my voice to my mother. I still don't know how or why you did it, but fuck you up to your neck.

Tim Jinks

P.S. Enclosed is a picture of Little Tim. I thought you'd want to see what he looked like.

P.P.S. Happy Halloween, Wanda. Trick or treat.

"Who is this guy?" Robert asked.

Wanda had been dressing in the bedroom and had just returned to the living room. She was wearing a navy blazer and a new pair of gray pants. "Oh," she said, "you found that letter."

"It was here on the coffee table," Robert said. "I couldn't keep from reading it. Who is he?"

"One of my patients," Wanda said. "I had him the last five months I was in Miami."

"Why would he send you this picture?"

"We talked about his childhood," Wanda said. "I guess he sent it to make me feel bad."

The picture was a wallet-sized portrait that said "Wrentree, Ark." across the top and "First Grade, 1945–46" across the bottom. In between, a little boy in overalls stared at the camera as if he hated it. He had bangs and freckles and the glummest mouth Wanda had ever seen.

"He was kind of cute," Robert said. He folded the letter, which was scrawled in pencil on a large sheet of drawing paper, and put it back in the envelope. "Is he dangerous?"

"I don't think so," Wanda said. "He's upset because I left him before the therapy was finished. He'll get over it." She stepped directly in front of Robert. "How do I look?"

"Fine," Robert said.

Wanda wished she could say as much for him. He was wearing the same corduroy jacket he had worn all week, and his sport shirt—he seldom wore a tie—was frayed at the collar. As usual, his feet were encased in battered Hush Puppies.

Driving through a blizzard of red blowing leaves, they took a narrow road out of town to an old farmhouse that had been converted into a plush restaurant called the Hilltop Inn. Because the dinner crowd had not yet arrived, they secured a table overlooking Lake Windward. They sipped martinis and talked about the weather.

"Fall's our best season around here," Robert said.

They looked out the window and admired the leaves again. "It looks like a postcard out there," Wanda said. "Or a painting." Then, as the last of the daylight faded, it occurred to her that this was going to be the best fall and winter of her life. Windward, New York, with its population of 30,000, its hills and trees, and its breathtaking gorges, was a pleasant change from the large cities she had lived in. She was a country person now, and she felt good about it.

She was suddenly aware of being stared at by a couple off to her right. They were staring, she was sure, because of her and Robert's size. Robert was a beefy six five; Wanda was exactly six feet. There had been a time when she dreaded to appear in public, but since going through therapy with Sarah Pitkin a few years ago, she felt better about being big. It was true that sometimes, looking in the mirror, she could still catch a glimpse of the fat teenager she used to be. When this happened she shuddered in revulsion and fasted for a few days. Mostly, though, what she now saw in her mirror was a dark-haired young woman with large dark eyes, a straight nose, good cheekbones, perfect teeth and skin, and a pretty though slightly crooked smile—altogether a very attractive young woman, large but not really fat, who dressed well and carried herself with some of Sarah Pitkin's own cool elegance. She looked defiantly at the other couple and they turned their attention to each other.

"What's the matter?" Robert asked. "Why so quiet?"

"Little people," Wanda said. "They were staring."

Robert looked at the little people. "I don't think they were staring. I think they were just glancing around the room."

"Maybe," Wanda said. "Or maybe," she added with a smile, "they were staring because we're such a handsome couple."

"I doubt that," Robert said. He blushed as if embarrassed.

The waitress brought their steaks and they began to eat.

* * *

Wanda had moved to Windward a month ago to be near Robert and decide whether to marry him or not. She had met him last Christmas. Her roommate in Miami, a post-doc RET specialist named Barbara Snell, had invited Wanda home with her for the holidays. Wanda, who was just coming out of a brief, distasteful affair with an aggressive doctor, jumped at the chance to get away for a few days. They were met at the Syracuse airport by Barbara's boyfriend, who was a graduate student at Windward University, and by Robert, who owned a small electronics company.

5

At first Wanda was miffed that Barbara had arranged a date without telling her about it, but on the hour's drive from Syracuse to Windward she found Robert increasingly attractive. After spending so much time with psychiatrists and psychologists, she was taken with his down-to-earth style, not to mention his reddish hair, freckled nose, and all the other features that added up to what she thought of as his rugged good looks. Over the next few days she came to appreciate him even more. Maybe he wasn't as sharp or sophisticated as other men she had known, but he was nicer. He was considerate in bed and big enough for her to cuddle up to.

After she returned to Miami, she and Robert wrote to each other and talked on the phone. Twice he came to see her. The first time he came, she took him to a party of psychology interns, psychiatric residents, and faculty members. Although he was out of his element, he handled himself surprisingly well. With his quiet good manners and bashful grin, he was even something of a hit, especially with the women at the party. On his second visit, they decided that Wanda would take an apartment in Windward to finish rewriting her dissertation. That would give them a chance to get to know each other better—to let the relationship develop at its own pace, as Wanda had explained it—and to make a sensible decision about marriage.

When she came to town to see about renting an apartment, she learned that a new county hospital, including a mental health facility, was being built and would be open in the spring. The director of the facility, a psychiatrist named Epperson, turned out to be a bland, seemingly disorganized man of fifty or so. After an hour of rambling conversation, repeatedly interrupted by the roar of bulldozers and the shouts of workmen, he offered Wanda a job at a good salary.

Three days later she received a letter, sent in care of Robert's home address (Wanda was staying at the Collegetown Motor Inn), informing her that although contracts would not be drawn up until April, she could consider herself a member of the Windward County mental health team. A handwritten P.S. provided a nice touch: "I will deem it a great honor to be associated with the daughter of Dr. Hiram North."

That same afternoon she found a two-bedroom furnished apartment, almost new, that was convenient both to the Windward University campus and to the Community Shopping Center. With its low ceilings, stark white walls, and uncomfortably low-slung furniture, beige in color, the apartment seemed a bit sterile. Wanda kept meaning to personalize it with a couple of throw rugs and a nice lamp or two and by replacing the framed Fredric Remington reproductions with some contemporary posters. She also intended to keep an eye out for a used easy chair to read in and watch television. So far she had done nothing about these plans, and they were already becoming vague in her mind.

Thinking back, Wanda was amazed at how well things had turned out. If, as seemed likely, she and Robert got married, she would have two of the things she wanted most: a rewarding job and a quiet life with a man she could count on. Beyond these rather modest goals, she wanted, eventually, to switch from clinic work to private practice. The time to start doing this would be in a couple of years, after her experience at the clinic qualified her for a state license. This too was a modest goal, though one that would require some time to achieve. Her further aims were not so modest. She wanted to write books and she wanted to overcome her father's prejudice against women psychoanalysts. If everything worked out, she would eventually become an analyst herself.

* * *

"You tried to help him," Robert said between bites of apple pie. "Why would he turn on you like that?"

"Who?" Wanda had not eaten so much as a bite of dessert in more than a year. To avoid temptation she was looking down into her coffee.

"The guy that wrote the letter."

"It's a transference," Wanda said. "He thought he loved me. I had to leave before he was ready for me to. So now he thinks he hates me."

"Well," Robert said, "don't let it get you down."

Wanda laughed. "Why would it get me down? It comes with the territory, doesn't it?" Although her coffee contained neither cream nor sugar, she stirred it compulsively.

"I don't know," Robert said, "but I'm impressed with your attitude. If I got a letter like that, I'd be worried to death. You're an amazing girl, the way you can be so calm." He picked up a large piece of pie crust in his fingers and stuffed it into his mouth.

"Woman," Wanda said. She was twenty-eight years old and didn't like being called a girl. Her father was always saying, "How's my girl?" or "That's my girl," and Wanda couldn't stand it.

On the way back to town Robert decided he wanted to drink beer at Denny's, a main hangout for successful men of thirty or thereabouts. Denny's was decorated with fake leather paneling and fake candles that gave off a dim yellow light. The long bar and also the booths were painted to look like mahogany. Wanda sat on a wobbly stool and sipped Scotch. Robert stood beside her. He and the bartender watched a football game on television. The bartender wore a bow tie, sleeve garters, and a derby hat, and he was chomping on a fat cigar. The acoustics were so poor that Wanda had to listen not only to the announcer and to the two men but to an echo as well.

"I played in high school," the bartender said. "How about you?"

Robert shook his head and gave Wanda a grin. "I was always afraid I'd hurt somebody. Besides, I'm too clumsy. The only game I play is golf."

When the bartender turned away to wash some glasses, Robert said to Wanda, "I was hoping some of the guys would be here." He surveyed the almost empty room and then downed an entire glass of beer without removing it from his lips.

At eight-thirty Floyd Robbins showed up with a young woman. Wanda knew Floyd—he was a lawyer and Robert's best friend—but she had not seen the woman before. Robert had told her that Floyd had more girls than you could shake a stick at, and she guessed this was one of them. She didn't much like Floyd. He was short and wiry, had a thin mustache, and used hair spray. He wore dapper, tight-fitting suits and wide ties, and he liked to stand with his thumbs in his vest pockets.

While the men watched the ball game, Wanda talked with the woman. Her name was Marie Becker. Her pretty face was smeared with rouge, and her jet-black hair hung in tangled curls halfway down her back. In her shiny white blouse, gray shawl, and long red skirt she could have passed for a gypsy. She was in fact a social worker.

"And you're a therapist," Marie said. "That's so exciting."

Wanda explained that she had finished her year as an intern and was rewriting her dissertation. "Next spring," she said, "I'll start at the clinic." The bar was filling up fast and getting noisy. She had to talk loud to make herself heard. She was glad when Robert suggested they move to a booth.

When they were seated, Floyd leaned over and said, "I've been meaning to ask you—are you into psychic phenomena?"

Wanda shook her head. Other people had asked her that question, and it always annoyed her. It made her wish she'd gone to med school and become a psychiatrist. No one would think of asking a psychiatrist such a question.

"The next war will be fought with psychic energy," Floyd said. "Telekinesis, astral projection, stuff like that." He motioned to the waiter to bring another round. When the drinks had been delivered, he said, "Would you psychoanalyze me sometime?"

"I'm not taking patients now," Wanda said. It didn't seem worth the effort to explain the difference between psychoanalysis and psychotherapy.

"What would I do if you psychoanalyzed me?" Floyd asked. "Come in and talk about my sex life?"

"That's all he ever thinks about," Marie said. She put an arm around Floyd's neck and pressed herself against him.

"It's too complicated," Wanda said. "I couldn't possibly explain it now."

"You hear that?" Floyd said to Robert. "She thinks my sex life is too complicated."

"That's not what she meant," Marie said with a giggle.

"I don't need to be psychoanalyzed," Floyd said. I read *You Be You, I'll Be Me,* and then I took the quiz at the end. I did okay . . . Have you read it?" he asked Wanda.

Wanda shook her head.

"How about the sex manual?"

"What sex manual?"

"The *You Be You Sex Guide,*" Floyd said. "It's all in those two books."

"What is?" Robert asked.

"Everything," Floyd said. He looked at Wanda. "I read other stuff too. Masters and Johnson, stuff like that. I'd like to have one of those screwing machines in my apartment."

Wanda smiled. She was glad she had resisted the temptation to talk about her work. People tended to interpret what you told them in terms of their own preconceptions. Or else they told you about a book they'd read.

"How about rats?" Floyd said. "Have you done much with rats?"

"That's the experimental part," Wanda said. "I had to learn it, but it's not my main interest."

"I've heard rats are smart," Floyd said.

Wanda shrugged.

"I've heard they're as mean as people," Floyd said, "and also as horny."

Robert and Marie laughed.

"My rats were pretty tame," Wanda said.

"I don't think I could work with live animals," Marie said.

"It's creepy at first," Wanda said, "but you get used to it. I wrote my master's thesis on rats. It was about the effects of random reinforcement."

"Far out," Floyd said, but Marie made a face.

Two more of Robert's friends came in and joined them. One was Rick and the other was Carl. Floyd made the introductions. "Wanda's a psychologist," he said. "She's been telling us some weird things."

The men discussed the new by-pass. Wanda and Marie listened politely. The booth was too small for six people, and Wanda was uncomfortable. After a while, Floyd steered the conversation around to the *You Be You* sex book. Then he got started on the Masters and Johnson screwing machines.

"The shafts are hollow," he said, "and made of clear plastic. If you were inside one, you'd have a ringside seat."

"Maybe you should have been a gynecologist," Carl said.

"I thought he was," Marie said. The men laughed.

Wanda got Robert's attention and told him she wanted to leave. "It's so loud in here," she said.

"I think I'll stay," Robert said. "I'm having fun." He took his keys out of his pocket and handed them to Wanda. "One of the guys'll drop me off later," he said.

Floyd got up and took Wanda's hand and helped her out of the booth. "We'll talk about all of this some other time," he said.

"Sure," Wanda said. She pulled her hand free and hurried for the door. She was angry that Robert was sending her home alone, but she didn't want to appear immature by making a scene.

When she reached the apartment she swallowed an aspirin and made some coffee. She drank half a cup and then took a shower and put on her pajamas and a robe. She read a chapter of her dissertation. Robert came in about one o'clock. Considering all the beer he'd had, he was in pretty good shape. He poured a cup of coffee and joined Wanda on the sofa.

"Are you staying all night," she said, "or going home?"

Robert grinned and put a hand on her knee. "It's Friday," he said. His large fingers massaged her thigh. He continued to grin. Presently he removed his hand from her leg and became serious. "I hope you won't ever take Floyd as a patient," he said.

"I could handle Floyd," Wanda said.

"Him and his girls," Robert said. "He gets some doozies. Did you notice how she does her eyes?"

"The way she bats them? I thought at first there was something wrong with them."

"And the way she throws herself around . . . Is that what they talk about?"

"Who?"

"Patients. Is sex what they talk about?"

"It gets to that."

Robert picked up Tim Jinks' letter. "Is that what this fellow talked about?"

"Sometimes."

"I couldn't do it in a million years," Robert said.

"What?"

"Talk about sex with some strange woman."

Wanda smiled. "After a while you couldn't *help* talking about it."

Robert looked at the letter and then at Wanda.

"It was nothing personal," Wanda said.

Robert put the letter down and kissed her. The last of her anger vanished. Presently Robert led her to the bedroom. He was usually a subdued lover, but tonight he got carried away. The bed broke and tilted sharply to one side. Robert didn't seem to notice. He kept going until, at last, he threw his head back and let out a loud cry, unlike anything Wanda had heard from him before.

2

Nov 7

Dear Wanda,

I'm ashamed about the letter I sent you last week. I hope you can forgive me. Your going was a much greater shock than I thought it would be, and it left me with no heart for therapy or anything else. But that isn't your fault—whatever was strong and decent in me was lost a long time ago. I learned from working with you what a hopeless piece of shit I really am, and I guess that's something. I'll probably continue to write to you—you're all I ever think about—but I'll try not to mail the letters. I don't expect to be bothering you again.

Have a good life; I'm sure you deserve it. It will be an elegant life, I know, full of romance and fire and perfect moments. A life that well befits the only truly glamorous woman I ever met. Interesting word, "glamorous."

Love,
Tim

At the top of the page was a letterhead:

MAGNOLIA RETREAT
Elmerton, Arkansas
"A Therapeutic Milieu for the Disturbed Individual"
Arthur Bonds, M.D., Director

"It must be some kind of halfway house," Wanda said. "Or a private home. There won't be much there in the way of therapy, that's for sure."

"At least he won't be bothering us again," Robert said. "What was the matter with him, anyway?"

"Oh, I don't know. Things got too much for him."

"What things?"

Wanda thought a minute. "One of his sons got killed in a car wreck. He hadn't seen the son in years and he felt guilty about it. His sister, with whom he'd been close, tried to kill herself, and he felt guilty about *that*. Then his wife tried it. They were all killing themselves at once. On top of that, he hated his work. He was burned out."

"What was his work?"

"He was a philosophy teacher."

Robert looked impressed. "What else happened to him?"

"He had an affair with a student. It was all very messy. She was the daughter of one of his colleagues. His wife left him over it. He tried to live with the student. He was drinking too much, and falling apart, and after a couple of weeks *she* left him. He went to school in a rage and broke her father's nose with a book."

"Jesus," Robert said.

"That's when he came to the hospital. At first he had a male therapist, but he didn't make much progress. I didn't have a patient at the time, so they switched him to me for intensive therapy. I was supposed to be a substitute-nurturant figure."

"A what?"

"A mother replacement," Wanda said. She stepped over to the bookcase and took down the dictionary.

"What are you doing?" Robert asked.

"Looking up 'glamorous.'"

13

"It means beautiful," Robert said. "Like a movie star."

"It must mean more than that," Wanda said. "Let's see, 'glamour' means 'alluring and often illusory charm . . . magic or enchantment . . . spell . . . witchery.'"

"That guy's a real dope," Robert said.

"You don't think I'm glamorous?"

"I still say it means like a movie star."

Wanda put the dictionary away and went to the kitchen. She returned with a bottle of beer and a bowl of pretzels. "Here," she said, "this will hold you till I can get ready." They were going to Robert's house for dinner with his parents.

"I feel sorry for him," Robert said. "He had a lot happen to him. How old is he?"

"Forty-five, forty-six."

"One of those mid-life deals," Robert said. "There's something I don't understand, though. How could you be his mother replacement when he's old enough to be your father?"

"It would take too long to explain," Wanda said. "You'd have to understand how therapy works. You'd have to understand about transference and regression and the Oedipus complex. That's his basic problem, is the Oedipus complex."

Robert glanced at his watch, whistled between his teeth, and said she was right.

"About what?"

"About it taking too long to explain. Mom's expecting us in forty minutes. She gets upset if you're the least bit late."

* * *

Wanda had never met Robert's parents, so this was a night of some importance. Driving over, Robert was nervous.

"I want everything to go all right," he said. "I want everyone to like each other."

"Why wouldn't we like each other?"

"I don't know. Sometimes people don't."

The Martins lived in an old, predominantly working-class section of town. The two-story house was freshly painted and appeared to be immaculately maintained. Wanda remarked on this, and Robert told her his father did all the work himself. She was impressed. She doubted that her own father had so much as touched a paintbrush or lawnmower in his entire life. Nor would old houses—at least old houses like this one—appeal to him. He was, as he had said one night on the Johnny Carson program, "an afficionado of the flashy."

Mr. Martin, wearing a blue cardigan sweater and khaki pants, was waiting inside the door for them. Wanda knew he had recently retired from his maintenance job at Windward University, but he looked younger than his sixty-five years. He was bigger than Wanda but not as big as Robert. With his full red mouth and thick gray hair, he reminded Wanda of Dr. Campbell, her dissertation chairman.

"Welcome, welcome," he said. He shook her hand and then helped her out of her coat. He grabbed her hand again and looked her up and down. "So you're Wanda," he said.

"It's nice to meet you," Wanda said. She was relieved by his friendly manner.

"You didn't have to get dressed up for our benefit," he said, "but I'm glad you did." He continued to hold her hand. "She's a feast," he said to Robert. "A feast for sore eyes."

"Dad," Robert said.

"Why don't I go get Ma?" Mr. Martin said. "She's in the kitchen."

The inside of the house was not as impressive as the outside. The furnishings were color coordinated and there were knick-knacks everywhere. Most of them were little glass dogs.

Mr. Martin came back with Robert's mother, a thin woman in white double-knit pants, a red and white pullover, and an apron. Her hair, as gray as her husband's, was done up in a permanent so tight it gave her whole face a pained expression.

"It was nice you could come," she said. "We've heard about you."

"All of it was good, though," Mr. Martin said.

"You'll have to watch him," Mrs. Martin said. "He'll talk your ear off."

"Sit down," Mr. Martin said. "I'll get Bob and me a beer."

"He always calls Robert Bob," Mrs. Martin said. "I always called him Robert."

"Maybe you'd like a beer too," Mr. Martin said.

"Or coffee," Mrs. Martin said. "That's what I'm having."

Wanda decided to allow herself a beer, and Mr. Martin went to get it. Robert pushed her over to the sofa and sat closely beside her. Mr. Martin returned with the beer, and Mrs. Martin excused herself to go see about dinner. Mr. Martin pulled a chair up directly in front of Wanda and asked if she had ever eaten a Zounds.

"You know," Robert said. "The candy bar."

Wanda nodded. She had once eaten twelve Zounds bars in the space of an hour.

"I got one the other day," Mr. Martin said, "and it had *milk* chocolate on it."

"Dad's been talking about this all week," Robert said.

"What gets me," Mr. Martin said, "is now you can't tell a Zounds from a Cashew Treat."

"Except for the cashew," Robert said.

"Yeah," Mr. Martin said, "but who's going to buy a Zounds when you can get the same thing plus a cashew to boot?"

Mrs. Martin came in and stood directly between Wanda and her husband. "Dinner'll be ready in a minute," she said. "Is he talking about that candy bar?"

"Get out of the damned way," Mr. Martin said.

"Dad," Robert said. He moved over and let his mother sit between him and Wanda.

"Why bother to put out a Zounds bar," Mr. Martin said, "with milk chocolate on it?"

"I see what you mean," Wanda said.

"Don't egg him on," Mrs. Martin said, "or he'll talk your leg off."

"I'll tell you one thing," Robert said. "They didn't decide to make that milk-chocolate Zounds overnight. A lot of research goes into a decision like that."

Mr. Martin took a pipe out of his sweater pocket and put it in his mouth.

"Don't light that," Mrs. Martin said. "We're going to eat here in a minute."

Mr. Martin returned the pipe to his pocket. A buzzer went off in the kitchen. Mrs. Martin jumped to her feet and hurried out of the room.

"You don't throw away a name like Zounds," Robert said. "What you do is change the product but keep the name."

"And end up duplicating everything," Mr. Martin said. "Pretty soon every candy bar in the country will taste exactly alike."

"But they'll have different names," Robert said. "That's what counts."

"He went to school four years," Mr. Martin said, "to learn a dumb thing like that."

Wanda was laughing when Mrs. Martin came in and said dinner was ready.

While he was carving the roast, Mr. Martin started telling a story that lasted well into the meal. It was about a dog and a boy who were separated for seven years. Overcoming unbelievable obstacles, the dog finally managed to find the boy again. The only trouble was that, in the intervening years, the boy had grown up to become a medical student. Instead of welcoming the dog back, the boy put him to sleep and carved him up for practice.

At the beginning of the story, Mrs. Martin ostentatiously tore a paper napkin into two pieces. She stuffed the pieces in her ears. She pursed her lips and stared at a spot across the room.

"He tells that fool story all the time," she said to Wanda later. "I don't know why."

"Some people are like that dog," Mr. Martin said.

"This is right down Wanda's alley," Robert said. "She studied this kind of stuff in school."

"I thought you people didn't study anything but sex," Mr. Martin said. He gave Wanda a wink.

"Who wants dessert?" Mrs. Martin asked. She stood up and moved toward the kitchen.

"Not me," Wanda said. "I have to watch my calories."

"A big girl like you needs lots of calories," Mr. Martin said. "Besides, it's Ma's Dutch chocolate cake."

"Please . . . no . . ." Wanda said. To her vast annoyance, Mrs. Martin returned from the kitchen and placed a large piece of cake in front of her. On the dish with the cake was a dip of vanilla ice cream. "Really," Wanda said, "I told you—"

Robert and his father started talking about CD's and interest rates. Wanda told Mrs. Martin how good the roast had been. Mrs. Martin complimented Wanda's dress and said she was glad the longer styles were back in. During the agonizingly long time it took the others to eat, Wanda, with her hands in her lap, watched her ice cream slowly melt and soak into the cake.

When they finally finished, the two men, each carrying a beer, returned to the living room. Wanda remained seated while Mrs. Martin cleared the table. Then she followed Mrs. Martin into the kitchen and watched while she scraped the leftovers, including Wanda's cake, into the disposal and then put the dishes into the washer.

"I can't get over how good that was," Wanda said.

"You ate like a bird," Mrs. Martin said. "You didn't have any gravy or bread or dessert."

"What I did eat was delicious," Wanda said. "Especially that roast."

"It's nice you could come." Mrs. Martin spoke without enthusiasm. "I don't know why Robert was so slow about asking you."

"I don't either," Wanda said.

"Oh I do too know. He was afraid I wouldn't like you."

"Why's that?"

"He has it in his head that I don't want him staying out all night. He does it two or three times a week."

"I'm sorry if that bothers you," Wanda said.

"He's never done it before," Mrs. Martin said, "except sometimes with that awful Doreen—" She clapped a hand over her mouth. "I shouldn't have said that."

"It's all right," Wanda said. Robert had already told her about Doreen Dalton, the woman he'd broken off with a few months before he met Wanda.

"You should have *seen* that girl," Mrs. Martin said. "Skirts up to here and I don't know what else. I don't know what Robert was thinking about."

"Well . . ." Wanda said.

"Mr. Martin liked it though," Mrs. Martin said. "They used to sit and talk like there was no one else in the room. Robert and I felt right out of it sometimes . . . I never did know why Walter carried on like that."

"It's hard to say," Wanda said. It seemed important not to take sides.

Mrs. Martin frowned and started the dishwasher. Then she removed her apron and, without so much as a nod in Wanda's direction, led the way to the living room.

"Did you give her the tour of the house?" Mr. Martin asked.

"She wouldn't be interested," Mrs. Martin said.

"It's a lovely house," Wanda said. "I told Robert how nice I thought it was."

"It's not that nice on the inside," Mrs. Martin said. She sat down in an easy chair and put her head back and closed her eyes.

Wanda looked at Robert and saw that he was staring at the floor.

"How about the dogs?" Mr. Martin said. ""Are you going to show her your dog collection?"

"There certainly are a lot of them," Wanda said.

Mrs. Martin opened her eyes but didn't look at Wanda. "He buys the fool things," she said, "and then says my collection." She picked up some needles and yarn and started knitting.

"Well," Mr. Martin said, "maybe I'll show her the workshop."

"She wouldn't want to see a thing like that," Mrs. Martin said.

"Yes I would," Wanda said. "I'd like to see it."

"I'd better tag along too," Robert said.

The workshop smelled pleasantly of oil and wood. Mr. Martin pointed out the various tools and machines and told Wanda what they were for and how much they cost. Wanda put her hand on one of the machines he had not yet come to, and Mr. Martin told her not to fool with it or they might end up in a Texas chain-saw massacre.

"This is a chain saw?" Wanda ran a finger along the blade. "You certainly keep it shined up."

"You bet," Mr. Martin said. "If it wasn't so cold I'd take you outside for a demonstration. You come over some afternoon and we'll cut us some wood. A big girl like you could handle that saw. It used to scare Doreen half to death."

"Dad," Robert said.

"I guess I shouldn't have mentioned her," Mr. Martin said.

"It's all right," Wanda said. "Mrs. Martin was just talking about her."

Mr. Martin's face darkened. "I'll bet she was. No one would ever let that girl be herself."

"Dad," Robert said.

"Everybody wants to legislate somebody's morals," Mr. Mar-

19

tin said. "I say you can't do that. You've got to let people be themselves."

"That seems sensible," Wanda said.

"I think we've seen everything," Robert said. "Let's go upstairs."

"Let's drive a nail first," Mr. Martin said. Ignoring Robert's protest, he placed a thick piece of wood on a worktable. Then he took down a hammer from a rack on the wall and got some large nails out of a drawer. "You're going to be impressed," he told Wanda. He tapped a nail lightly so it stood up by itself. "Watch this," he said. He brought the hammer down hard and drove the nail all the way into the wood with one blow.

"Hey," Wanda said, "that's pretty good."

"I told you," Mr. Martin said with a grin. He set up another nail and handed the hammer to Robert.

Robert, frowning, gave the nail a glancing blow that sent it flying across the room.

"He won't even try," Mr. Martin said. "That's what gets me. Now it's your turn."

"Me?" Wanda said. "I couldn't do it in a million years."

"You might fool yourself. Be sure to hit it center."

Wanda took her time and aimed carefully. To her amazement, the nail went straight down and all the way in.

"She's a natural," Mr. Martin said. "I never saw anything like it."

"It was luck," Wanda said, but she felt proud of herself.

Robert turned and headed up the stairs. Mr. Martin put away the hammer and nails, and he and Wanda went up too. Back in the living room, they found Mrs. Martin asleep in her chair.

"Poor old thing," Mr. Martin said. "She had a hard day at the beauty parlor."

"That was a pretty big dinner she fixed," Wanda said.

"I did most of that," Mr. Martin said.

"Crap," Robert said.

"Talk real low," Mr. Martin said. "She's crabby if you wake her." He turned off all the lights except the lamp by the sofa. With his pipe in his hand he sat facing Wanda. He leaned forward with his elbows on his knees. "Tell us all about yourself," he said.

"If you let him get started," Robert said, "he'll give you the third degree."

"There's not a lot to tell," Wanda said.

"Don't give me that," Mr. Martin said. "I saw your father on television a while back. They called him the psychoanalyst of the stars, but they didn't say which ones."

"They never do," Wanda said. "It wouldn't be proper for Daddy to capitalize on somebody's name."

"What's he like in person?" Mr. Martin asked.

Robert stood up and yawned. "Guess I'll get a beer," he said.

Mr. Martin checked his own bottle, saw that it was empty, and said to bring him one as well. It seemed to Wanda that he had consumed a good many for a man his age. He struck a kitchen match and lit his pipe.

"To tell you the truth," Wanda said, "I don't see Daddy very often. We're not what you'd call close. I've been on my own for several years."

"I admire that in a girl," Mr. Martin said. "How about your mother? Is she alive?"

Wanda shook her head. "She died when I was four. Daddy raised me."

"That's a shame," Mr. Martin said. "I mean about your mother."

Robert handed him a beer and went over and looked out the window. Wanda wished he could stop being so nervous. In spite of Mrs. Martin's moodiness, the evening was not going badly.

"I guess you must like your father okay," Mr. Martin said, "the way you've followed in his footsteps."

"I haven't *exactly* followed in them. He's a psychiatrist and so is my brother. That's enough for one family. I'm a psychologist."

Robert turned from the window and stared at his father's back. Then he looked so intently at Wanda that she almost squirmed.

"I guess they live in California," Mr. Martin said.

"I think Eric does, but I'm not sure. He moves around a lot. Daddy's based in Chicago."

"But you're all therapists," Mr. Martin said. "That's what Bob told me."

Wanda nodded. Robert was still looking at her, and she wondered what was bothering him now.

"What do people do in this psychotherapy?" Mr. Martin asked. "Come in and plop down on a couch?"

"They would if they went to Daddy," Wanda said. "If they came to me, they'd sit in a chair."

"Like I'm doing now?"

"That's right."

Mr. Martin gave her a once-over. "I can tell you something," he said. "You're going to be a big success."

"Why's that?"

"There's plenty of guys out there," Mr. Martin said, "who'd pay good money to talk to a girl like you." For the second time that night, he gave Wanda a wink.

She struggled to keep from sounding angry. "That doesn't have a thing to do with it."

Mr. Martin sat back and puffed his pipe. "Don't kid yourself," he said with a leer.

Robert, to Wanda's great relief, announced that it was time to be going.

* * *

Back at the apartment, the first thing Robert did was chug-a-lug a beer. Then, while Wanda was getting into her pajamas, he wandered about looking glum and irritable.

"It's been a strain," Wanda said, "but we're home now. Can't you relax?"

"I'll try," Robert said.

He went to the kitchen for another beer. When he returned, Wanda sat him on the sofa and stood behind him and massaged his neck with her thumbs.

"It's like a knot in there," she said, "but I can feel it dissolving. Say, did you see me drive that nail? I've never been so surprised in my life."

"For God's sake," Robert said. "He put your nail in a hole that was already there. You could have pushed it down with your finger."

Wanda thought about this and realized that it must be true. She stopped massaging and sat down. "Why would he do that?"

"To get you on his side," Robert said. "The first day Doreen came to the house, he had her thinking she was the greatest carpenter since Jesus Christ. Doreen was so thin she could barely lift the hammer. What did Mom tell you about Doreen?"

"I got the impression she didn't like her."

"That's not true. Mom and Doreen were like that." Robert held up his right hand and crossed his fingers tightly.

"You're kidding," Wanda said.

"They used to go shopping together, take long walks together, go up in the bedroom and talk for hours. All kinds of stuff like that."

"Your mother told me," Wanda said, "that it was your *father* Doreen was close to."

"She must have said that for your benefit," Robert said. "Doreen was scared to death of my father."

"The way your mother talked," Wanda said, "Doreen threw herself at him. Inflamed him with miniskirts and spent all her time entertaining him."

"She did wear short dresses," Robert said. "That was her style. But she stayed as far away from Dad as she possibly could. As a matter of fact"—Robert threw his head back and laughed bitterly—"you gave Dad more undivided attention in one night than Doreen did the whole six months she knew him."

"What was I supposed to do?" Wanda said. "No one else would talk . . . I'm sorry your mother didn't like me."

Robert shrugged. "You're too high-toned or something. You should have helped with the dinner. You should have eaten some gravy. You should have had some of that damned cake. You should have made a fuss over the dogs. You should have gone upstairs and talked about how men are. You should have— It doesn't matter."

"I said I was sorry. I tried to make a good impression."

"Well, you did. You made a big impression on Dad."

They sat in silence for a while. Then Wanda said, "Why wouldn't you even try to drive the nail?"

"I did try. You want to hear a funny story?"

Wanda nodded.

"One afternoon a few months ago, when Mom and Dad were out of town, I spent an hour trying to learn to drive those nails. I never even came close."

"I don't think that's too funny," Wanda said.

"Not really." Robert's beer can was empty, and he tossed it at the wastebasket. It missed and rolled across the floor.

"Why do you live with your parents?" Wanda asked.

"To take care of Mom. Dad used to beat on her. When I got big enough, I more or less put a stop to it, but he's still mean to her. He's run her off five or six times, but she keeps coming back."

"She's the dog in the story," Wanda said. "I'm glad I figured that out."

"She's the what?"

"The dog. At first I thought it might be you, but now I can see it was her. She's the dog in your father's story."

"She's not a dog," Robert said fiercely. "She's the best mother in the world and don't you forget it." He went over and picked up his beer can and slammed it straight down into the wastebasket.

3

Nov 19

Darling Wanda,

Why did you say I couldn't write to you? Weren't you interested? What kind of letters did you think I'd send? Do you imagine that I'm not capable of composing decent, friendly letters to my former therapist? To the woman I love. You whore.

I've been having good memories of you recently. I close my eyes and there they are, like snapshots. Here, for example, is your funny little smile with just the corners turned up—the one that draws a guy in. Here's the big one that knocks a guy out. The wistful one, the merry one . . . If I'm going too fast, let me know. I keep forgetting that you aren't as familiar with these pictures as I am. Now here—my favorite maybe— here's your lopsided, quizzical grin. God bless that grin. Here we have your eyes, those gorgeous eyes, flashing the time you got so mad (you denied you were angry, but you couldn't fool me). In this one, you're tossing your head, the way you did at the beginning of a session. (Until I commented on it—remember?—and then you stopped doing it. I could have cut out my tongue.) Here's the spoiled Daddy's-girl expression you sometimes got, and here's that look of God damned pure compassion. You did that look very well.

Here's another picture, a dandy—you in the cocktail dress you wore to one of our meetings. A blue party dress. I almost believed you wore it for me. Later, I saw you leaving the ward with a twirpy doctor who was also dressed to the nines.

The other guys on the ward teased me for finding you so attractive. One of them—asshole!—even referred to you as "that cow." I wanted to kill him. Sure, your belly's too big and your hips too broad. (If you'd run with me every morning, Wanda, you'd get rid of the gut. I used to have fantasies about that. I used to think how yummy it would be, afterward, to lick the sweat from around your eyes. Do you know how good you'd look in a blue warm-up suit?) But so what if you're a little heavy in the middle? You have those marvelous long legs, and that's the important thing. I loved the way you sat, not five feet from me, your delectable shoulders squared just so and your head (after that preliminary toss) perfectly still, slightly cocked. Was it hard for you to hold your head so still? Was that why you crossed your legs so often? Because of your height, your knees were right in my face, and I got a big flash of thigh every time you crossed those beauties. Except when you wore pants. Then I got something else—the faintest outline of your most secret part. As a matter of fact, the outline wasn't that faint. Those pants were pretty tight.

The same guy who called you a cow made fun of your hair. He nick-named you "Sailboat" because of the way it flared out at the sides. But I loved it. It gave you a slightly saucy air that matched your cockeyed grin. I am, by the way, an expert sailor.

Good memories all right. But who was it that said the best are also the worst? Me, probably—that's my style. Anyway, they bring me nothing but tears. Of grief or rage, I can no longer tell the difference. Two nights ago I smashed my glasses against the wall. Grief or rage, doesn't matter, they're broken. I can't get new ones because I can't drive without glasses, and the nearest place I could get them is twenty miles away. Actually, I could hitch a ride if I wanted to. But being nearsighted I don't need glasses for reading or, if the mood should strike me, for writing someone a letter.

You ought to see where I'm living, Wanda. When I left the hospital, I drove nonstop to my hometown. I thought maybe there, in Wrentree, in the place of my birth, in the bosom of my family, I might tap into some long-forgotten strength, might at least find some solace. But nothing much happened. Although everyone was as sweet as could be, they regarded me with suspicion. They kept an eye on me. If I didn't stay right on schedule, they thought I was going crazy again. We all walked around on tiptoes. I thought about you and cried all the time. Buckets of tears, Wanda. My mother was terrified, my father embarrassed. In the end, I couldn't quite connect with that town and those people. If you live with your family, it's almost essential that you connect. Connect or confront. I could do neither, and the role of polite stranger wasn't comfortable. One day I threw some things in the car and headed south. I drove a hundred miles or so, then stopped in Elmerton for cigarettes. I've been here ever since—about a month now.

This whole region is what's called depressed, and we're right in the middle of it. A weather-beaten, rock-battered sign on the edge of town announces "Elmerton—Home of 400 Lively People," but I hope you don't believe everything you read. The town is in fact as dead a place as you could ever want to find. Main street runs for a block and a half, then becomes a narrow dirt road that winds into the hills beyond. (Or maybe the road takes a turn, so as to get out of sight, and then stops. I don't know.) The stores are uniformly gray and falling down, and so are the houses. So are the people. So are the dogs, cats, chickens, and cows. The whole feeling of the place is of nothing doing, and being here is like having vanished from the earth. I don't seem to mind. Connection, or anything like it, is not required or expected; it might be frowned upon. That seems to suit my mood. You're my only connection, Wanda.

I'm staying in a large house about a half mile from town. Although it's rotting steadily away, it must once have been elegant. Maybe it was a plantation house or a fancy hotel. Maybe it was used as a hospital during the Civil War. The house has a history—I'm sure of that—but like everything else around here, it has outlived itself. I think of it as the Arkansas Home for the Disappointed.

There are six of us in the house. The proprietors, Doc and Mrs. Bonds, have quarters on the first floor; the four "guests"—Jack, Bill,

Millie, and I—have rooms on the second. Besides the Bonds' quarters,
the first floor contains rooms we're all permitted to use—a large front
room (the lobby, as I call it), a kitchen, and a bathroom. There's a third
floor, but it's not in use right now. Until a couple of weeks ago, all of us
at the Home spent a lot of time on the front porch, sitting in wicker
chairs and staring toward the road. Now that the weather has become
cooler, we've moved into the lobby and do our staring through the big
front window. Doc Bonds, who is retired I guess, is a drinker. So, I sus-
pect, is Mrs. Bonds, or maybe a doper. Or maybe both. Anyway, they
can stare with the best of us. If there were a passing scene, you might
think we were sharp observers of it. We're not. We're merely a band of
shabby little people, lost in our shoddy, second-rate selves. I know
you're curious about these folks, so I'll give you a rundown.

Jack is about thirty, built like a fireplug but drooped in spirit. Wanted
to be a ballplayer but couldn't hit the curve. Not much with the glove
either, and he faded fast. In his job with the hardware company, he de-
manded one raise too many and got the ax instead.

Millie, thirty-eight. Wispy little blonde. Miss Perkins County of
1965. Badly wilted but still a looker. Sold real estate, was big in com-
munity affairs. Four years ago, at what she calls her peak, she was
rendered insane by a spell of religious excitement. When it passed, she
was unable to resume her old active ways. On top of that, she's con-
vinced that people circulate stories about her.

Bill, bearded and frail, is forty-one. The son of an immigrant, he
says he thinks in one language and speaks in another. The connection is
bad and nothing comes out right. If he could say what he meant, he
could be an inventor and make money. He bears his disappointment
with dignity and will leave a note saying no one was to blame but
himself.

Tim, forty-six. A phony from an early age, thanks to an uncontrol-
lable urge to please. A while back he suffered a total breakdown in such
vital areas as confidence, charm, intelligence, and sense of humor. Few
significant interests and no realistic desires. Although he taught philoso-
phy for years, he doesn't know the meaning of the word "will." Probably
hopeless, he likes to imagine he could be smiled back to life. Last night

he burned holes in his legs with cigarettes. The places are white now,
but in a few days they'll explode into big red blossoms. He'll think of
them as a bouquet from the smiler. If she's a good girl, he might send her
the scabs. He doesn't mean to sound bitter. He never could stand that in
a person.

Once, Wanda, when I was about seven, I accidentally burned my fin-
ger. My grandmother plunged it into a dish of vanilla ice cream she hap-
pened to be eating. I have never forgotten how good that felt.

Love,
Tim

Unlike the other letters, this one was neatly typed. To Wanda's surprise, Robert read it without comment. When he finished, he folded it carefully, returned it to the envelope, and said he was hungry. They drove to the Chinese restaurant on Caldwell Road. Wanda had sweet-and-sour shrimp and Robert had pork twice cooked. They both had a couple of egg rolls.

"The food here's not as good as it used to be," Robert grumbled. "A few years ago you couldn't beat this place."

"Tastes change too," Wanda said.

"Maybe that's it," Robert said morosely.

Later they went to Tremensville, a town ten miles away, to a bar that featured live music every Saturday. Tonight, instead of the usual rock group, a bluegrass group was playing. The members of the band were college students who wore overalls and straw hats. One of them chewed tobacco and spat on the floor.

Wanda didn't especially like bluegrass, but Robert, who claimed to like all kinds of music, tapped his foot and appeared to have a good time. Wanda could tell, though, that something was bothering him. After he'd had several beers, he started calling the waitress honey, a sure sign that he was getting drunk. Once when he went to the men's room, he surprised Wanda by doing a few dance steps across the floor. Coming back to the table, he almost fell. He tried to make a joke of it, but his laugh was not successful. A few minutes later he said he wanted to go home.

Wanda drove and Robert slept. When they reached the apartment house, Robert said he was going to spend the night in the car. He had some thinking to do, he said. Wanda said if he changed his mind to come on up, and after a while he did. He went to the bathroom and then fell on the bed and passed out. When it became apparent that he wasn't going to wake up, Wanda removed his shoes and pulled his pants off. He was wearing white knit briefs. It occurred to Wanda that although she had known him intimately for the better part of a year, she had never seen him naked. Out of curiosity, she tried to pull his shorts down, but Robert growled and rolled away from her. Since, as she well knew, there was nothing inadequate about his penis, she decided that he was shy because of his weight. It was a feeling that Wanda could well understand: she too was pretty bashful when it came to undressing all the way. She made up her mind to lose another ten pounds just as fast as she could.

Knowing that Robert would snore and toss the entire night, she threw a blanket over him and went to the living room to sleep on the sofa. The sofa was narrow and short and hard as a board. Pretty soon she returned to the bedroom. Although Robert was beginning to snort and grit his teeth, she fell quickly asleep. In the morning, feeling more sympathetic, she made him some toast and coffee. She sat on the side of the bed while he ate.

"I wish you'd tell me what's wrong," she said.

"Nothing," Robert said. He pawed furiously at the Sunday *Times*.

"What are you looking for?" Wanda said. "The sports page? I'll find it for you in a minute." She took the paper out of his hands and put it on the bed. "I know what's bothering you. It's the letter from Tim."

Robert finally admitted that it was. "I never read anything like it in my life," he said without looking at her. "Parts of it are dirty and insulting. Parts of it are like a love letter. He knows you better than I do."

"No he doesn't," Wanda said. "He's making it up. He's inventing me, is what he's doing."

Robert crammed the last of his toast into his mouth and washed it down with coffee.

"I hope you don't think," Wanda said with a laugh, "that I sat there putting on some kind of a floor show for him."

"I don't know what to think," Robert said.

Wanda gave him a little talk on the therapeutic relationship and the concept of transference. She had done nothing, she explained, to provoke Tim's feelings. She had merely sat there, cloaked in professional anonymity and carefully observing the rule of abstinence. Her attitude had been one of sympathetic (but purely professional) interest and calm receptiveness. It was nothing *she* had done, but rather the situation itself, that had given rise to the transference. Tim's reactions—strange as they might seem to Robert—were perfectly natural and predictable. As Freud had pointed out a long time ago, transference feelings had a peculiarly compulsive quality and a special intensity. Caught up in these feelings, a patient was subject to all manner of wild imaginings and was prone to project, on the blank screen of the therapist's presence, precisely those qualities he was at the moment most desperate for. When Tim wanted a mother, Wanda appeared to him as a mother; if he wanted a sexpot, she appeared to him as a sexpot; if he had gotten around to wanting a father, she might have appeared to him as a man—

"Crap," Robert said.

"Don't you believe me?"

"Not the part about appearing as a man."

"There's a case like that in a book by Frieda Fromm-Reichmann," Wanda said. "A patient saw his female therapist as his bearded father."

"I'd come nearer believing you," Robert said, "if I hadn't seen the floor show for myself. Remember when you were at the house for dinner?"

Wanda nodded.

"Well," Robert said, "all the time you were talking to Dad, you were putting on the floor show."

"I was not."

"He's mentioned it to me two or three times. I finally told him if he didn't shut up I'd break his jaw."

"You'd take *his* word?"

"I don't have to. I told you, I saw it for myself."

"You did not." Wanda's neck was tingling.

"I got tired of hearing you two talk," Robert said, "so I went over and looked out the window. Then I turned and watched you and Dad. In about five minutes you ran through twenty smiles and crossed your legs four or five times. Tim's right—you show the works every time you do it. I thought Dad was going to crawl up your dress. You're a bigger flirt than Doreen ever thought of being."

Wanda blushed hotly.

"If you'd do it for Dad," Robert said, "it stands to reason you did it for Tim."

"You know what you are?" Wanda said. "All three of you— you're little boys peeking up mommy's skirt and thinking you see something you don't."

"Your eyes are flashing," Robert said, "just like Tim described."

Wanda stood up, but Robert grabbed her wrist and jerked her onto the bed and rolled her over on her back. The breakfast tray crashed to the floor.

"No," Wanda said.

"If you can show it to the whole world," Robert said, "you can by God show it to me." He held her wrists tightly and pressed a knee between her legs.

"God damn you," Wanda said. She clamped her mouth shut and shook her head from side to side, but this did not prevent Robert from getting his other leg between hers. She was losing ground in a hurry.

Robert hesitated, then rolled off and fell heavily backward. "I could never do it against your will," he said. He threw an arm over his eyes and groaned.

"You don't have to do it against my will," Wanda said. "All you have to do is ask nicely."

She went to the bathroom and took a shower. When she came out Robert was gone. He had left a note that said he was meeting Floyd at the Country Club. They were going to work out on the weights and talk. He would return about five o'clock.

Wanda slipped into the green dress she had worn to the Martins'. The hemline reached well below the knee. She put on a pair of shoes with medium heels and moved a chair in front of the full-length mirror on one of the closet doors. She sat down and crossed her legs a few times, looking carefully in the mirror as she did so. Although she wondered if it would be noticed by anyone not already inclined to peek, she had to admit that there was a definite flash of thigh each time she crossed them. She thought about this for a while, then crossed her legs a few more times. The more often she did it, the more noticeable the flash became. She had never seen herself from this angle, and she had to admit that she was more sexy than she had imagined herself to be. She couldn't worry about Tim. Tim was a thing of the past. Anyway, she could have worn a nun's habit and he would have accused her of being stark naked. Mr. Martin was a different story. She would have to watch herself around him from now on.

She took the dress off and put on pants and a sweater. She went outside and began to walk. A few weeks ago, when she first came to town, the air had been crisp and light; Wanda had savored it with her nose. November had brought heavy clouds and days of constant drizzle. But although the air had turned thick and gray, and seeped through her clothes and into her skin, it was no less pure than it had been in October. Wanda gulped it gratefully down. She had never felt as alive as she felt in Windward, New York.

She stopped in the Community Shopping Center and bought two steaks and a package of crescent rolls. Although she seldom cooked, she felt like doing something special for Robert.

Walking back, she thought again about transference. What she had outlined for Robert was the classical position of Freud and his followers, including her father—the idea that transference feelings developed automatically and were extremely powerful. This seemed to be true in Tim's case: there could be no question about the sheer strength of his feelings. Her own experience with transference had not been so intense. During her third year of graduate school, she had developed a crush on a faculty member who led a practice group. She had a couple of dreams that, when she interpreted them, clearly referred to this man and were full of sexual content. She also had some dreams that seemed to require no interpretation. Sometimes she thought about him and masturbated. When she finally got up the nerve to discuss her feelings before the group (she did not, of course, mention the masturbation), someone pointed out that she was having a transference. Almost as if by magic, the feelings evaporated. She had hoped the same thing would happen with Tim, but it didn't. For him, the word "transference" held no magic. He would listen carefully and then say, in his quiet desperate voice, that although he understood what she meant, it didn't help a bit—he still loved her. And there they stalled. One day, after she had memorized a passage from Freud and quoted it almost verbatim to Tim, he looked at the ceiling and said, "Please make her stop. Please." He regarded her with sadness and pity. He looked at the floor and shook his head. Then he pulled himself together, sat up straight, and, fixing Wanda with a hard stare, poised himself on the edge of his seat. It suddenly occurred to her—the feeling was one of absolute certainty—that she was about to be kissed and that there was nothing in the world she could do about it. She had never felt so cornered in her life. At that moment, a loud disturbance broke out in the hall. They both glanced at the door. When their eyes met again, Tim's features crumpled; his shoulders sagged; he put his face in his hands and wept. Soon afterward, with her departure from the hospital still two months away, he went into a deep regression during which he alternately made veiled suicide threats and gazed at Wanda with the mute adoration of a five-year-old. This was the stage he was in when she left.

She felt bad about leaving a patient in such a condition, but of course she had no choice. Furthermore, her supervisor assured her that having a tough case early in her career would make things easier for her later on. "It's from the hard cases," he said, "that we draw our greatest strength. Anyway, from what you've told me, the man's impossible to work with." Wanda appreciated the pat on the back.

* * *

"I've been giving it some thought," Robert said at dinner. "It doesn't matter what he thinks about you. It's what *you* think that's important. If you don't love him—"

"Why would I love him?" Wanda said. "I couldn't love him if I wanted to. He was my patient."

"That's what counts. How *you* feel." Robert poured more wine, and they held up their glasses in a toast. "I'm sorry I said that stuff about the floor show," he said.

"Maybe I had it coming."

"You were just nervous. First time meeting Dad and Mom. That's what Floyd said."

"I guess he's an expert," Wanda said.

"He's always been sharp about women," Robert said.

"Let's not talk about Floyd," Wanda said. "Floyd gives me a headache. Did you really tell your father you'd break his jaw?"

Robert looked sheepish. "It's the only way to shut him up sometimes. I always feel guilty about it, though . . . This was a good idea, eating at home."

"Thank you."

"I was afraid you wouldn't even let me back in. I was surprised to see you cooking dinner . . . Say, do you think he actually burned himself?"

"Who?"

"Tim. He says in the letter he burned his legs with cigarettes."

"He probably did," Wanda said. "He did the same thing in the hospital. The burns were an attempt to resist the transference."

Robert winced.

"Another time," Wanda said, "he carved a message on his arm with a razor blade."

"That's pretty crazy," Robert said. "What did it say?"

"Teach us to care and not to care," Wanda said.

"What did that mean exactly?"

"Who knows?" Wanda said. "I think it was poetry or something."

They ate in silence for a few minutes, then Wanda said: "It isn't fair for you to have to read those letters. They seem to upset you."

"Don't they bother you?"

"I'm trained to deal with people like Tim. You're not."

"If you're going to get the letters," Robert said, "I'm going to read them."

After dinner they decided to stay home and play backgammon. Later they would watch television. Wanda was setting up the backgammon board when Robert said:

"There's one other thing that's been bothering me. I won't mention it if it's going to make you mad."

"How will I know," Wanda said, "unless you mention it?"

"It's that twirpy doctor Tim talks about. Did you go out with him or what?"

Wanda had to think a minute. "I remember now," she said.

"The reason I ask is this," Robert said. "That would have been after you and I knew each other and agreed not to see other people."

"What it was," Wanda said, "was a cocktail party for the interns and residents. That's why I was wearing the blue dress. The twirpy doctor gave me a ride." This was true as far as it went. Wanda could have said a lot more, but it didn't seem wise to open another can of worms right now. "Let's roll to see who goes first," she said.

* * *

A couple of days later Robert came to the apartment with two expensive-looking running outfits. He had bought a black one for himself, a blue one for Wanda. Both suits had white stripes down the legs and arms.

"You got them because of that letter," Wanda said.

"What if I did?" Robert said. "It's still a good idea."

They went jogging twice. The first time, they did a full mile, the second time a half mile. Neither time, as Robert pointed out, did any sweat appear around Wanda's eyes, perhaps because of the chilly weather. On the third day they were so sore they could hardly get out of bed.

"That does it," Robert said, and threw his suit far back in the closet.

Wanda decided to keep hers handy. She did look good in it, and it would be a nice thing to wear around the apartment.

4

Nov 28

Dear Sailboat,

After our last session together, I returned to the ward and paced the halls. My group-therapy leader, Lorna Beane—remember her, the psychiatric nurse with the layered look?—fell in beside me. After we had walked for a while in silence, Lorna asked me how I felt, now that my marriage to you was over.

Lorna was prone to extravagant metaphors. I could never tell whether she was missing the point entirely or going to the very heart of the matter. Maybe she was doing both. Maybe I'm becoming very Hegel-Freud. Maybe you better bring me a double order of reechie-poochies with a little hot sauce. Slim Gailliard said that on a record with Charlie Parker and Dizzy Gillespie. I used to love jazz. My only interest now is you. If you have any use for 2,000 jazz albums, I can arrange to have them shipped to you, postpaid from Wrentree, Arkansas. You can also have my books, I don't care. You took the best, why not take the rest?— that's how I look at it. Do you know the Billie Holiday version?

Anyhow, when I didn't answer, Lorna said, "That's what it was, you know—a marriage." I loved that metaphor and hated it too. "So how do you feel?" Lorna asked.

What I felt, Wanda, on that last day, was cheated on a cosmic scale. With your leaving, I had been kicked out of the heaven of being and back into the hell of existence. Nausea, in Sartre's sense of the word— that's what I felt. Hence my ambivalence about the marriage metaphor. Contrary to popular superstition, real marriages are not made in heaven. They are, indeed, among the baser manifestations of the great slime of existence. My "marriage" to you was entirely different, reflecting as it did—nay, it embodied—the old ideal of uncontaminated being. All I ever wanted from you, Wanda, was more and more therapy. My love for you is the purest you'll ever know.

Could one, by the way, argue that, in Freudian categories, the passage from repetition to recollection just is the passage from existence to being? Frankly, Sailboat, I neither know nor care, but if you'd like to explore the question in an article, I'd be glad to lend a hand. We could start, perhaps, by rephrasing Freud's dictum, "Where id was, there ego shall be," to read: "Where existence was, there being shall be," and go on from there.

Or maybe you're more at home with Heidegger, in which case we'll talk first about the world of das Man—the ho-hum workaday world of one does and they say, the world that gives rise, as you know, to that profound boredom that drifts hither and thither in the abysses of existence like a mute fog. Exact quote, Wanda—ain't it purty? Boy, do I know that boredom. And then we'll talk about how, in therapy, one can pass from that world to a state of perfect joy in the presence of another, etc. So they say. I never completed the passage, but I could sense, in therapy with you, the possibility of completing it. I am so sick Wanda please help me. Anyway, the paper would be a post-Freudian, neo-existential synthesis, with dashes of Barthes and Derrida. A paper like that could do wonders for a girl's reputation.

What a crock. We both know, don't we, that what I really wanted from you was some serious fucking? I did feel cheated when you left— but only because I realized, once and for all, that despite your come-ons, I would never get the chance to wallow and pant with you in the primal muck.

That's wrong too, damn it. What I really wanted was to exist and be—to fuck and do therapy—at the same time. That goes against your so-called principles, but have you ever tried it? A lot of things would damage a patient more than that. This patient, anyway.

It was sweet of Lorna to walk the hall with me. I wish you'd ever done it. You probably don't believe this, but if I'm with the right person, and if I'm in the right mood, I can turn hall walking into a regular adventure. Do you know what I think? I think if you'd hold me for two minutes this world would be redeemed. I guess I'm as extravagant as Lorna.

I am haunted by your dear face.

Love and kisses,
Tim

"I don't understand a word of it," Robert said angrily," except that now he's practically married to you. It's *me* you're going to marry. *Isn't* it?"

"I'm thinking about it." Wanda spoke softly but firmly.

"Mom says it's cruel to keep me in suspense," Robert said.

"Have you forgotten our agreement? We were going to give ourselves time. We were going to be sure."

"Maybe I am sure."

"And maybe I'm not. It's as simple as that." Wanda went over and clasped Robert's face in her hands and kissed him. "You're sweet though," she said. "You're really sweet . . . How is your mother, anyway?"

"Same as always. You know."

"Not really. I've only seen her that one time."

"She's exactly the same as she was then." Robert picked up Tim's letter. "What's this stuff about existence?"

"He's just showing off," Wanda said.

As a matter of fact, talk about existence made her uncomfortable. She had nothing to say on the subject—didn't even know, really, what the subject *was*—and she couldn't understand why some people found it exciting. Early in his therapy with her, Tim had talked a lot about it—intellectualizing, which was one of the worst forms of resisting. This talk had shaded into talk about the meaninglessness of life, which in turn had led to talk about how life wasn't worth living. By this time, Wanda felt herself on firmer ground. As the transference took hold and his defenses fell, Tim decided that maybe it was only *his* life that wasn't worth living. Wanda had considered this a definite advance. Then, to her horror, her apparent gains were swept away in Tim's continued regression and episodes of self-mutilation. Now that he was out of therapy, he had obviously gone back to square one and was reading his private misery into the world as a whole.

The only other people Wanda had known who were hung up on the meaninglessness of life were two young psychiatrists at the hospital. They were married to each other and were exactly alike. "Life," they were fond of saying, "begins on the other side of despair." Like Tim, they called themselves existentialists. Unlike Tim, they were unfailingly cheerful—to the point, indeed, that no one could stand to be around them. They had a perfectly ordinary baby named Joy. They were always bringing Joy on the ward and waving her around in patients' faces. They thought this was therapeutic. "The joy of existence," they said to the patients one day, "is the existence of Joy." Some of the patients liked this and some of them didn't. After the couple left, taking Joy with them of course, the patients who didn't like it went around repeating "The joy of existence is the existence of Joy" in sarcastic voices. This made the other patients angry, and an argument broke out. Within an hour, the entire ward was sunk in a deep general depression.

Robert was still puzzling over the letter. "Could I ask you something?"

"Sure."

"Well—" Robert hesitated. "Would it be out of line if you accepted those records?"

"I can't accept anything from him. Besides, you don't like jazz."

"I like all music," Robert said. "It's you that doesn't like it. It's you that turns it off every time it comes on the radio."

"It's out of the question," Wanda said, "to accept those records."

"Anyway," Robert said, "that's not what I wanted to ask. I wanted to ask whether he's right about the other thing."

"What other thing?" Wanda had encouraged Robert to be more direct in his dealings with people, but so far with little success.

"About not being able to make love and do therapy at the same time."

"Well sure."

"I guess I'm glad to hear that. The way you and Tim and Floyd go on about sex, I wasn't too sure."

"*Me?*" Wanda laughed. "Don't lump me in with those guys."

* * *

That night, at Robert's insistence, they went to see the Amazing Kreskin in person at the Grand Theater. Robert went up with some other people and got himself hypnotized. Wanda had to smile at the sight of him hopping around the stage, flapping his arms and clucking like a hen.

"It was the damnedest thing," he said after the show.

They went to Denny's and had a couple of drinks. Robert told everyone who would listen about being hypnotized by Kreskin. "It was the damnedest thing," he kept saying.

Floyd Robbins came in with the social worker, Marie Becker.

"We've been to see the Amazing Kreskin," Robert said. "I got hypnotized."

Marie was impressed, but Floyd wasn't.

"Nobody could hypnotize me," he said.

"Kreskin could," Robert said.

"Not me," Floyd said. "How many people went up?"

"About twenty," Robert said. He looked at Wanda.

"About that," Wanda said.

"And all of them were hypnotized?" Floyd asked.

"Sure," Robert said.

"About two thirds," Wanda said.

"See?" Floyd said. "I'd have been one of those who wasn't." He slapped Robert on the back. "Let's face it, big fellow—you're a pretty suggestible guy."

"Oh he is not," Marie said. She grabbed Robert's arm and pressed against him. "Anyway, stop picking on him. I think it's sweet to be hypnotized."

Robert blushed and pulled his arm free and ordered a round of drinks. "Tim's an existentialist," he blurted out.

"Who's Tim?" Floyd asked.

"A man who writes to Wanda," Robert said.

"A patient," Wanda said.

"That's so exciting," Marie said.

"Not really," Wanda said. "The letters are pretty bitter."

"Oh," Marie said.

"He'll say anything," Robert said. "He's an existentialist."

"Me too," Marie said. "I'm one too."

"I don't even know what one is," Robert said.

"I thought you were a feminist," Floyd said.

"Me?" Robert said.

"Marie," Floyd said. "I thought she was a feminist."

"You can be both," Marie said. "You don't have to be one or the other."

"I don't even know what one is," Robert said.

"It means you live for the moment," Marie said. "Doesn't it, Wanda?"

"Well—" Wanda said.

"Maybe I'm one," Floyd said, "if that's all it means."

"I don't think you're intense enough," Marie said. "You not only have to live for the moment, you also have to be intense."

"I'm a lot more intense than I let on," Floyd said.

"Maybe Doreen was one," Robert said. "She was pretty tense sometimes."

"*In*tense," Marie said. "Who's Doreen?"

"A girl I used to know," Robert said. "She was always living for the moment and was kind of *in*tense." He set his drink down and went to the men's room. When he returned, he started talking football with Floyd.

"He must have been an interesting person," Marie said to Wanda.

"Who?"

"That fellow Tim. Being a professor and an existentialist."

"Not to me," Wanda said. "I had my fill of professors in graduate school. Never knowing where you stand with them or what to expect."

"I think *I* always knew," Marie said with a smile.

"You're lucky," Wanda said. "Anyway, it's true that Tim *tried* to be interesting. Then, when I wouldn't be impressed, he'd get down on himself."

"Maybe you should have pretended to be impressed."

Wanda shook her head. "It would have been too much gratification. It would have ruined the therapy."

"It was ruined anyway, wasn't it? Otherwise you wouldn't be getting those letters."

"He was the kind of person who ruined everything he touched," Wanda said. "It was his biggest problem."

* * *

In the car driving home, Robert said he hoped Wanda wasn't mad because of the way Marie had grabbed his arm and batted her eyes at him.

"That's her way," he said. "I didn't do a thing to provoke it. I like to hear her talk though. She's pretty interesting."

When they got to the apartment, he started going on about the Amazing Kreskin.

"You didn't have to go to *him* to be hypnotized," Wanda said. "I could have done it myself." She took off her coat and threw it on a chair.

"You could not," Robert said.

"Sure I could."

"Crap," Robert said. "It takes somebody like Kreskin to hypnotize *me*."

"I'll do it right now if you'll let me."

Robert looked alarmed. "Can't a guy just enjoy himself?"

"It's in my field," Wanda said. "Naturally I know about it."

"You're not going to do it to me," Robert said.

Wanda stepped out of her shoes and mussed her hair with her hands. She struck a seductive pose and gave Robert a smouldering look.

"You'd like to do it." Robert's face had become deeply flushed.

"You're the one who likes it," Wanda said. She unbuttoned the top of her blouse.

"Have me hopping around here like a chicken," Robert said. "You'd enjoy that, wouldn't you?" He stood up and went to the door. "I'm going home," he said.

"No you're not," Wanda said softly. "You're going to remain perfectly still. You're going to obey my every command." She moved slowly toward him. "Look deep into my eyes, big boy," she said in a thick foreign accent.

"No!" Robert shouted.

"I'm *kidding* you," Wanda said, but it was too late. Robert had ducked out the door and slammed it behind him.

Next day he showed up with six roses and said he was sorry for the way he'd acted. "But you still couldn't hypnotize me," he said. "I don't want you thinking you could."

"Let's forget it," Wanda said.

"You could probably hypnotize poor Tim, but you couldn't hypnotize me."

"It doesn't matter," Wanda said.

"You're just not the type," Robert said.

5

Dec 5

Dear Wanda,

I've been remembering how you could never open the door to the room where we had our sessions. You did open it, of course, but only after a lot of fumbling around with different keys. Besides that you were always late. I used to think it was funny, the trouble you had getting into that room. Now I'm unbearably depressed. You hated me, didn't you?

We have a new guest here at the Home. He looks like a cartoon hill-billy—tall and stooped and cruel of lip, walks with a shuffle, etc.—but I understand he's a high-school math teacher. Or was till the blues got him. Welcome, Loy, to the world of the disappointed.

I wish you'd write and tell me you didn't hate me. Or tell me you did. I just wish you'd write. I wish you'd come back and resume. I'd rather be with you and have you hate me than not be with you at all. You could shit in my mouth. You could kick my balls three feet up my ass and I wouldn't care. Or carve them off, if that's your pleasure. I never use them.

Your zever,
Tim

P.S. When I realized how much you detested me, I couldn't stand it. But I have, this minute, seen everything in a new light. Fact is, you must have loved me very much. Why else would you sit there and pretend, day after day, that you didn't hate me? Maybe it's time we made some plans. Maybe you ought to get yourself down here at once.

Hold on, I've had the gloomiest thought imaginable. There's yet another reason why you might have disguised your hatred for me. Maybe you wanted to stay with me in order to do me as much harm as you possibly could.

This is a question of some urgency. Please phone me immediately and let me know whether you stayed as long as you did out of love or in order to destroy me. I will not rest until I have heard from you. Then, depending on your answer, I'll either kill myself or clean my room.

P.P.S. Do you think I don't feel stupid loving you? That I don't feel stupid writing these stupid letters? That the stupidity of my whole stupid life doesn't make me want to puke? You could change all that if you would. But hell no, you won't do it. You won't do anything. I don't know which is more painful, writing the letters or burning myself, but I do know which is more degrading.

"You've sure got him wrapped around your finger," Robert said.

"He's got himself wrapped," Wanda said. "That's the way sick people are. They wrap themselves around other people's fingers."

"You said it was to be expected. You said the therapeutic situation—"

"I didn't know he'd wrap himself so tightly," Wanda said.

Robert looked at her for a moment, then shrugged. "Beats me why he'd do it. I don't understand a bit of it . . . When are you going to decide about marrying me? Mom keeps asking."

He had been talking about marriage all week, and Wanda was tired of it. "Tell her it's none of her business. She doesn't like me anyway. Why does she even care?"

"She wants what I want," Robert said. He glanced at the letter again. "*Were* you always late?"

"I can't remember," Wanda said. "Maybe I was. An intern's nothing but a flunky for a bunch of psychiatrists. When you get through doing stuff for them, you don't have time for your patients." She was surprised by the bitterness in her voice.

"I just asked," Robert said.

"I was probably late sometimes," Wanda said, "but I don't remember. I had other patients, too, you know."

"I wonder why we never hear from them."

"Maybe they weren't so stupid. He says himself how stupid he is. Maybe the others wanted to get well. Maybe they weren't hellbent on getting as bad as they possibly could. If I'd let him, he'd have dragged me right down with him."

* * *

Robert played poker at Floyd's that night, and Wanda, who had turned her spare bedroom into a study, sat at the typewriter and tried to work. Her dissertation, which at one time had excited her, had become pure drudgery—a thing to be gotten out of the way so that she could move on to her real work, which was therapy. Based on fifty-five questionnaire responses and twenty-seven personal interviews, the dissertation was about big women and their characteristic modes of coping and noncoping. It was called—Wanda was still proud of the title—*Ugly Ducklings, Cows, Earth Mothers and*

Amazons. The subtitle, which was required to be descriptive and specific, was *Patterns of Development and Neuroses in Women 5'10" and Over and Weighing More than 200 Pounds.*

Her first bad experience with the dissertation had come at the meeting of the American Psychological Association two years ago. She had assumed, naively she could now see, that the work would be of interest to the publishers' representatives who conducted the book exhibits at the meeting. Carrying an outline, the first three chapters, and ten of the questionnaires, she spent a whole day going from one booth to another, inquiring about the prospects of having the dissertation published in book form. Most of the editors gave her a quick brush-off—it was against their policy, they said, to consider unrevised dissertations, let alone unfinished ones. Others, who at least looked at the title and the outline, told her that the topic was too specialized. One editor spent a few minutes leafing through the sample chapters and then informed Wanda that the entire project was ill-conceived, poorly organized, and badly written—as if he could tell all that from such a brief inspection.

After this incident, Wanda started introducing herself as Hiram North's daughter. This gained her a certain amount of respect, and several editors expressed an interest in any future work she might do, especially if—as one editor put it—she became as proficient as her father at producing case histories that read like thrillers. One man offered to take her dissertation sight unseen if Dr. North would sign a contract with his company. When Wanda told him she had no control over her father's plans, he said for her to bugger off and stop bothering him. All things considered, it was one of the worst days of Wanda's life.

That evening she sat in a bar with some other graduate students who had also been rebuffed by the editors. They were as shocked as Wanda by the editors' lack of interest and general cynicism—by what one of the more articulate members of the group called the iron curtain of prejudice against anything new. The shock turned quickly to despair, and they all did some serious wondering about their futures and the future of psychology as a whole. After a while, when they had a few drinks under their belts, they started joking about the sheer *anality* of the publishing business, and this put everybody in a better mood.

Later, in her room, Wanda thought about the editor who had

spoken of case histories that read like thrillers. She remembered that a reviewer had once referred to one of her father's books as "a moving human document." She had always liked that phrase. She saw no way of turning the dissertation into a thriller, but she didn't see why, if she made her characters interesting enough, she couldn't produce a human document. When she returned to school, she re-wrote the first three chapters with this idea in mind. She was so pleased with the results that she continued on in the same vein. This led directly to her second bad experience with the dissertation.

Two weeks after she handed in the complete draft, her committee chairman, Dr. Campbell, called her to his office and practically threw it in her lap. "Won't do," he said gruffly. "Won't do at all."

As he spoke, he looked not at Wanda but out the window. He had always done this, but that day Wanda found the habit especially annoying. It seemed suddenly to symbolize his whole attitude to-ward her and toward life in general—his lack of interest in teaching; his often expressed desire to be out chasing butterflies instead of being cooped up in his drab little office; above all, his failure to su-pervise Wanda's dissertation in a responsible way. The freedom he had given her was not, she could now see, the trust she had taken it for. It was laziness, was what it was.

She fought back a surge of resentment, then asked what was wrong with the dissertation.

The problem, Dr. Campbell told her, was that—judging from the questionnaire responses and from Wanda's interview notes—she had stumbled on the dullest bunch of fat slobs that ever lived and had tried, sometimes with hilarious results, to make them sound in-teresting. It not only didn't work, he said, it went so far beyond the data as to be an obscenity. He produced two of Wanda's question-naires and read from them. Even allowing for his flat tone of voice, Wanda had to admit that they were dull. Then he compared what he had read with what Wanda had written. "You can't do that," he said. "You can't turn people into what you want them to be. Not in a piece of research. These fatties of yours aren't struggling with inner conflicts. They're struggling with a weight problem."

Wanda hung her head and bit her lip again.

Dr. Campbell went on to give her a lecture on academic integrity and basic research writing. Stick to the data, he kept saying. Stick to the data and drop the rich-inner-life stuff and the fancy prose and the Freudian hypothesizing. If Wanda would drop this stuff and stick to the data, she would be okay. She had done it in her thesis on rats, and she could do it with people as well.

At this point, Wanda remembered that Dr. Campbell had become increasingly behavioristic over the three years she had known him, and she realized that this accounted for some of his more extreme criticisms. She wished she had worked with someone more in tune with her own psychoanalytical orientation. But it was too late to think of changing chairmen; her best course, and certainly the easiest, was to rewrite the damned thing to Dr. Campbell's specifications.

When he finished tearing her apart, Dr. Campbell described, in loving detail, a butterfly he had seen a few days earlier. Then he talked about the ways of the common field mouse and the striped squirrel. Wanda wanted to yell at him to shut his stupid old trap, but, as always, she sat there and listened politely.

Then, as she rose to leave, Dr. Campbell told her he was sorry about the dissertation. It was because he had expected more of Wanda that he had spoken so harshly. He hadn't meant to imply, he said gently, that she had deliberately falsified her materials. What had happened was that she had lost her objectivity. When you dealt with personal issues, you tended to do that. Wanda had to remember that these women she had gathered data on had not had a famous psychiatrist for a father, and they had not gone through analysis with Sarah Pitkin. Wanda had to see them as they were and stop projecting her own good fortune onto the subjects of her inquiry . . . He wished her well at the hospital in Miami, and he looked forward to seeing the dissertation again, suitably revised.

After this speech, Wanda found it impossible to be angry at him. She thanked him and backed out of the room, clutching her manuscript to her chest.

* * *

She had intended to work on the dissertation while she was an intern, but she could never find the time. That was why she was having to rewrite it now. Unfortunately, this was not one of her good nights. She kept thinking of Robert. Maybe he was right, maybe it wasn't fair to keep him in suspense; yet she didn't feel ready to make a decision. More or less on impulse, she went to the living room and phoned her father in Chicago and told him she might get married.

Dr. North ignored this statement and said he was glad she had called, he was afraid that Eric—Wanda's brother—might be visiting her in the next few days.

"That's fine," Wanda said. "I'd love to see him."

"You *think* you would," Dr. North said. "He's traveling with a crazy man. They left here yesterday on their way to New York City."

"Who's the man?" Wanda asked. "One of his patients?" Eric, she knew, was the kind of doctor who sometimes took patients on trips with him. He had learned about such things from Sándor Ferenczi, and he did them as a way of rebelling against Dr. North's policy of strict limit setting in the therapeutic relationship. According to Dr. North, Ferenczi was a paranoid cretin who had shit on the floor of Sigmund Freud's mansion.

"Patient hell," Dr. North said. "He's a God damned doctor. Name's Smith, of all things. Well known, I understand, on the West Coast. He's—"

"Lester Smith," Wanda said.

"That's the one."

"Eric's in the big time," Wanda said, "if he's traveling with Lester Smith."

"He's a quack, if you ask me, and Eric's getting to be one too. Besides that, I think they're a couple of faggots."

"Eric?" Wanda started to question him about this, but then remembered that her father often thought people he disliked were faggots. He was one of those Freudians who managed to regard homosexuality as both a dread disease and a serious moral defect. She had seen him tackle the subject on a talk show one night. Afterward he was roundly jeered by a hip young audience. The same audience would have applauded anything Lester Smith said, even if—as seemed likely—he said that watching or attending talk shows was the most psychotic thing he had witnessed in his twenty years of practice.

"They actually think," Dr. North said, "that I might give them some money." He emitted a tight little laugh.

"What do they want the money for?"

"They want to buy an old house in Los Angeles and furnish it with a bunch of God damned schizophrenics. It's that R. D. Laing bullshit all over again, only worse. I didn't go for it the first time around and I won't go for it now. Freud said—"

He explained Freud's views on psychotics at some length. Wanda, having heard it all before, tuned him out and reviewed what she knew about Lester Smith. He was famous for his unorthodox—some would say outrageous—treatment of schizophrenics and anorectics, and he had written some influential books. Although his reputation had declined in recent years, he remained a cult hero for younger members of the therapy professions. He was just the kind of man that Eric would latch onto.

"Freud wouldn't fool with them," Dr. North concluded, "and by God *I* won't fool with them . . . What's this about you getting married?"

Now that he had returned to the subject, Wanda wasn't sure what to say.

"What does he do?" Dr. North asked.

"He's a businessman," Wanda said.

"That's good," Dr. North said. "Some of my best patients have been businessmen."

Wanda knew what kind of businessman her father had in mind—some highpowered executive—and how far short of this standard Robert fell.

"He owns a small electronics plant," she said.

"How small?"

"Nineteen people."

Dr. North gave his tight little laugh. "Why don't you finish that degree—you've come this far, you might as well finish it—and then let me send you on a world cruise?" He had been wanting to send Wanda on a cruise since the day Sarah left. If he had had his way, Wanda would have been on a cruise for the last eight years instead of going to college.

"And forget about Robert?" she said.

"He sounds pretty forgettable," Dr. North said.

Wanda had a sudden picture of her father sitting there at the other end of the line. He looked like an older version of Floyd Robbins. They had the same little mustache and the same smug expression, and they talked in the same know-it-all way.

"I haven't decided yet about marrying him," she said. "I like him though, and I like Windward."

"I was there once," Dr. North said. "I gave a lecture at the university. It's the pits, if you ask me."

"I like it."

"That's a rationalization if I ever heard one."

"It is not."

"Now it's denial," Dr. North said. "Your defenses are pathetically obvious. How did you end up in a place like that? Are you there for the convenience of Mr. Computer Parts?"

"I have a job. I'll be working at the mental health clinic. I'll be doing therapy."

"I wish you'd give that up too," Dr. North said.

"I don't know why I have to keep taking the blame for Sarah," Wanda said.

"I will not discuss Sarah Pitkin. But let's not fight. I hate it when we fight."

"I'm not fighting."

"You're such a good girl when you want to be."

"I'm not a girl."

"You'll always be a girl to me," Dr. North said softly. "You'll always be my little Wanda . . . You do these things to spite me."

"What things?"

"Marrying a salesman. Living in Windward. Becoming a therapist."

"You're bitter because of Sarah. She's the reason you don't want me to be a therapist." Wanda wished she had not made the call. She might have known it would turn out like this.

"I saw her on the street the other day," Dr. North said. "She's still with her nigger—"

"I don't like that word," Wanda said.

"She's still with her nigger and still talking about her soul every minute. The soul's the bottom line with Sarah Pitkin."

Wanda could sympathize with her father about the soul business. When she gave up psychoanalysis and started running around with jazz musicians, Sarah became a real pest about the soul.

"Your salesman's not a nigger, is he?" Dr. North asked.

"Please."

"There are a lot of niggers going into sales these days."

"I won't listen to you talk this way. It's degrading."

"That clinic of yours will be crawling with niggers," Dr. North said. "They think it's the thing to do, is have their head examined."

Wanda had not thought about it, but she supposed she would indeed have to do therapy with black people. She had to admit that the prospect was not a pleasant one. She had worked briefly with a young black woman named C. C. at the hospital. Realizing that the girl was not verbal enough for anything very deep, Wanda had adopted a supportive, client-centered stance—just being herself, creating an atmosphere of unconditional acceptance, doing a lot of reflective listening and repeating back. Each session began with C. C. spewing forth her contempt for every motherfucking honky bastard who ever lived. She would go on for ten or fifteen minutes, speaking so fast that Wanda could not get in a word. Then she would fall into a defiant silence. Wanda would smile warmly and say something like "My goodness, aren't we hostile today?" or "The world seems like a very cruel place to you right now, doesn't it?" C. C. would assume the pose of a spoiled, bored little girl, putting her feet on the chair and her thumb in her mouth. Wanda would begin to paraphrase C. C.'s speech: "I hear you saying that you're the victim of inexorable fate . . . I hear you saying that people are out to get you . . . I hear you saying that you're in considerable pain . . ." After a couple of minutes of this, C. C. would jump up and run back to the ward and spend the rest of the day crying in her room. This went on for a couple of weeks, and Wanda despaired of ever reaching the girl.

Then one morning a nurse who didn't like Wanda greeted her by saying, "Well, well, if it's not Smiley Burnett." The other nurses laughed. "That's what C. C. calls you," the nurse explained.

The next day, after C. C. had delivered her customary diatribe, Wanda leaned forward and put her hand gently on the girl's knee. She hoped to establish a feeling of intimacy between them. "Nurse French tells me you have a nickname for me," she said. "I think it's an amusing name, and I was wondering if maybe you could share your feelings about it with me. That way I could get to know you better. We might even become friends." She squeezed C. C.'s knee. "So tell me, C. C.—why do you call me Smiley Burnett?"

C. C., who had been shrinking back in her chair with her thumb in her mouth, suddenly sprang to her feet. "I'll tell you why I do it," she screeched. "I do it because that's what my daddy calls fat honky grinners." She stepped forward and gave Wanda a stinging slap across the face and then spat in her eye. Then she marched out of the hospital and was not heard from again. A week later Wanda was assigned to Tim Jinks. After their first interview, she went to the women's room and wept for joy. With his civilized manner and his capacity for deep insight, he seemed—compared at least to a C. C. Barnes—like the answer to a young therapist's prayers.

"Are you still there?" Dr. North asked.

"Yes," Wanda said. "I was thinking about a case I had in Miami."

"What kind of case?"

Not wishing to get back on the subject of black people, Wanda told him about Tim. Thinking her father might be impressed, she bragged about the strength of the transference that had developed. "Freud was right. I still get letters from the guy. It's a funny thing—"

"Letters of gratitude?" Dr. North asked.

"Not exactly of gratitude." Wanda described the letters to her father. She wanted to hear him say they went with the territory.

"Why do you say it's funny?" Dr. North asked. "There's nothing funny about it."

"I didn't mean ha-ha funny. I meant strange."

"It isn't strange either. Haven't you ever heard of a transference neurosis? No wonder you're getting the letters . . . Poor devil."

Wanda smiled at the way he said the last two words. A couple of months ago, she and Robert had watched an old horror movie on television. The movie was set in Haiti. At one point, the hero, a muscular young anthropologist, discovered the body of a colleague who had died as a result of a Voodoo curse. "Poor devil," the hero said. His tone was very much like the one Dr. North had just used.

"This wasn't psychoanalysis," Wanda said. "It was face-to-face therapy. Transferences aren't as important as in psychoanalysis."

"But if you *get* one," Dr. North said, "you've got to work through it. Don't they teach you people *anything?*"

"I was a God damned intern!" Wanda shouted. "I *couldn't* work through it."

"Ask yourself," Dr. North said quietly, "the meaning of that outburst."

Wanda fought off an impulse to show him what a *real* outburst would sound like. "I'd better hang up," she said.

"To let a transference develop in a situation like that," Dr. North said, "was some kind of countertransference."

"It was not."

"Ask yourself why you want to deny something so obvious."

"I won't ask myself anything."

"I don't know why you want to be a therapist in the first place," Dr. North said. "Why don't you go into sex education? That's a nice field. Or psychic phenomena. Why don't you explore psychic phenomena? There's a ton of money in psychic phenomena."

"You're as bad as Floyd," Wanda said.

"Freud? He didn't write much on the subject, but he was interested."

"Not Freud. *Floyd*. He's this guy I know."

"Your nigger salesman? That's a nigger name if I ever heard one."

"I'm going to hang up."

"Don't go away mad. I can't bear for you to go away mad."

"I'm sorry," Wanda said.

"That's my girl," Dr. North said.

"Listen," Wanda said, "if I promise not to get married—"

"Yes?"

"Will you help me get into one of the institutes?"

"You know my feeling about women in psychoanalysis," Dr. North said. "I won't bargain with you about psychoanalysis."

"I could go through my training," Wanda said, "and then we could work together. We could both have offices in the house. I could be like Sarah."

"I told you," Dr. North said, "I will not discuss Sarah Pitkin."

Wanda knew the conversation was over, and she didn't bother to reply. She could only hope that she could someday change his mind.

"I'm going to hang up now," Dr. North said, "but before I do, I want you to promise me one thing. When your brother and that man get there, you tell them my answer on the money is a firm no."

* * *

Wanda had no sooner put down the receiver than the phone rang. It was Floyd. "Robert's in pretty bad shape," he said.

"What do you mean? Drunk?"

57

"He's had a few," Floyd said, "but that's not the problem. He's been trying to call you for thirty minutes and the line's been busy. He's got it in his head that you've been talking to some guy who wants to shit in your mouth."

There was a loud burst of laughter in the background, then Robert yelled, "Knock it off, you guys." Wanda supposed he was talking to his poker buddies.

"It's the other way around," she said.

"What is?"

"He wants me to do it in *his* mouth."

"Whichever way it is," Floyd said, "it's pretty funny." There was another burst of laughter, and then Floyd said: "I'm going to let Robert go in the bedroom and talk on the extension. Okay? Marie's in there, but it won't bother her."

Presently Robert came on the line. Wanda didn't hear a click, and she guessed Floyd was listening in.

"I was talking to Daddy," she told Robert.

"You sure?" Robert sounded as if he was about to cry.

"Of course I'm sure."

"You're going to ditch me," Robert said. "I can feel it . . . Here's Marie. She wants to say hi."

"Wanda?" Marie said. "Robert's in bad shape. He thinks you're going to say no and go off to Arkansas."

"He does not. Does he want me to come and get him?"

There was a pause while Marie conferred with Robert. Then Marie said, "He doesn't want you to see him like this. Poor guy."

"He's in pretty bad shape," Floyd said.

"I'm trying to comfort him," Marie said. "Don't you worry about a thing."

It was another fifteen minutes before Wanda could gracefully hang up. She was pouring herself a drink of Scotch when she realized that she was excited about seeing Eric and his Dr. Smith. Although she had not read Smith's books, she was intrigued by his reputation. More than that, she was tired of Marie and Floyd, and she guessed she was tired of Robert as well. It would be nice to see some people she could talk to. Whatever she did, she must not let Robert's needs force her into a hasty marriage.

6

Dec 12

Wanda—

I hate to be the one to bring bad news, but Bill hanged himself last Thursday. He didn't come down for breakfast, but nobody thought much about it—missing meals is pretty common around here. When he didn't show up for lunch, Doc Bonds went to his room to check on him. The doc was back in less than a minute, his face pale and sweaty, his hands trembling more than usual. "You boys help me," he said. "Bill's killed himself." Millie moaned and would have fallen from her chair if Mrs. Bonds hadn't caught her.

Bill had done the job with a piece of clothesline rope, attached to a pipe on the ceiling. His suit, a tie, and a fresh white shirt lay neatly on the bed. Perhaps he had planned to wear them and then changed his mind. At any rate, he was dressed in jeans and a tee shirt. The fingers of his left hand were trapped between the rope and his neck, as if he'd decided, too late, to try to save himself. His bare feet were no more than three inches from the floor. I won't try to describe his face. Jack and I held the body, which was still warm, and Loy cut the rope. We put the body on the bed and looked at the note pinned to the tee shirt. Bill had first written "No one to blame but myself." Then he had crossed this out

59

and scribbled a second message: "Wife and kids completely responsible. Also father for not teaching me to say what I mean. Also the food in this awful place." He had crossed out this message as well, but he had still pinned the paper to his shirt. I've never known what kind of message to leave either.

Loy is a hunter. I saw him early this morning, shotgun in hand, tromping off to the woods behind the house. I run in those woods several times a week. Let's hope he doesn't mistake me for a deer. Have I mentioned his cruel mouth?

Speaking of cruelty, why did you manipulate the transference and set me up so high? Knowing the trouble I had already had with women, and knowing how vulnerable I was, you could surely see what the effects of your leaving would be. It's as though you were out to really teach him a lesson this time. And I'm supposed to sit back and take that shit? Talk it out with another shrink? I trust shrinks about as much now as I trust women. I still trust you though, Wanda—I trust you either to make it all up to me or to pay the price. I could tear your wings off without batting an eye, you despicable, infinitely corrupted sow.

Is it possible you hated me only because you believed I didn't love you enough? Perish that thought. I love you a lot more than enough.

Sincerely,
Tim

"That guy Tim is madder than hell," Robert said. "I'm afraid he might sue Wanda."

"No he won't," Wanda said.

"Maybe I ought to look at the letter," Floyd said.

"Maybe you ought to," Marie said.

"There's no need for that," Wanda said.

It was Saturday afternoon, and they were drinking beer at Denny's. The men were watching a football game.

"One of his friends killed himself," Wanda told Marie, "and he's feeling disillusioned with therapists. He says he's going to tear my wings off."

"For heaven's sake," Marie said. "Does he still love you?"

"I keep telling you, it's not *me* he loves. He's transferring feelings from his past, from his childhood."

"According to an article I read," Marie said, "all love is that way. Girls go for the same type as their father. Either that or the opposite type."

"He doesn't even know me. All I did was sit there and let him talk."

"There's a quotation in the article about that," Marie said. "Something about when a man starts telling a woman everything, you know he's in love. A Frenchman said it."

Wanda sipped her beer. Because of the calories, she was drinking slowly. The beer was so hot and flat that she almost gagged. She wondered why she was bothering to explain anything to an ass like Marie. Anyone who would go out with Floyd Robbins couldn't be very bright.

"And you just sat there?" Marie asked.

Wanda nodded.

"You know what you were doing, don't you? You were playing hard to get."

A sharp pain shot through Wanda's head. "Let's talk about it some other time. It's pretty complicated."

"Oh it is not," Marie said. "It's when a guy doesn't know what he's getting that he falls the hardest. Maurice Chevalier said—this was in the article too, let me see if I can get it right . . . something about men falling in love with women in a light so dim they wouldn't buy a suit in it."

"I suppose he's an authority," Wanda said coldly.

"Are you kidding? That guy—"

"Never mind." Wanda motioned to the bartender to bring her another beer. She turned again to Marie. "Look at it this way— what Tim saw in me wasn't the *real* me."

"It's always that way," Marie said. "The article says that poets have known that for centuries. 'If Jack's in love, he's no judge of Jill's beauty.' That's an exact quote."

"Who said it?"

"Benjamin Franklin."

"Maybe we can discuss this later," Wanda said, "when we're not both drinking."

"Beauty is always in the eye of the beholder," Marie said.

"Please."

"Love is blind," Marie said.

"And stupid too," Wanda said. "That's the trouble with men like Tim. All they ever think about is love. Or what they *call* love. No wonder they're so screwed up."

"I think about it too," Marie said.

"I don't," Wanda said. "I *never* think about it."

"You don't have to bite my head off," Marie said.

"I don't want this damned beer either," Wanda said. "Beer makes me fat. I want some Perrier."

When the football game ended, Floyd said Robert would never guess who he'd seen in Albany a couple of days ago.

"Who?"

"Doreen Dalton."

Robert blushed and said so what.

"You know about Doreen, don't you?" Floyd asked Wanda.

"Oh sure," Wanda said.

"I don't," Marie said. "Robert mentioned her the other night."

"Before Wanda," Floyd said, "Doreen was Robert's big heart-throb. Everybody thought they'd get married for sure." He glanced at Wanda and poked Robert in the ribs. "I bet now you're glad you waited, eh big fellow?"

Robert put an arm over Wanda's shoulders and said, "If she'll ever say yes."

"Let's not start that again," Wanda said, and Robert removed his arm.

"Wanda's in a bad mood today," Marie said. "She's a real bitch."

"It's a headache," Wanda said.

"Doreen's married," Floyd said. "She looks like death warmed over."

"She can *be* dead," Robert said, "far as I'm concerned."

"She asked about you," Floyd said. "I told her about Wanda and she became alarmed."

"Still carrying a torch," Marie said.

Floyd shrugged. "She said she wanted to talk to Wanda before it was too late. I told her no, of course."

"Before *what* was too late?" Marie asked.

"Beats me," Floyd said.

"She was being crazy," Robert said angrily. "She's always been crazy and always will be."

* * *

Three nights later, Wanda was playing cutthroat rummy with Robert and Floyd when her brother showed up. Although Eric's features were a masculine version of her own, she almost didn't recognize him. The last time she had seen him, a couple of years ago, he was heavier than she was; now, as she embraced him, she could feel his ribs under the unseasonably light jacket he was wearing. The beginnings of a beard scraped her face.

"I've about quit eating," he said, "but I never felt better."

"You're a skeleton," Wanda said. She looked over his shoulder and saw the man she guessed he was trying to look like.

"You're Dr. Smith," she said, putting out her hand.

"Lester," the man said. Like Eric, he was dressed in sneakers, jeans, and a checked flannel shirt.

He shook Wanda's hand with no particular warmth. His eyes, a startling blue in color, flickered briefly and then lost interest. Wanda, who had been thinking about him all week, hung on to his hand and stared at him. This was the man who had dangled anorectic girls out of a helicopter by their ankles, holding them there until they ate large quantities of trail mix. This was the man who had shaped a group of waxy flexibles into the words "FUCK YOU DAD" and photographed them. A poster version had become popular during the Vietnam war. Later, in a celebrated attempt "to cure just one schizophrenic," Lester had moved in with a large middle-class family in London for an entire year. His designated patient was the oldest son in the family. At the end of this experiment in "nude marathon live-in group interactional analysis," he pronounced his patient worse, the family unchanged, and himself completely cured. He then vanished into the heart of Africa. From there he had issued no statements, but occasionally, in a magazine, you would come across a picture of a ravaged white man surrounded by starving black babies. This was that same man, and Wanda could not help feeling overwhelmed.

If anything, he was more ravaged now than he was then. His straight brown hair and his short, snow-white beard looked as if they had been hacked at with garden shears. His long forehead was lined and scarred. His clothes hung on him. One of Wanda's teachers had said in a lecture that Lester had burned himself out and was lost in the "therapeutic despair." Looking into his dead blue eyes, she had no doubt that this was true.

She pulled her hand free and gave it to a third man, who turned out to be Burt Epperson, the psychiatrist who had hired her to work at the clinic. He was wearing a suit and an overcoat, and he looked apologetic.

"I hope I'm not a bother," he said.

"Oh no," Wanda said.

"I went to school with this guy"—he slapped Lester on the back—"and he insisted on dragging me over here. I hope that's okay."

"Of course," Wanda said.

She introduced the doctors to Robert and Floyd, then went to the kitchen to make drinks. When she returned, the doctors had formed a triangle on the floor. Robert and Floyd were sitting on the sofa. Although she wanted to be with the doctors, she decided she ought to stay by Robert, who was obviously uncomfortable. She and Eric managed to get in a few words with each other, but gradually Eric paid more and more attention to Lester and Dr. Epperson, and Wanda was shut out entirely.

Lester, who did most of the talking, spoke in such a low voice that she could hear almost nothing of what he said. He seemed to be talking about somebody's "whang," but she couldn't be sure. She gathered, though, that he was explaining his work in California to Dr. Epperson, who listened with a bemused expression. Wanda had the feeling that he liked Lester but didn't approve of a thing he said. For his part, Lester didn't seem to care what Burt might think. He seldom stopped talking except to laugh or to light a cigarette. After a while, he began to give Wanda an occasional glance. She wished he would speak a little louder.

Floyd, who was sitting closer to Lester than Wanda was, leaned far forward and hung on every word. Now and then he turned to Wanda and Robert and said, "Did you hear *that?*" or "God, this is deep."

Robert sat stiffly upright and looked straight ahead. After about an hour, he whispered to Wanda that he wanted to talk to her. As she followed him to the bedroom, she had the idea that Lester was watching her.

"You're miserable," she said to Robert.

"Those guys give me the creeps. They're not like the doctors I met in Miami."

"Burt is."

"Yeah, but those other two . . . I don't care if he is your brother."

"You're tired," Wanda said. "Why don't you go home? If I know Eric, they'll talk half the night. I'll probably go on to bed myself."

"Well—" Robert said.

Wanda helped him into his coat and walked him down to his car and kissed him. She knew she was being brusque, but she might not have another chance to talk with Lester Smith.

She hoped Floyd would leave too, but he didn't. When she returned to the apartment, he had joined the doctors on the floor and was telling them about *You Be You, I'll Be Me.* Wanda sat down between Lester and Eric. Burt was looking at Floyd with a patronizing smile, but Lester seemed genuinely interested in what he was saying.

"It strikes me," he said when Floyd finished, "that no self-respecting normal psychotic American ought to be without that book."

Floyd took this as praise. "I told you," he said to Wanda, "These guys are sharp."

Wanda laughed. Lester touched her chin with his fingers and looked her square in the face.

"My God," he said, "it's really you."

"Who?" Wanda said.

"Dorothy Denmother," Lester said.

Eric laughed and Burt gave a small tolerant chuckle. Floyd looked puzzled.

"Why do you call her that?" he asked.

"She's a psychologist, isn't she?" Lester said. He was still looking at Wanda and shaking his head.

"Well yeah—" Floyd said.

"He's kidding me," Wanda said. She didn't know what Lester was getting at, but she was not surprised by his hostility. It was well known that psychiatrists, with their sense of superiority to the non-medical people in the field, resented the growing prestige of clinical psychologists. She had hoped that Lester would be above such pettiness, but apparently he wasn't. She smiled at him to show that she understood his hostility and could be a good sport about it.

"I'm not exactly kidding," Lester said.

"Maybe you should ask yourself why you feel that way," Wanda said in a bantering tone.

"When I see a psychologist," Lester said, "I think of textbooks with pastel covers. The covers have drawings on them. The outline of a head maybe, with little gears and wheels representing the parts of the mind. Below that a diagram illustrating the dynamics of group relations. Over to the left, we have a series of faces: grandpa, grandma, mom and pop, a couple of teenagers—right on down the line to the cutest little baby you ever saw in your God damned life. The pictures represent human development, the continuity of the generations, the holiness of the family unit, the entire psychotic bullshit. Right in the center of the cover, larger than the other pictures, is a drawing of two dedicated psychology students, a boy and a girl for Christ's sake, earnestly surveying the horizon of a better future. The content of the book is at one with the cover—the whole thing a collage of bourgeois ideology parading itself as scientific humanism. I hate psychology."

Wanda guessed he was going to be as bad as C. C. Barnes, but at least he was a better speaker. Like her father, he had a way with words. Although she was blushing, she continued to smile.

"I read other things too," she said. "I've read most of Daddy's books."

"Oh God," Eric said.

"What do you know about them?" Wanda said. Her anger blazed up from deep within her. "You probably haven't even read them."

"I don't have to read them," Eric said. "I know the piece of shit that wrote them."

"I pity you when you talk like that," Wanda said. "Besides," she added spitefully, "when you sneer you look exactly like him."

"I do not," Eric said. "Fucking bitch."

"Now you *sound* just like him," Wanda said.

They glared at each other. Wanda remembered that Eric had once thrown a dish of potato salad through a plate-glass window. This happened at a restaurant in Chicago, after he had quarreled bitterly with his father about Sándor Ferenczi. He looked as angry now as he had then, but Wanda was determined not to back down.

"Sibling rivalry," Floyd said to Lester. "Right?"

"You got it," Lester said. "You should have been one of us."

Floyd beamed and said, "Thanks. That's what Wanda's always saying."

Burt snickered.

Wanda glared at all of them. She wished Marie was here. Marie could keep these other guys occupied while Wanda concentrated on Lester Smith.

"When I see a psychologist," Lester said, "I think of school nurses, county health officers, scoutmasters, and unitarian ministers. I think of sex educators. I think of alcohol counselors. I think of experts on the Donovan show. Sometimes—" He looked at Wanda and his smile became shy and warm. "Sometimes," he said, "I think of den mothers."

"Thanks a lot," Wanda said.

"It was meant as a compliment," Lester said softly.

"What's wrong with school nurses?" Floyd asked. "I liked my school nurse."

"So did I," Wanda said. She gave Lester a defiant look.

"I liked my scoutmaster," Burt said.

"I hated all of them," Lester said. "All but Dorothy Benson. She was my den mother. I sure didn't hate Mrs. Benson."

"My school nurse was pretty hot stuff," Floyd said.

"I hate psychologists," Lester said savagely, "almost as much as I hate psychiatrists and rich psychoanalysts."

Wanda guessed this was a reference to her father. She had hoped to have a good talk with Lester, maybe even to learn something from him. She had hoped to be impressed by him and to impress him in turn. But she guessed it wasn't possible. She might have known he'd be on Eric's side. Or maybe he was one of those people who hated everything. Or maybe this wasn't the real Lester Smith she was hearing; maybe it was the therapeutic despair that was talking.

"I'm going to bed," she said. She couldn't keep the disappointment out of her voice.

"Mrs. Benson had that same frown," Lester said.

Wanda, knowing he was laughing at her, looked at the floor.

"I didn't even notice it at first," Lester said.

"What?" Floyd asked.

"The resemblance," Lester said. "I walk around in such a daze sometimes. I didn't notice it till she sat down on the couch. Something about the way she moved . . . I should have known she'd come back as a psychologist." He glanced at Floyd. "And I should have known she'd be as unavailable as ever." He sighed heavily and leaned back against the wall.

There was a pause and then Burt said to Floyd: "He's as full of crap as he ever was. Don't pay him any mind." He looked at his watch, drained his glass, and announced he was leaving.

"It's only ten o'clock," Eric said. "Wanda's going to break out some dope here in a minute." He gave Wanda a look that was almost friendly.

"I don't have any dope," Wanda said irritably. She didn't want Dr. Epperson to think she was the kind of psychologist who experimented with drugs. She remembered that Lester had once had a reputation for taking hallucinogens.

Burt looked at his watch again and stood up. "I'm not on vacation," he said, "like the rest of you fellows. Besides, Jane's expecting me."

"You still with *her?*" Lester asked.

Burt nodded and slipped into his coat. Wanda let him out and went to the kitchen and got the Scotch bottle and a bowl of ice. She turned off most of the lights to make the room cozier. She had decided to give Lester one more chance. If he persisted in making fun of her, she would go to bed. When she sat back down, he was saying what an asshole Burt was.

"I've known him for twenty-five years," he said. "He's always been an asshole."

"A lot of those university people are assholes," Floyd said.

"I didn't know he was connected with the university," Wanda said.

"He's the head shrink," Floyd said. "He's also on the city council. He's got a finger in everything. I see him at the Country Club all the time. I've always said he's an asshole."

"I like him though," Lester said.

"I didn't mean I didn't like him," Floyd said.

Lester put his head against the wall and took a long drag from his cigarette. His eyes, Wanda noticed, were fading out again. At least he had stopped talking about den mothers.

"Lester even likes Dad," Eric said.

"I like him a lot," Lester said, blowing out smoke. "Hell, I like everybody."

He was about fifty, Wanda decided. Looking at him now, you wouldn't know that he was famous for his slam-bang, highly physical methods. He didn't look as if he could hold his own with one of his anorectic girls, let alone with some stocky schizophrenic. But he still had a presence. His eyes, even when dead, were the kind you could jump right into. She picked up the bottle and freshened everybody's drink.

"Where's that dope you were going to break out?" Eric asked.

"I don't have any," Wanda said.

"Shit," Eric said. "I thought you said that for Epperson's benefit."

"You want some dope?" Floyd said. "I can get some, but it might take awhile."

"Get it," Lester said. He waved toward the door as if shooing a fly.

"Sure," Floyd said. He put his coat on and left the apartment.

"What an asshole," Lester said.

"I know," Wanda said.

"You like him though," Lester said.

"I can't stand him," Wanda said.

For some reason this struck Lester as funny. His eyes sparkled and he gave a rich loud laugh. "She doesn't like him," he said.

"She can't stand him," Eric said.

They laughed so hard that Wanda couldn't help joining in.

Lester leaned forward and said to Eric: "Did you see Burt's face when I was telling him about Jesse?"

"Oh God," Eric said.

"I didn't hear the story," Wanda said. "Who's Jesse?"

The men laughed again.

"Jesse's the most famous schizophrenic on the West Coast," Lester said.

"For being unreachable," Eric said, "and for having a hard-on."

Wanda laughed.

"I had him for two months," Lester said, "with no success at all. He just sat there, with that awful dead face and that God damned hard-on. Then, a couple of weeks ago—out of frustration more than anything else—I reached over and unzipped his pants and hauled out his whang and squeezed it."

"That's all he did," Eric said.

"I just held it and squeezed it," Lester said.

"God," Wanda said.

"His face came to life," Lester said.

"Tell her the rest," Eric said.

"He spoke," Lester said. "He actually said something."

"God," Wanda said. She had a little more Scotch.

"When Lester told the story to Burt," Eric said, "do you know what Burt said?"

Wanda shook her head.

Lester mimicked Burt's prissy voice: "It sounds to me as if you acted out a countertransference fantasy."

"That's exactly what he said," Eric said.

The two men almost fell over laughing.

"That's good," Wanda said. "Daddy would have said the same thing."

"He did say the same thing," Eric said.

"You *told* him?" Wanda said.

"You should have seen his face," Eric said.

"All I care about is reaching Jesse," Lester said. "That's all that counts in that kind of case." He put his head against the wall and shut his eyes.

The story was over, Wanda realized, and he was about to fade away again.

"I had a funny case when I was interning last summer," she said. She poured herself some more Scotch. "This guy begged me to shit in his mouth."

"You're kidding," Eric said.

"Luckily that wasn't his main thing," Wanda said. "Mostly he was like Jesse. Very withdrawn."

"Schizophrenic?" Lester asked.

"No," Wanda said. "Psychotic depression."

"Melancholia," Lester said. The word rolled off his tongue in a way that made Wanda shiver.

"He was a middle-aged intellectual," Wanda said. "Polarized, sick of life. Besides the depression, I had him down as a DSM-III, 301.4."

Lester looked at her in amazement. "What the hell is that?"

"Compulsive personality," Wanda said. She was amused that he didn't know his *Diagnostic and Statistical Manual* as well as she did.

"Shit," Eric said. "Everybody that ever did anything is a compulsive personality."

"Besides that," Wanda said, "he had a passive-aggressive streak a mile wide. Sometimes he was suspicious and aloof. The psyche tests showed strong schizoid tendencies. Sometimes—"

"A lot of intellectuals are schizoid," Lester said.

Wanda felt rewarded. "I thought so," she said. "He also liked to burn himself with cigarettes."

"Borderline syndrome," Lester said.

"That's what I thought," Wanda said. Borderline was a popular category those days, and Lester had helped to invent it. His book on early mothering and object relations was widely referred to in the literature. "They didn't encourage that diagnosis at the hospital," Wanda said, "or I'd have used it." She reached over to the bookcase and took out the DSM-III and opened it to the section on the borderline disorder.

"Read to us," Lester said. He looked intently at Wanda.

"Well," she said, "let's see . . . 'Instability in a variety of areas . . . impulsive and unpredictable behavior that is potentially physically

71

self-damaging . . . inappropriate, intense anger . . . lack of control . . . profound identity disturbance . . . chronic feelings of emptiness or boredom' . . . That's Tim all right," she said.

"Read some more," Lester said.

"'Frequently this disorder is accompanied by many features of other Personality Disorders such as Schizotypal, Histrionic, Narcissistic, and Antisocial Personality Disorders . . . social contrariness and a generally pessimistic outlook.' That's Tim to a T," Wanda said. "I hadn't realized how bad off he was. He was a mess." She remembered an article she had read about how, in therapy, borderline patients alternated between clinging love and absolute rage. Tim's letters were perfect examples of this. She closed the book and put it aside.

"Is that all you're going to read?" Lester asked.

"It's all I need to. He was definitely borderline."

"Just as well," Lester said gloomily. "It drives me up the wall."

"What does?"

"The way you read. Mrs. Benson used to read like that. She used to read from the Cub Scout Manual. She used to read about clean and manly. It used to drive me right up the wall."

"God damn you," Wanda said. "I thought you were interested."

"I am," Lester said.

"I don't want to hear any more about Mrs. Benson," Wanda said. "If you talk about Mrs. Benson, I'll go to bed."

"Tell us some more about your patient," Lester said.

"You'll just laugh."

"I won't."

"Promise?"

Lester nodded solemnly. "Scout's honor," he said. He held up his hand in what Wanda guessed was the cub scout salute.

"You son of a bitch," she said. She threw a piece of ice at him and they both laughed.

"Where's the damned dope?" Eric said.

"It'll be here," Wanda said.

"I'm serious," Lester said. "I want to hear about your patient."

"I worked with him for five months," Wanda said.

"This is the guy that wanted you to shit in his mouth?" Eric said.

Wanda nodded. "Fortunately I didn't have to do that or hold his whang either. What I did was deliberately play the seductress."

72

Lester looked at her with respect.

"I put on a real floor show for him," Wanda said, "just to reach him and keep him alive." If being controversial was the order of the day, she guessed she could do it as well as anybody else.

"He was suicidal?" Eric asked.

"Very," Wanda said.

"You could have lost him," Lester said.

"I didn't though," Wanda said. "I played the seductress and kept him alive."

"You won't know what it's all about," Eric said, "till you've lost one."

"God," Wanda said.

"I lost one my first year," Eric said.

"I didn't know that," Wanda said. "I'm sorry."

"Lester's lost seven," Eric said.

"Seven?" Wanda said.

"I've been at this a long time," Lester said. He gave her a wan smile. "Anyway, maybe they were just being authentic. That's the main thing." The smile took on a sly quality. "Wouldn't you say?"

"I don't know," Wanda said. She wished she could tell when he was kidding and when he wasn't. If he could joke about suicide, she guessed he was indeed in the therapeutic despair.

"Mine took pills," Eric said.

"I had two take pills," Lester said. "Another one swallowed Drano. Another one used carbon monoxide. Another one jumped from the eighth floor. Another one ripped his veins out with a pair of surgical scissors. Another one hanged himself. Another one—"

Wanda's temples throbbed. Her head filled with an image of Bill hanging from the ceiling with his feet three inches off the floor. Tim was in the shower, carving messages on his arm. Everything turned red.

"—burned himself to death," Lester went on. "It was during the Vietnam War. I was standing right there when he did it. It was a protest. I never knew whether to count that one or not."

"I think I'd count it," Eric said.

"You all right?" Lester asked Wanda. He put his hand on her knee.

"I'm a little dizzy," Wanda said. Bill's body swayed and turned.

"What happened to yours?" Eric asked.

"My what?"

"Your patient, stupid. What happened to him?"

"I cured him," Wanda said. "He got completely well."

"You're going to sit there and tell me," Eric said, "that you cured this psychotically depressed middle-fucking-aged borderline in five months? Jesus Christ."

"Maybe I shouldn't have said cured," Wanda said. "Cured was too strong. But I got him through his crisis. I gained his trust. You've got to do that with borderlines." She said this in a superior tone, as if she were instructing Eric on a matter of technique.

"You've got to gain their trust," she went on, "and that's what I did. About a month before I left the hospital, he came out of his shell and had an affair with a dietician. Two weeks later he checked out of the hospital and returned to work."

"A hospital dietician?" Lester said. "I thought they smelled like tuna fish."

"She was a part-time model," Wanda said.

"Do you think it'll last?" Eric said.

"They already broke up," Wanda said. "It was a temporary thing."

"I mean his improvement," Eric said. "Do you think he'll continue to improve?"

"Oh sure," Wanda said. "I'm treating him now by mail. He keeps me posted on everthing he does. I got a letter from him a few days ago. He feels fine and says he can never repay me. I'm going to keep in touch with him as long as it's necessary. You've got to do that with borderlines. You've got to stay available." She was pretty sure she had read this somewhere. In any case, she thought it would sound good to Lester, and apparently it did. He continued to regard her with what appeared to be respect.

"He'll probably kill himself yet," Eric said.

"Maybe not," Lester said. "Maybe she's handling it exactly right."

"Thank you," Wanda said. She poured them all a fresh drink and noticed that her hand was trembling.

Lester lit a cigarette and began a meandering, half-humorous discussion of psychological theory. Every other word seemed to be either "phenomenological" or "existential," and he said several times that schizophrenia was the only strictly authentic response to the terrors of life. Except, of course, for suicide, which was even more authentic. Wanda couldn't follow all of what he said, or even tell how much of it he meant, but she thought it was fascinating. She was irritated when Floyd pounded on the door and yelled to let him in.

"There's your boyfriend," Lester said.

"Thank God," Eric said.

"*He's* not my boyfriend," Wanda said. She stood up and realized she was drunk.

"I thought he was," Lester said. "That's why I laughed when you said you couldn't stand him."

"The other one was my boyfriend," Wanda said.

"The one that left?"

"That's right. Robert."

Lester smiled. "Robert's an asshole," he said.

"But you like him," Wanda said.

"I'm crazy about him," Lester said, "now that he's gone."

Floyd knocked again and Wanda went over and let him in.

"Got some grass," he said. He tossed a plastic bag to Eric.

"No coke?" Eric asked.

"No," Floyd said. He produced another plastic bag. "Poppy seeds," he said.

"Poppy seeds," Eric said. "I've never had fucking poppy seeds."

He rolled a joint, lit it, and offered it to Wanda. She declined and he gave it to Lester. Wanda had some more Scotch. Before long they were all talking at once and laughing at everything that was said. After a while Floyd and Eric began to prepare the poppy seeds.

"Come work with us," Lester said to Wanda.

"You've kidded me enough already," Wanda said.

"He's serious," Eric said in a disgusted voice.

"I already have a job," Wanda said.

"I heard about that," Lester said. "I guess it's your business if you want to work for an asshole like Burt."

"Also," Wanda said, "I might get married."

Eric looked at Lester and smiled.

"It figures," Lester said morosely. "Unavailable as ever . . . Well, if you change your mind . . ."

"Sure," Wanda said. The idea of working with someone so eminent was definitely appealing. On the other hand, she had little interest in doing therapy with schizophrenics. They might be even tougher to handle than Tim. If Tim was a borderline, she didn't care if she never saw another borderline, let alone a schizophrenic, in her entire life. Her father had warned her that the clinic might be crawling with black people. For all she knew, it would also be crawling with schizophrenics and borderlines. She would be glad when she had her own practice and could, like Dr. North, be selective about the patients she accepted. The idea, as he had explained it to her, was not to waste your time with people that couldn't be helped.

Lester put his hand on her knee again. "We could use a good den mother," he said.

"Oh go to hell," Wanda said vehemently. Then, because she was feeling so good from the Scotch, she burst out laughing. Lester removed his hand from her knee and looked hurt.

The poppy seeds were ready, and Floyd offered some to Lester. Lester said he'd pass.

"Just as well," Floyd said. "There's not enough here to really do much." He and Eric ate the seeds.

Another joint came around, and Wanda took a drag. She had not smoked for a couple of years and had forgotten how quickly it always hit her. She took another drag.

At some point, Eric said to Floyd: "How are these seeds supposed to make me feel?"

"Well," Floyd said, "how *do* you feel?"

"Everything's blurry," Eric said.

"Boring?" Floyd said. "That's the way it's supposed to be."

"*Blurry,*" Eric said.

"Oh," Floyd said. "Blurry."

Wanda started giggling and couldn't stop. She squinted her eyes and looked at the three men. "You're all blurry," she said. Lester smiled at her. "Scrinch yours up," Wanda said, "and I'll be blurry too." Lester squinted his eyes. "See how blurry we are," Wanda said happily. They pressed their noses together and squinted at each other.

Lester kissed her, and Wanda pulled away. "Don't," she said. She brought her glass to her lips to protect them. Lester's eyes were wide open now, and Wanda had to turn away to keep from jumping in.

She decided to be serious again. "You never did tell me what Jesse said."

"Jesse?" Lester said.

"Tell her," Eric said. He and Floyd were sitting in identical poses and grinning stupidly. Wanda had forgotten they were in the room.

"When you squeezed his whang," Wanda said.

"What he said—" Lester began.

"Get ready," Eric said.

"What he said was—'Ouch that hurts.'"

Lester's laugh was pure and rich. Eric and Floyd howled. Wanda began to laugh too, but hers was the laughter of hysteria. She tried to stop but couldn't. The laughter was being jerked from her mouth in long thin ribbons. The ribbons fluttered in the still air. The room filled with thin red ribbons of sound. Some of the ribbons stuck in Wanda's throat and she gagged. Lester pounded on her back. Then he held her close against him. She put her head on his shoulder.

"What did we expect?" Lester said. "The secret of the universe?"

"I'm exhausted," Wanda said. "I think I might be sick."

Lester pulled her head down in his lap. "Rest a minute," he said.

Eric and Floyd were grinning stupidly. Lester was smiling down at her. The room tilted and she closed her eyes. Floyd started talking about Masters and Johnson.

* * *

The next thing Wanda knew, it was beginning to get light outside. It took her a minute to figure out that she had been asleep on the floor. Then she realized that Lester was lying beside her. He had a hand in her blouse and was kissing her neck. She tried to pull away, but he moved in closer and kissed her mouth. She jerked her head back and shut her lips tightly. Out of the corner of one eye she saw Eric asleep on the sofa. She pushed against Lester's shoulders and tried to sit up. "Please," he whispered. "You got away once because I was eleven years old. *Please.*" He held her down with what seemed like enormous strength. Wanda wanted to say something to him—she wasn't sure what—but at the same time was afraid of waking Eric. They struggled in silence. Lester got her brassiere off and began licking her breasts. Then he put his hand high on her leg. The hand was steamy hot. Although Wanda's long thighs were strong and heavy, they swung open as if run by a motor. She gave a little gasp and pressed her lips against Lester's. The hand moved up to the waist of her pantyhose. She lifted her hips and felt the panty-hose slide over them. A moan formed in her throat. She swallowed it and felt its heat settle in her loins. She started to suggest that they go in the bedroom but instead drew her legs up and let Lester move between them. "Dear God," he said as he entered her.

Afterward, he lay in her arms and talked about his life. Before long, Wanda realized that what he was saying now was a person-alized version of the theoretical talk he had given earlier. He had dedicated himself to schizophrenics, he said, because he was dan-gerously schizoid himself. He spoke at length about the double mes-sages he had received from his schizophrenogenic mother and the double binds she had laid on him. He talked about his alienation, his despair, his ontological insecurity, his false-self system, the loss of meaning in his life, and the necessity, in both his life and his work, to subordinate his feelings to his will in order to create rela-tionship where none seemed possible. His head was resting in such a way that his lips brushed Wanda's right nipple as he talked. The whole speech, rambling and repetitious, was delivered in a mono-tone scarcely distinguishable from Eric's rather labored breathing. For the first thirty minutes, Wanda knew with absolute certainty that she was going to pledge her life to this lean, quietly desperate, unconventionally handsome man with the startling blue eyes. To-gether they would map the contours of the sometimes garishly hec-tic, sometimes catatonic cosmos whose secret meaning he had dared to challenge. For the next thirty minutes, with the room getting lighter and lighter, Wanda wondered how in the world she could get rid of the gray-faced, yellow-toothed, intolerably vain and ugly middle-aged scarecrow who had unaccountably managed to screw her and now threatened to bury her in words she didn't understand.

When at last he fell asleep, Wanda extricated herself and went to the bathroom and showered and douched. Then she went to the bedroom and saw that there was someone in her bed. She looked closer and saw that it was Eric. She returned to the living room and discovered that the body on the sofa belonged to Floyd Robbins.

She got a blanket from the hall closet and carried it to her study. When she awoke, at two in the afternoon, she felt as if she had been on a long binge. To her great relief, the men were gone. She soaked in the tub for an hour and brushed her teeth three times. In the living room she found a note from Eric that said he was sorry they hadn't had more time to visit. On the same piece of paper Lester had written: "My Sweet Mrs. Benson, You were everything I expected and more besides. If you change your mind, the offer's still open." Trembling with rage—for, after all, Robert might have come in and found the note—Wanda burned it in the kitchen sink. She made a cup of coffee and sat down at the table. Her rage gave way to panic as she began to wonder whether Floyd had seen her making love to Lester, and, if so, whether he would tell Robert. She hoped not. She wanted, suddenly and desperately, to marry Robert just as soon as she possibly could.

part two

7

Dec 19

Dear Glamourpuss,

Today in the lobby I was glancing through a book about cats and ran across some interesting stuff. Did you know, for example, that one of the main responsibilities of a mother cat is to wean her kittens? Well of course you knew it, but it's the kind of obvious fact we take for granted and then forget. According to the book, weaning starts about six weeks after the kittens are born. The mother becomes less and less available. If the kittens insist on suckling, the mother may refuse to lie down, in which case they must suckle while she's sitting or even standing. But the less encouragement the mother gives them, the more eager, the more persistent, I daresay the more desperate, the kittens become. Sometimes when the mother terminates a feeding session and starts to walk away, the kittens are still clinging to her tits—hanging there, the book says, "like little sausages."

All this has me thinking of Little Tim. (Remember?—I sent you a picture.) As you may or may not recall, after the early, highly erotic (for me anyway) stages of therapy (the things I did to you in my head, Wanda!), I passed rapidly into being a God damned little boy. I hated that boy, that sniveling sissy. No I didn't. I only wish you could have seen him at his best. Very appealing kid most of the time. Extremely well be-

haved, you couldn't have helped liking him. But you never got to see this aspect of Little Tim; what you saw was always the scared father of the devastated man. You don't know what it's like, Wanda, to want to impress a person with your maturity, wit, and poise, and then to find yourself, every time you're in that person's presence, reverting into the worst part of the child you were. No wonder you hate me. If you'd stuck around, though—the way you were supposed to—you'd have seen, eventually, the appealing side of Little Tim. And you'd have seen him grow up, right before your eyes, into the very man you've always wanted. You could still love me, Wanda, if you'd let yourself. It's not too late. The trouble with being Little Tim was that Little Tim had no concept of your leaving. He thought you'd stay forever.

I chose that particular picture, by the way, for a good reason. Out of the dozens of pictures in my real mother's collection, it's the one that most resembles the child we, you and I, conjured up between us. The one you're the mother of. He's your child, Wanda, you can't get out of it.

To turn to news from the home, I was still awake at four this morning and decided to go downstairs for a cup of coffee. In the hall I saw Jack, the fireplug, coming out of Millie's room. I guess the stories you hear about that woman are true. Maybe she and Jack are easing out of their depression. Maybe he's getting back the old desire and determination. Maybe she'll join the auxiliary again. They say that interest in sex is a good sign, don't they?

We have another new guest. They brought her in a couple of days ago. I was out running, and I haven't seen her yet. She hasn't been down for meals or anything. There are three empty rooms on the second floor, but for some reason they put her on the third. In fact, she's right above my head. I can hear her stirring around up there sometimes.

I don't like this place. Can I come live with you? I am clean and no trouble. I could sleep by the side of the bed or even in the closet. You would not know I was around. Maybe after a few months you'd want to adopt me or make me your mascot. Hoping to hear from you, I remain,

Your little sausage,
Tim

84

P.S. You'll be interested to know that the first annual Great Wanda Festival of the Arts (Children's Division) has just ended. Your judge is pleased to award first prize to me for the following poem:

> *My precious Wanda precious*
> *You mean the world to me*
> *I would like to eat you*
> *Like a dish of vanilla ice cream*

You have always reminded me of v.i.c., Wanda—I guess because it's my favorite—so the poem is highly appropriate. And, of course, you're also a "dish," so the poem is doubly appropriate. That's why it's a prizewinner.

P.P.S. I don't mind being a little sausage. You're nothing but a lousy weaner yourself.

P.P.P.S. Big Tim would like to eat you too, while we're at it. If you go for that kind of thing, glamourpussy, don't hesitate to write for details and a list of references.

Other Mother, sweet Mother Other—why did you betray me

"This is a hell of a thing to come home to," Robert said. "Especially after a honeymoon." He glanced at the letter again and shook his head. "It's a hell of a thing."

"It's nicer than most of them," Wanda said. She carried their luggage into the bedroom and came back and sat on the sofa. It was Christmas day and they had just returned from New York City.

"I'll tell you one thing," Robert said, pacing around the room. "He's not moving in here with us."

Wanda laughed. "Is *that* what's bothering you? Of course he's not."

"That's not what's bothering me."

"What is?"

"You know."

Wanda shook her head.

"I don't know either. It's just the whole tone of the thing. The whole tone."

"Good lord," Wanda said. "He's written worse letters than this one."

"Maybe so, but I wasn't married to you then." He waved the letter in Wanda's face. "This is awfully personal stuff."

"I think you ought to stop reading the letters," Wanda said.

"Then I'd *wonder*," Robert said. "That would be even worse."

* * *

They had gotten married four days after the incident with Lester. The ceremony was performed by a justice of the peace with Floyd, Marie, and Robert's parents in attendance. Robert looked handsome in a new suit, and for once he didn't wear his Hush Puppies. Marie cried when the justice of the peace pronounced them man and wife. Then, as Robert and his mother embraced, Mr. Martin gave Wanda a kiss on the mouth that she was still trying to forget.

Afterward they went to the Hilltop Inn to drink champagne. The party was spoiled by Mr. Martin, who told some newlywed jokes and a long story about a mysterious "sleeve job." When he finished the story, he asked Wanda and Robert to move in with him and Mrs. Martin.

"There's all kinds of room," he said.

"There is not," Mrs. Martin said.

"We could drive nails all day," Mr. Martin told Wanda, "and talk and cut wood."

"She'd be bored sick," Mrs. Martin said.

"A lot you know about it," Mr. Martin said.

"Anyway," Wanda said, "I need privacy so I can work on my dissertation."

"We'd have plenty of privacy," Mr. Martin said. "Ma spends more time at the beauty shop than she does at home."

"I do not," Mrs. Martin said. "I never leave the fool house."

"I'll tell you what," Mr. Martin said. "You can keep the apartment as a kind of office but live with us. That way you'd have people around you at night. You'd have a daddy in the next room while you slept."

Marie choked on a piece of food, and Floyd hit her on the back.

"We'd better live in the apartment," Wanda said.

"Your own daddy didn't even come to the wedding," Mr. Martin said.

"He couldn't get away," Wanda said. "This was all pretty sudden." As a matter of fact, she had not bothered to tell him about the wedding, let alone ask him to attend.

"Nobody would want to come all the way to Windward for a little old wedding like this one," Mrs. Martin said.

"I still think it's too bad," Mr. Martin said. "A nice daddy's the most important thing a girl can have." He swilled down another glass of champagne.

"Bull," Mrs. Martin said.

"The trouble with families these days," Mr. Martin said, "is that they don't live together the way they used to."

"That can work both ways," Floyd said. "Sometimes it's as bad to be too close as it is too far. I see that at the office all the time. Half your murders start right there in the home."

"I've heard that too," Robert said.

"You believe everything you hear?" Mr. Martin said. To lighten the mood, he told another joke.

By the time he finished, Mrs. Martin's face had hardened into a mask of absolute contempt. Marie, sitting next to her, held her hand to try to comfort her.

At the airport, Mr. Martin pulled Wanda aside and told her he was looking forward to teaching her how to operate the chain saw. Then he winked and said he hoped she wouldn't do anything in New York that he wouldn't do. Off to Wanda's left, Floyd was shaking Robert's hand and slapping him on the back. Behind them, in a corner by the vending machines, stood Marie and Mrs. Martin. Marie had an arm around the older woman and was talking earnestly into her ear. Mrs. Martin looked straight ahead. Her face was still hard, but it appeared to Wanda that she was blinking back tears.

When they were finally on the plane, Robert asked Wanda what his father had said to her.

"He wants to show me his chain saw," Wanda said.

"I wouldn't plan on spending a lot of time over there," Robert said. "It makes Mom nervous to have strange women in the house."

"I'm not a strange woman," Wanda said with a laugh. "I'm your wife."

"You know what I mean," Robert said. "You sure bring out the worst in Dad. For some reason he thinks he can say anything around you he wants to say."

* * *

They were in New York three days and nights. In the hotel room, which seemed very small, Robert was tense and easily distracted. If he wasn't complaining about the noise out on the streets, he was complaining about the noise in the halls. Now that they were married, Wanda had assumed that he would be a little less shy around her, but he wasn't. When they made love during the day, he insisted on doing it under the covers. When he left the bed to use the bathroom, he slipped quickly into a robe. When he took a shower he locked the bathroom door, just as he had always done at Wanda's apartment. One morning Wanda woke up first and threw back the sheets, thinking at least to get a look at him naked, only to find that he had got up sometime in the night and put on pajamas. Later, when she mentioned his shyness, he became angry and defensive, and Wanda backed off. Although she was a bit disappointed in their lovemaking, she wasn't really worried. She supposed that Robert seldom came to the city and that the strange environment and cramped quarters had amplified all the normal anxieties of a honeymoon.

Outside the room, Robert quickly became relaxed and amiable. He squired Wanda around the streets of Manhattan with no trouble, and he seemed to enjoy hanging out in the hotel bars and in the lobby. Several times Wanda caught him eyeing the women, and she finally remarked on it.

"Hey," she said in a tone of mock jealousy, "you're on your honeymoon."

"It's the clothes they wear down here," Robert said with a grin. "Some of them are really outlandish." Once he thought he saw Marie, but it turned out to be a young Spanish woman with the same long kinky hair that Marie affected. "I'd bet anything that girl's a hooker," he said.

"How can you tell?"

"You just can."

"Marie's not a hooker."

"I know," Robert said, "but she looks like one. I don't know where Floyd digs 'em up." He watched as the Spanish girl entered an elevator. "She's going up to some guy's room right now," he said.

Apart from the mediocre lovemaking, the trip was a success. They went to restaurants. They shopped. They watched the animals at the Central Park Zoo. They saw a Knicks' game at the Garden, a circus at the Felt Forum, and a stage show called *Rock, Rock, Rock,* which they agreed was the highlight of the honeymoon.

* * *

Knowing the trip would be expensive, they had decided not to exchange gifts for Christmas. This had seemed like a practical decision, but now that they were home they wished they had some presents to open. They sat and watched the lights on their small tree blink on and off.

"This is depressing," Robert said. He picked Tim's letter up and read it again. Wanda was afraid he would go into another rage, but he didn't. "I don't understand this Little Tim business," he said.

"Regression," Wanda said. "It happens with most patients in the transference. When they see the therapist isn't going to respond to their customary ways of behaving, they revert to more primitive patterns. They more or less relive the past. If their egos are weak, the regression can go pretty far." The speed and depth of Tim's regression had in fact amazed her. Reading about it, or hearing a professor lecture about it, was one thing; seeing it happen in front of you was something else again. Her supervisor took the line that Tim's regression was another way of avoiding serious therapeutic work, but of course he had never himself interviewed Tim. Wanda was not even sure he had ever *seen* Tim. Thinking about the regression, she remembered something funny from her childhood. She considered telling it to Robert, but she decided it was too complicated and that anyway he might not see the humor of it.

Robert returned the letter to the envelope and looked pensively at the Christmas tree. After a while he said he was hungry. "I thought Mom might call and ask us over, but I guess she's not going to. She knows we're back."

"I'm too tired to cook," Wanda said. "Anyway, there's nothing here."

"We could go out," Robert said.

Wanda said no, she was too tired for that too. They sat awhile longer, and then Robert said he'd go get a pizza. "I've never had pizza on Christmas," he said. "Mom always cooks turkey or ham. Last year she cooked both."

"Next year *I'll* cook both," Wanda said.

Robert was gone about two hours. When he returned, Wanda had long since unpacked and was working on her dissertation. He was carrying a pizza and two gift-wrapped packages.

"Presents," Wanda said. "What store was open?"

"I didn't go to a store," Robert said. "I went to Denny's and got the pizza. Denny's is always open on Christmas. I had a couple of drinks and decided to say hi to the folks. They gave me the presents."

"They shouldn't have done that," Wanda said. "I thought the champagne was their gift."

"Mom said she wanted to give us something else," Robert said. "She picked them out herself."

"Shall we open them?"

"Go ahead and eat. I'll get us a beer."

Wanda set the pizza on the coffee table. "Aren't you having any?"

"Naw," Robert said. "Mom insisted that I have a plate of turkey and dressing. I loaded up pretty good. I didn't think, or I could have brought you some."

Wanda picked up a piece of pizza. "This is cold," she said.

"That's because I got it before I went to the folks'," Robert said.

"I can't eat it," Wanda said.

"You could heat it up."

"I don't like it heated up. Anyway, I shouldn't be eating pizza. I gained three pounds in New York City."

"We might as well open the presents then," Robert said. "Mine'll be underwear, but yours might be something special. Mom said it was a combination."

"Combination what?"

"Honeymoon and Christmas," Robert said. He opened his package and took out six pairs of white cotton briefs. "Every dang year," he said. "I've got enough underwear to last till the day I die . . . Open yours."

Wanda removed the wrapping paper and saw that the box was from the Big Girls Shop in Syracuse. She opened the box and saw a nylon garment that was day-glo orange in color. "It's a peignoir, I think," she said. She had never seen anything so ugly in her life.

Robert took it out of the box and stood up with it. "It's awful bright," he said. He handed it to Wanda and told her to try it on.

"I can't," Wanda said. "I'm too tired."

Robert said his mother had bought it and she had to try it on. "It wouldn't be right not to," he said.

Wanda went in the bedroom and put it on. It was several sizes too large. She wore it into the living room and said, "Look, it's too damned big."

"It sure is," Robert said. "I told Mom your size, but I guess she forgot."

"It would fit an elephant."

"Or at least a cow. Are you crying?"

"I'm about to."

"That's silly. We can have it exchanged. Anyway, it's the thought that counts."

"That's why I'm crying," Wanda said.

She returned to the bedroom and took the peignoir off. She was standing naked, trying to locate a robe, when Robert came in and pushed her onto the bed. He opened her legs and put his head between them and performed oral sex as if it were going out of style. He had not done it to Wanda before and she was surprised how good he was.

When she could stand no more of it, she pulled his head up and held it against her chest. "I think the honeymoon just started," she murmured.

"Are you happy?" Robert asked.

"God, am I ever," Wanda said. "I'm still tingling. I feel more married or something. I'll sleep like a log."

"Consider it a present," Robert said.

"I will," Wanda said. She rolled him over on his back and put her head on his shoulder and snuggled tightly against him. "You smell good," she said. She nuzzled his ear and his neck. She unbuttoned his shirt and licked his chest and his belly. "Yum," she said. She unbuckled his belt. "I'm going to see if you taste this good all over," she said.

"Consider it a present from old Tim," Robert said.

Wanda jerked away from him. "I can't believe you said that."

"All I meant," Robert said, "is that he gave me the idea. I might not have thought of it otherwise."

Wanda got up, found her robe, and went to the living room. She thought Robert might come and apologize, but after a while she heard him snoring. No longer sleepy herself, she poured a drink and went to the big glass door and looked out and saw that it was snowing. Although the snow could not have begun more than an hour ago, the street and the roofs of the surrounding houses were already covered. She had heard that winters here were bad, and she supposed this one was beginning in earnest.

She sat on the sofa and sipped her drink. Her eye fell on Tim's letter and she remembered the paragraph about Little Tim being her child. This made her think again of the funny story from her own childhood. Because it was so funny, she had often been tempted to tell the story to Dr. Campbell or to some of her fellow graduate students. Knowing it would get a big laugh, she had even been tempted to tell it in some of her practice groups, but she never had. In fact, she had never told it to anybody, not even to Sarah Pitkin.

* * *

Her father had always conducted his practice at home. Because her mother was sick and seldom out of bed, Wanda spent much of her childhood playing in the vicinity of Dr. North's office. Dr. North had no receptionist, and sometimes, especially with nice Mrs. Jaffe, Wanda assumed this role. "Good afternoon," she would say. "Won't you have a seat? The doctor will see you promptly at four." Her prim manner and businesslike little voice would bring a smile to Mrs. Jaffe's face, and the woman would remark how cute Wanda was. Wanda would wait until Mrs. Jaffe had disappeared into the mysterious inner office, where Wanda herself was not permitted to go, and then she would run off to the kitchen and eat cookies and ice cream.

When she was five, Wanda became curious to know what her father did in there with all those different people. All those women. She knew it was psychoanalysis, but she didn't know what psychoanalysis was. One day, when her father stepped into the waiting room to greet a patient, Wanda slipped past him, unseen, into the inner office and hid in the storage part of the window seat. Presently her father and the patient—not Mrs. Jaffe but a snooty woman named Mrs. Winslow—came in and began to talk. Their voices were muffled and Wanda could not make out the words. After a while, she became bold enough to push the seat up and peek out. To her surprise, Dr. North was not sitting at his desk but had rolled his chair to a spot at the head of the couch. To her even greater surprise, Mrs. Winslow was *lying* on the couch, her head near Dr. North and her feet pointing directly at Wanda. It occurred to Wanda that the woman might be dying; but, if so, why was her father looking, not at the patient, but at a painting on the far wall?

By the time Wanda had taken all this in, the doctor and the patient had stopped talking and were in the middle of an awkward pause. Finally, after a good deal of tension had built up, Dr. North demanded to know what was going on. "What is it you don't want to talk about?" he asked.

There was another pause, and then Mrs. Winslow said it was a dream, and yes, it was hard to talk about, she wasn't sure why.

Dr. North suggested that the dream might pertain to him.

There was a man in the dream, Mrs. Winslow admitted, but she didn't know who it was. All she knew was that, in the dream, she kept receiving presents from this man. Her doorbell was always ringing. She would open the door and find a present. The man himself was always disappearing around the corner of the house. It went on and on, throughout the dream. One present after another. Always from the same man. The presents frightened her and made her ashamed, but she also felt flattered. She was scared and ashamed and pleased, all at the same time . . .

As she talked, Mrs. Winslow became more and more agitated. She kicked off one shoe and then the other. She put her hands over her face and moaned. She rubbed her feet together. Then, with a loud sob, she threw a leg out to the side and pulled her other leg up. Her dress fell back around her hips, and Wanda found herself looking directly at the shiniest, pinkest pair of panties she had ever seen. Her father turned his head in Mrs. Winslow's direction, and Wanda quickly lowered the lid of the window seat and sat huddled in total darkness. When she lifted the lid again, her father was saying something about giving Mrs. Winslow a baby. "Is that it?" he demanded. "You want my baby?"

"Yes!" Mrs. Winslow screamed. "Yes! Yes! Yes!"

Wanda let the seat fall shut and sat with her eyes closed and her hands over her ears till she was sure the session, the last one of the day, was over. From that time on, she steered clear of her father's office.

Not long after the experience in the window seat, Wanda started to school. One day some of her classmates began speculating about where babies came from. Sally Bloom said they came out of the mother's stomach. A boy named Leon sneered and said sure, everyone knew that, but how did they get *in* the stomach? Wanda informed them, with a superior air, that it was all done by psychoanalysis. The children were impressed, but the teacher, who had overheard the exchange, burst out laughing. Although she laughed for a long time, she would not explain what was funny. In an odd way, Wanda was comforted by the laughter. It made psychoanalysis seem not quite as frightening as it had seemed that day in her father's office.

A few weeks later, Wanda and her father were walking in the park and saw a pregnant woman. Wanda smiled and said that the woman had been psychoanalyzed. Her father laughed and asked why she had said such a thing. "Well," Wanda said knowingly, "she's going to have a baby, isn't she?"

Dr. North jerked Wanda to a halt and slapped her. Then he grabbed her shoulders and shook her till she thought her neck would break. "You little bitch!" he yelled. "Don't you ever say that again. Not *ever*." Then he started crying. He clasped Wanda tightly to him and said he was sorry. He brushed her hair with his hand and dried her tears and then his own. When he finished, he picked Wanda up and carried her across the street to a drugstore and bought her a triple-dip banana split with all the trimmings.

Soon afterward her mother died. She had been sickly for years and finally died of cancer. Eric, who had been a problem child, was sent off to some special school or academy. Dr. North was beginning to make a name for himself as an author and usually devoted his evenings to writing. Wanda spent many hours alone.

When she was in the fourth grade, she learned the truth about babies. "Fucking," the boy named Leon said. "That's how it's done." He described in graphic (though, it turned out, highly inaccurate) detail what fucking was. He made it sound like the worst thing in the world. Wanda went home and felt confused and vaguely ashamed in the presence of her father.

By the time she was twelve, Wanda was reading from her father's library. She didn't understand much of what she read, but she was relieved to discover that it didn't sound like what Leon had described. On the other hand, the words "penis" and "vagina" appeared fairly often, and this disturbed Wanda no end. Psychoanalysis was not, it seemed, the same as fucking, but it had to do with penis and vagina and a few other words that Wanda had picked up at school. Before long, she became obsessed with the idea of being psychoanalyzed. Every time she mentioned it to her father, he told her she was too young and in any case *he* couldn't do it. If she asked why he couldn't, he told her it would be inappropriate. If she kept on about it, he told her she was too young to understand. If she persisted further, he told her to shut up, he was thinking about his writing or about one of his patients.

During her early teens, Wanda could do nothing to please him. If he was not angry about psychoanalysis, he was angry about something else. He was always yelling at her to put her feet down, for God's sake, and sit like a lady. Or he would become angry about the way she wouldn't look at him when he talked to her. Then, if she looked at him, he would tell her to quit staring at him all the time. If she asked to be sent away to school, like Eric, he would stomp around for an hour, raving about how people thought he was made of money. It was costing him a fortune to keep Eric out of trouble, he would shout. Couldn't people see that? Every time he yelled at her, Wanda ran to the kitchen and ate everything she could find.

When she turned fifteen, she was five feet nine and weighed two hundred ten pounds. One day, after returning home from a lecture tour, her father looked at her in surprise and disgust. "Jesus Christ," he yelled, "do you have any idea what a *pig* you are?" He turned on his heel and stomped out of the house, ignoring the pie that Wanda had baked as a welcome-home present. When he came back, about an hour later, he told Wanda to please sit up for a change—he was tired of her lying on the divan all the time—and to please put her feet on the floor like a lady and not behave like some kind of slut. If she would do those things, he would tell her something important. Wanda sat up. Her father knelt in front of her and clasped her hands in his and spoke to her in a voice that was quiet but full of emotion. He had been a bad father, he said. He had not realized how bad until this very day, but he was going to make it all up to her. He was going to get her some professional help, he said, and Wanda would turn out okay. When he finished talking, he hugged Wanda and cried. Two days later, he introduced her to Sarah Pitkin and explained that Sarah was going to be her therapist for as long as it took to get Wanda straightened out. All Wanda had to do was to put her trust in Sarah, and before she knew it she would be a different person entirely . . .

* * *

What was funny about the story, of course, was that Wanda—herself now a professional therapist—would once have thought that babies were produced by psychoanalysis. Smiling to herself, she finished her drink and went to the bedroom. Robert was sound asleep. She put on her pajamas and got in bed and looked at his serene, rather boyish face, which was clearly visible in the light from the window. The last of her anger drained away. She had known, after all, that he was sometimes slightly gauche. On the other hand, he was basically a considerate person, and Wanda was confident that he would, in time, learn to be more cognizant of her needs.

She lay down, closed her eyes, and slept like a log.

8

Dec 26

Dear Wanda—

Why don't you write to me God damn you never write and I can't bear it I tell you everything and you don't seem to understand we're not playing therapy now this is serious business you'd better understand before it's too late and quit sitting there with your fat cat grin and elegant life and interesting friends and no time for the only one who cares enough to destroy us both if we're not careful fuck you fuck you fuck you fuck you fuck you fuck you fuck you fuck you fuck you fuck you fuck you fuck you fuck you

I wrote that yesterday. I have a better grip now, but I'm despondent. I sure miss you during this holiday season. Did you have a white Xmas up there in the frozen north? Up there in the region of ice? All we've had are a few flurries.

White or not, I'll bet you had a marvelous Xmas—of course you did, nothing but the best for Her Loveliness—and I can't wait to hear all about it. Our celebration here at the home was on the quiet side. After Bill killed himself, Millie and Mrs. Bonds scrapped their plans for decorating the lobby, and we voted unanimously against swapping gifts. The rather impressive tree the doc chopped down never got past the front porch. I expect it'll still be there come summer. Mrs. Bonds had prom-

*ised us a turkey dinner, but she and the doc started drinking early in the
morning and were in bed by noon. The guests, including me, passed the
day staring out the big window. You might have thought we were waiting for someone, Santa perhaps, but we weren't. We know better than
that. I got it in my head that you might call, but you didn't. Maybe you
tried and the circuits were busy. On Xmas day, Wanda, you have to stay
right by the phone and keep dialing dialing dialing, every minute or so,
if you really want to get through. The phone rang once, about seven
o'clock, and I jumped out of my skin. Wrong number, of course. I went to
my room and wept. Don't ever hesitate to phone me, day or night,
doesn't matter if you wake the whole house. I have your number but not
the courage to dial it. If I called and you were unfriendly I couldn't stand
it. Why don't you let me know how friendly you'd be and then I'll decide
about calling.*

*So then, no Xmas call from you and no gift, not even a card. I'm glad
I didn't send you anything.*

*You might—I doubt it—be interested to know that I have solved the
mystery of the third-floor guest. I was lying on my bed one afternoon,
looking at the ceiling, when I heard her moving around and decided to
investigate. I expected to find a locked door at the top of the stairs, but I
didn't. It wasn't even shut all the way. I stepped into a dark hall full of
boxes and broken furniture. I turned left, went to the end of the hall,
opened the door to the room directly above my own, and discovered—
sitting there in a battered old easy chair, surrounded by books and
stacks of photographs—the woman I'm going to call Nelda.*

*She was sobbing, quietly and persistently. She seemed unaware of
my presence. Even without my glasses, which I've never bothered to re-
place, I could see that she was a good-sized woman (not as big as you,
but pretty close and built along similar lines). To get a better look I
stepped into the room and stood directly in front of her. Her eyes were
open but fixed in a vacant, sightless stare. I spoke to her; she did not
respond. She is, I would guess, no more than thirty-five and possibly
younger—grief, after all, takes its toll. Her greasy hair falls in thick
tangles. It is longer than your pretty hair, and light brown rather than
dark. Cleaned up, and with her hair combed, she might be a handsome
woman.*

I backed into the hall and went downstairs to find Mrs. Bonds. She was sitting, as usual, in front of the big window, along with her husband and my fellow guests. I knelt beside her chair and told her I had discovered the back ward.

She looked puzzled, and I said I meant the woman on the third floor. She shrugged and said it was no secret, they put her up there so she'd have her own bathroom. "She's blind," I said. Mrs. Bonds nodded and said she had been blind since her automobile accident a year ago. Before that she was a photographer in Little Rock. All she did now, Mrs. Bonds said, was sit and cry. I, for one, can understand that. Imagine, Wanda, being a photographer and not being able to see!

I expressed an interest in the books in the room, and Mrs. Bonds said not to remove them, she didn't want them scattered all over the place. So, Wanda, I've now gone to Nelda's room twice and sat on the floor and read from first one book and then another. Most of the books are popular novels, but that doesn't matter. What matters is that I have something different to do.

The second day I was there I started reading aloud, and I plan to continue this practice. Let me tell you, it's pretty eerie to sit up there in that dim dusty room and read to a woman who can't see and won't talk and for all I know can't hear either. Please understand, Sailboat—I would not want you to be jealous—that there is no real connection between Nelda and me. You're still my only connection.

One other piece of news. At dinner Saturday, Millie said that the stories about her were circulating again. Jack turned a bright red. Loy took it all in with a sardonic smile. He has yet to say a word at the table. He is even quieter than I am.

Love always,
Tim

P.S. What exactly is it you're doing in Windward, New York? Therapy, I assume, but in what context? Clinic? Private practice? Hospital? Maybe you're connected with the university. Remember how defeated I was when you said I couldn't follow you to your new destination? If you can fit me into your schedule, I'd still be happy to join you. It's only a question of time till we meet again; you might as well get paid for it.

Or maybe you'd rather I came on a more personal basis. I've been meaning to tell you that I understand the constraints you were under as an intern. It wouldn't have looked good, probably, if you had started an affair with one of your very first patients. But those constraints no longer apply, do they? All you'd have to do is drop me a line, say I love you Tim, come on up, let's live together, get married and so on and so forth. I'd be there in a flash. I'm at your disposal, is what it amounts to.

P.P.S. I don't want you to get the idea, from the way I sometimes go on about sex, that I think about you and masturbate. I don't. I get hard-ons sometimes, but I don't let them drag me into desire. Usually, I drive them away with a lighted cigarette. Other times—and I'm getting better at this—I simply stare them down. Do you want to know why I hate hard-ons? Probably not, but I'll tell you anyway. Of the twenty-three dreams I've so far had about you, two have been overtly sexual and very depressing.

In the first, we're in a dirty garage. You're lying naked on the floor, your back arched high. I'm standing between your legs, pumping it to you. I'm about four feet tall. I am, in fact, Little Tim. I can barely move, I'm so tired, but I keep going, I keep fucking you, because you can't get enough. I never saw anyone enjoy anything so much. I'm miserable and very scared. Tears run down my face, down my whole body; the floor is deep in tears, but you don't care. You keep telling me not to stop. You keep saying how much you enjoy it. That's the same thing you said when you shook my hand goodbye. You said it had been a great pleasure to work with me; you said you'd enjoyed every minute of it.

In the second dream, we're in bed. I'm lying on my back, you're straddling me. I keep trying to find your cunt, but I can't. I complain that I can't find it. You say never mind, you're enjoying it the way it is. I say all right, but I'm only doing it for you. And that's what I said on the day you left. You said what a pleasure it had been, how much you enjoyed it; I said what an ordeal it was and that I had done it all for you.

I refuse to be dragged into desire by dreams like those. You've humiliated me enough already.

The P.S. began a new page. Wanda, recalling Robert's reaction to the sexual references in Tim's last letter, removed this page and the subsequent pages and hid them in her desk.

When Robert came home, he read the abridged version of the letter two or three times. Wanda sat beside him on the sofa, trying to mend the sleeve of a blouse. She kept getting it crooked but was determined not to give up. It seemed like the kind of thing a married woman could handle.

"If you lop off the first paragraph," Robert said, "this could almost be from a friend."

"Almost," Wanda said. She thought of the pages in her desk and stuck herself with the needle. She popped her finger into her mouth and tasted blood. When the pain stopped, she returned the needle to her sewing kit and ripped the blouse into two pieces.

"You shouldn't have done that," Robert said. "Mom could have fixed it."

"I wasn't trying to fix it," Wanda said. "I was fooling around with a new stitch I read about."

After supper they turned off the lights and sat in front of the balcony window and looked out at the snow. There was at least a foot on the ground and it was still falling. It fell straight down, forming a heavy curtain between them and the lights of the street. Instead of obscuring the lights, it made them brighter.

"I wonder if it's snowing in Elmerton," Robert said.

"I'm sure we'll find out," Wanda said.

"It's nice of Tim to read to the blind woman. I wish he'd quit burning himself. I wish he'd do the things other people do."

"When he does do them," Wanda said, "he doesn't enjoy them."

"He would," Robert said, "if he was doing them with you. It makes me realize how lucky I am."

He turned on the radio and they listened to music. After a while the disk jockey announced that a snow emergency had been declared and that the streets were closed to cars. A half hour later, a snowmobile pulled up in front of the apartment house.

"I hate those things," Wanda said. "They make so much noise."

"Yeah," Robert said, "but that's Floyd and Marie."

"I liked it with just the two of us."

"They won't stay long." Robert flipped on a light and stood at the window and waved. Then he went to the door and waited till Floyd and Marie arrived.

"God," Marie said, "have we had fun." She wriggled out of her coat and shook the snow from her hair.

"Had the lights off, huh?" Floyd said.

"We were watching the snow," Robert said.

"I'll bet," Floyd said. "You want to try the snowmobile?" he asked Wanda. "I'll take you for a spin."

"No thanks," Wanda said.

"How about you, big fellow?" Marie said to Robert.

Robert blushed and said no, he didn't want to get bundled up.

"Spoilsport," Marie said.

"That's what getting married does for you," Floyd said. "You lose interest in outdoor activities."

Robert handed out beer and they sat around talking about their New Year's Eve plans. At Floyd's suggestion, they had decided to attend the Country Club dance. Marie thought it was great that they were going to do something "uptown" for a change.

"We can go to Denny's anytime," she said.

"That's true," Wanda said, "but I'm not much of a dancer."

"Anyone can dance," Marie said.

"You'd be surprised," Wanda said.

"At least we can see how the other half lives," Marie said. "Floyd says all the big shots and doctors hang out at the Country Club."

Floyd said he wanted to have a word with Robert in private, and they went in the bedroom and closed the door. Wanda could hear the drone of their voices, but she couldn't make out the words.

"What does Floyd want?" she asked Marie.

Marie shrugged. "Maybe he wants to borrow some money."

Wanda hoped so, but she was imagining a conversation in which Floyd told Robert about her and Lester Smith. At the end of the conversation, Robert came back and brained her with a beer bottle.

"I saw Robert's mother downtown," Marie said. "She's quite a person."

"I guess so," Wanda said.

"Why don't you two get along?"

"We will."

"I don't know about that," Marie said.

The men returned from the bedroom. Wanda was relieved when Robert said:

"It's that Doreen." He was very agitated.

"What about her?" Marie asked.

"She still wants to talk to Wanda," Floyd said. "She phoned me last night and said she had to see her."

"She's not going to," Robert said.

"Why does she want to see me?" Wanda asked.

"Who knows?" Robert snapped. "She's always been completely crazy."

He was still fuming when Floyd and Marie left. Although Wanda seldom gave advice, this seemed like a good time for it. She told Robert not to let himself get so worked up over Doreen.

"I know you're only trying to be protective of me," she said, "but I can handle myself. I can handle Doreen too, for that matter."

"You don't have to handle her," Robert said. "Floyd's going to do it."

"Do what?"

"See that she doesn't come to Windward."

"How can he stop her?" Wanda asked. Floyd's arrogance amazed her.

"I don't know," Robert said, "but he'll do it. He's always had a way with women."

Wanda laughed out loud.

* * *

On New Year's Eve, they presented their tickets to a woman at the door and were given some paper hats and noisemakers. They checked their coats and went into the dining room, which was decorated with red, white, and blue streamers and round yellow light shades with smiles painted on them. The tables had been pushed near the wall to provide a space for dancing. Wanda looked around and saw that the crowd was predominantly middle aged. Most of the women wore cocktail dresses, but here and there she spotted a blue or pink formal. The formals, which reminded her of a high-school prom, made her vaguely depressed.

Their table was halfway between the bar and the bandstand. Wanda sat with her back to the wall and Robert sat across from her, with Floyd and Marie on either side. The bandstand was empty, and Floyd said the musicians were taking a break. Two couples swayed listlessly to music from the jukebox.

As soon as they were settled, Floyd directed their attention to the bar and pointed out a rich dentist, a crooked lawyer, and the head of the anthropology department. Robert pointed out the president of the First National Bank.

"Now that we've seen the big shots," Marie said, "let's have some fun." She put on a red paper hat and began to blow into a noise-maker. Each time she blew, the gadget made a honking sound and a paper tube uncurled and shot forward about a foot. She caused the tube to hit Floyd's nose a few times and he told her to grow up.

"That's what we're here for, isn't it?" Marie said. "To have fun?"

"Yeah," Floyd said, "but don't forget where we are."

"Why'd we come here if we can't have fun?"

"Wait till other people start having fun," Floyd said. "Then you can join in. If you do it now, you'll be conspicuous."

"I like to be conspicuous," Marie said. "That's what I'm here for, is to be conspicuous." She placed the back of one hand against her cheek and batted her eyes, which, thanks to false lashes and a liberal use of liner, seemed unnaturally large. "Who knows," she said, "I might catch the attention of one of those big shots."

Robert grinned at Wanda as if to say "What a doozie."

"There's the mayor," Floyd said. "He just came in with his wife."

Wanda looked across the room and saw a pudgy man in a baggy suit. His wife, also on the pudgy side, was wearing a white formal with an orchid on it.

"Isn't he against the new mental health clinic?" Wanda asked. She remembered reading this in the paper.

"Yeah," Floyd said, "but that's just politics. There's nothing he can do about it."

"That's a relief," Wanda said.

"Mainly," Floyd said, "he hates that boss of yours."

"Dr. Epperson?"

Floyd nodded. "Epperson's on the City Council. The mayor would do anything to get him off. I don't know the story, but it was some kind of property deal. Apparently Epperson moved in and cut the mayor right out. Anyway, Epperson doesn't fit in with the rest of the guys on the Council."

"Let's go someplace else," Marie said with a yawn.

"We're staying here," Floyd said. "You can have fun here."

"How can I? You put the clamps on me the minute we walked in the door." She turned to Wanda. "I can't stand it when some guy puts the clamps on me . . . Where's the band?"

"They're at the bar," Robert said. "See? In the white coats."

"Oh yeah." Marie blew into the noisemaker and caused the paper tube to hit Robert in the forehead. Robert blushed.

Floyd waved to the mayor, who was standing with the crooked lawyer. After a while the mayor made a gesture that could be construed as a return wave. "He's quite a guy," Floyd said. "I worked in his last campaign."

"Floyd knows that whole downtown bunch," Robert said to Wanda.

A waiter came and took their orders for drinks. He was a slender young Indian who had trouble understanding what Floyd told him.

"I used to have breakfast with that bunch sometimes," Robert said, "when I was living at home."

"You still could," Wanda said.

"Where we live now," Robert said, "it's out of the way."

"You ought to keep your hand in though," Floyd said.

"Why should he?" Marie asked belligerently.

"You never know when you might need some clout," Floyd said. "Zoning ordinance or something."

The men discussed a recent zoning ordinance. Marie tried to interrupt, but Floyd told her to shut up, they were talking about the real world for a change. It didn't seem real to Wanda. Real was a funny word. Tim had once said that she was the only real person he had ever met. That was the transference talking—he was seeing her through his own confused feelings—but even so he had a point. Real was what interested you. When she went to work and had some patients, she would have a real world too.

The waiter came with the drinks, and Floyd proposed a toast to the New Year. They clicked their glasses and drank. Robert gave Wanda a kiss on the cheek. Floyd tried to kiss Marie, but she pulled away and said she didn't kiss people who put the clamps on.

106

"Don't give me any of your feminist crap," Floyd said.

"Keep it up," Marie said, "and I'll walk right out of here."

"If you embarrass me—"

"Look," Robert said, "here comes the band."

"It's about time," Marie said.

The band consisted of a rhythm section, a trumpet player, and a sax player. Three of the men were bald and paunchy; the other two had slicked-down hair and mustaches. Except that the players were all white, it looked suspiciously like a jazz band. Wanda was relieved when they started a slow rendition of "Rose Room." If this was jazz, it was at least bearable. It had nothing in common with the utterly intense music that Sarah listened to.

"Is that the kind of stuff they play?" Marie asked.

"I guess it's not good enough for you," Floyd said.

"Au contraire," Marie said. "I love that schmaltzy stuff sometimes." She was suddenly in a good mood.

"Well then," Floyd said as the dance floor filled up, "shall we?"

Marie laughed scornfully. "I wouldn't dance with you for a hundred dollars." She stood up and grabbed Robert by the hand. "I'll dance with the big fellow though."

Robert looked at Wanda.

"It's up to you," Wanda said.

"I guess I will then," Robert said, getting to his feet. "I can't stand this bickering."

To Wanda's amazement, he took Marie in his arms and whirled her gracefully away from the table.

"It's incredible," Wanda said. "He's always saying how clumsy he is."

"He wasn't much in sports," Floyd said, "but he was the best dancer in Windward High."

"I believe it." Wanda was pleased that Robert was capable of surprising her. It would not do, somehow, for a psychologist to be married to a man who was all surface. She watched as Robert and Marie glided around the floor.

"Don't worry about it," Floyd said. "Robert didn't marry you in order to dance."

"It's a good thing," Wanda said. "I'm terrible at it."

"Doesn't matter. You're what he was looking for. He said he was tired of the Hollywood type. He said he wanted a rock."

"A rock?" Wanda laughed.

"You know, somebody he could count on. When he started going with you, he said 'I've found her. I've found my rock.'"

"Like the Rock of Gibraltar," Wanda said.

"Sure," Floyd said.

"That's sweet." Wanda had dreaded being alone with Floyd, but so far it wasn't bad. "He's a rock too," she said.

Floyd looked over at the bar and happened to catch the eye of the crooked lawyer. This time he was rewarded with a definite wave. "That guy's totally corrupt," he said, "but you can't help liking him."

"They're dancing another number," Wanda said.

"If I know Robert, you won't get him off the floor again tonight. At least she's off *my* back." Floyd took a sip of his drink. "That was some party, wasn't it?"

"When was that?"

"The night your brother was here."

"What about it?" Wanda wished Robert and Marie would come back.

"Nothing," Floyd said. "One minute you were laughing your head off, and the next minute you were passed out cold. What did you do, sleep there all night?"

Wanda met Floyd's gaze but couldn't figure out what he was up to. "I slept there for a while. Then I woke up and went to my study."

"You knew I spent the night?"

Wanda nodded.

"I haven't said a word to Robert."

Wanda's heart fluttered. "What about?"

"About the dope and about me spending the night. I told him we sat up late and talked."

"That's what I told him."

"Robert doesn't go for wild parties these days. He might be upset if he found out I spent the night. He wouldn't like it if he knew we slept in the same room."

Wanda had trouble controlling her sense of relief. "You don't have to worry. I'm not going to tell him."

They sat back and sipped their drinks. They seemed to have nothing more to say. Floyd grinned for a while. Then he glanced over at the bar, where the mayor was still talking to the crooked lawyer.

"Go on over there," Wanda said, "if you want to."

"I shouldn't leave you alone."

"I don't mind."

"You're a good kid," Floyd said. He winked at her. As he stood up, he reached over and squeezed her hand.

Wanda watched as he walked to the bar. He said something to the mayor, and the mayor laughed and threw an arm around him. Floyd, in turn, threw an arm around the crooked lawyer, who also laughed. Then they all became serious again, as if settling then and there the fate of the city. Wanda surveyed the dance floor, looking for Robert and Marie, but all she could seem to focus on were the formals. Moving in slow, intricate patterns, they made her slightly dizzy. She looked up at the smiling lights, which hung from the ceiling like giant lollipops. They made her dizzy too. With lights like that, no wonder nothing seemed real. She looked down at her drink and listened to the people at the next table, who were trying to decide whether they wanted a swimming pool or a boat. Presently a man approached her. Wanda raised her head and saw the round face, prissy mouth, and gold-rimmed glasses of Burt Epperson.

"I'm not much of a dancer," she blurted out.

Burt laughed. "Do *I* look like a dancer?" He eased into the chair across from Wanda. "My wife has the flu."

"My husband's dancing."

"I didn't know you had one. Is it that Floyd person?"

"The other one. Robert."

"At least it's not Floyd," Burt said goodnaturedly. "He's a friend of His Honor. I can't stand either one of them."

The Indian waiter passed by and Burt signalled for him to bring a couple of drinks. "What was your impression of Lester?" he asked Wanda. "He can be overpowering, don't you think?"

"I only met him that one time," Wanda said.

"He's always been that way, even as a young man. Very idealistic."

"Why do you say that? He laughs at everything."

"That's only because of his disappointment. They let him down in a big way, you know."

"Who did?"

"Schizophrenics. He used to think they knew something deep. He thought they were oppressed. He thought they were potential rebels. He thought he could use them to overthrow the bourgeois family . . . Isn't that the craziest thing you ever heard of? The most idealistic?"

"Well—" Wanda said.

"Then, as evidence piled up that they suffer from brain damage or a chemical imbalance, he was shattered. He can't stand it that if you drug them up you can train them to watch TV and do the dishes and be polite. You can even train them to bowl. They take to bowling like a duck takes to water."

"Bowling?" Wanda said.

"Sure. Strikes and spares. Open frames. Gutter balls . . . But even so, I envy Lester. I envy him his dedication."

"Why? You don't agree with a thing he says."

"Officially no." Burt leaned forward and lowered his voice. "But deep down I've always wondered whether I wasn't rationalizing my own failure of nerve. Sitting here in my middle-class cocoon, living off the tuition of the privileged class, I almost have to be opposed to Lester. He lives like a pig, but he's got integrity. Every time I see him, I start doubting myself. I have some real conflicts about Lester."

"I think you do," Wanda said.

The waiter returned with the drinks. Wanda had barely noticed him before. Now she saw that he was outrageously handsome. No, he was beautiful. In fact he was gorgeous. Except that he had no breasts, you would have thought he was a girl. He handled the tray and the glasses with a breathtaking, almost insolent ease.

"Thank you, Mysore," Burt said.

Mysore lingered at the table. He was as slender as Marie. He had perfect dark skin and dark glittering eyes. His teeth sparkled. He put a knee on Robert's chair and gazed soulfully at Burt. He licked his lips. He slid the tray under his arm and made small, sylphlike gestures with his hands. Burt blushed and chuckled.

"That's enough now," he said. "You little pagan, can't you see I'm talking to this woman?"

Mysore bowed elaborately and backed away. He gave a dazzling smile and spun off into the crowd of dancers.

Wanda watched him until he was out of sight. "I've never seen anyone so . . . so graceful."

"They have that quality sometimes," Burt said. "That and those dark eyes . . . Where were we?"

"We were talking about Lester."

"He's a homosexual, of course," Burt said.

"Lester?"

"No. The waiter. Over there he's a prince; but over here he's just another faggot. I know all about him because he comes to me for light counseling."

"You shouldn't be telling me this," Wanda said.

"Why not? I know it won't go any further. It's common knowledge anyway . . . Where did you say we were?"

"You were telling me about your conflicts over Lester."

"Why should I have conflicts?"

"Well," Wanda said, "I don't think you should." It had dawned on her that Burt might be drunker than he appeared to be.

"You can afford all that integrity when you're dealing with schizophrenics," Burt said. "Nobody expects anything. Nobody's watching. When you're dealing with college kids and faculty wives, it's a different story. I've got parents breathing down my neck. I've got the board of trustees. I've got the president and the provost. Besides being a psychiatrist, I'm on the faculty. I've got students to face. Colleagues. I'm on the city council. I've got a wife and two kids. I can't go around squeezing somebody's whang every minute."

"Of course not," Wanda said.

"I have to watch myself," Burt said gloomily. "If I step out of line, it all gets back."

"I understand."

"I know too much for my own good. That's the problem. I hear it from the faculty wives, and then people imagine I blab it around. Maybe that's why Lester works with schizophrenics. They don't do a lot of gossiping."

"I guess that's right," Wanda said.

"See that guy at the end of the bar. The one in the bow tie? He beats his wife. The one next to him is impotent. I could go all around the room."

"I don't think you'd better," Wanda said.

"My head's full of crap like that. It'll cost me my job someday. The only reason they keep me on is they're afraid to let me go. They're afraid I might talk."

Wanda smiled. "Then you don't have to worry, do you?"

"Who worries? As far as I'm concerned, they can shove that job.

Maybe I'll go join Lester. Maybe I'll go somewhere and study Yoga. You wouldn't know it, but under this drab business suit there beats the heart of a Hindu mystic . . . Let's talk about something else."

"Fine," Wanda said. She looked up and saw Robert and Marie for the first time in about an hour. The band was playing a fast number and they were jitterbugging. The other couples had cleared a place for them and were clapping their hands. Floyd was still at the bar with his arms around people. Mysore flitted gracefully by.

"Speaking of bowling," Burt said, "do you do it?"

"Bowl?" Wanda shook her head.

"That's too bad. I'm co-editor of the *Bowling Therapy Newsletter.*"

"I haven't heard of it."

"It's just getting off the ground. The other editor works in Toledo. We're doing a research project on the therapeutic effects of bowling."

"That's interesting." Wanda spoke with as much conviction as she could manage.

"I recommend it to all my patients," Burt said. "It's going to be a big part of our program at the clinic."

"Bowling," Wanda said.

"Best therapy in the world," Burt said. "Hand-eye coordination. Body-mind. The excitement of being part of a team."

"A group," Wanda said.

"Exactly," Burt said. "There's the group aspect and also the milieu aspect. A bowling alley's a great milieu."

"I've never even been in one," Wanda said.

"You will be." Burt reached in his jacket pocket and pulled out a shiny green shirt, on the back of which was inscribed *Windward County Mental Health Clinic.* "I've got a grant that assures unlimited free bowling for the mentally ill in Windward County for the next three years. Every time they bowl, they'll get free hot dogs and Cokes. That'll be an incentive to people who need help but have been too shy to seek it. When word of our research gets out there'll be an upsurge of interest in bowling the likes of which this country has never seen." He stuffed the shirt back in his pocket and beamed triumphantly. "We're hoping eventually to hit *Readers' Digest,*" he said.

"I don't bowl," Wanda said. She was trying to figure out the implications of what Burt was saying.

"Doesn't matter. You can come and watch. You can be a cheerleader. You'll still get to wear a shirt."

"There'll be more to our program than bowling, won't there?" Wanda asked.

"Oh sure. What goes on in the consulting room is entirely between you and your patient. All I ask is that you put in a good word for bowling every now and then."

Wanda was relieved. As long as she had free rein in other aspects of therapy, she saw no objections to taking part in Burt's research. Every clinic director, she knew, had his pet theories, and she imagined a lot of them were worse than Burt's. There was no question but what the mentally ill needed more exercise than they normally got. Out on the floor, Robert and Marie were dancing to a tune she thought was called the "Tennessee Waltz."

"I saw your father on educational television the other night," Burt said. "He's another one who can afford integrity. He was blasting away at teaching hospitals."

Wanda took her eyes off Robert and turned back to Burt. "The son of a bitch," she muttered.

"What?"

"I said I must have missed it. Did he mention me?"

"I don't think so. According to him, those hospitals are hotbeds of unresolved transferences. The interns and residents induce transferences and then run off. They leave their patients wandering in a dark alley of distrust and despair. I think that's how he put it."

"I guess it could happen," Wanda said, "if a person wasn't careful."

"Careful's my middle name," Burt said. He glanced over his right shoulder and then his left.

"I did transference therapy with one patient," Wanda said, "but I made sure we had time to work through it. It was the most rewarding experience of my life."

"If you fool around with that stuff at the clinic," Burt said, "you'll have a bunch of nuts calling you at all hours and threatening to kill you."

"I sure wouldn't want that," Wanda said. "My patient wasn't that way at all. He was a philosophy teacher. Highly civilized. Extremely intelligent. Good ego strength. I wouldn't have started it if we hadn't had time. So it wasn't me that Daddy was talking about."

"You have to avoid transferences in a job like mine," Burt said. "How could I face my colleagues if their wives started falling in love with me? How could I face Jane? She's dead set against transferences."

"I got a letter from him the other day," Wanda said, "in which he said his therapy with me was like being reborn. God, it was thrilling."

"Or suppose some coed developed a transference," Burt said. "First thing she'd do is tell her father. Her father would turn out to be a wealthy alumnus. He'd tell the president. Next thing you know, I'd be on the carpet. If Freud had been in my position, you'd never have heard about this transference business. Psychoanalysis wouldn't even exist."

Wanda was sure this was false, but she didn't know how to argue the point. She looked up as Robert and Marie glided by. The band was playing "Embraceable You." Marie's head was pressed tightly against Robert's chest and her eyes were closed.

"Your father's in a position to do that kind of therapy," Burt said. "I'm not."

"It's more than position. It's a matter of principle. It's a matter of what's the best treatment."

"That's what I was saying," Burt said. "He's like Lester. He can *afford* to have principles. Private practice, rich patients, all the time in the world . . . How long has he had Mona Matson? Seven years? Eight?"

"I'm not sure." Wanda's mouth was suddenly dry. Mona Matson was her father's movie-star patient. It was her behind-the-scenes manipulations that had led to his becoming a television personality.

Burt finished his drink, set his glass down, and chuckled. "I'd *damn* sure believe in transferences," he said, "if I had Mona Matson for a patient."

Wanda's neck tingled, and she could feel her color rising. She knew now where the conversation was headed. Although the public didn't know that her father was Mona Matson's analyst, every psychiatrist and psychologist in the country seemed to be aware of it and they all wondered the same thing. "The answer," she said in a prim little voice, "is no." She remembered saying those same words to Dr. Campbell three years ago, and in that same little voice.

"What answer?" Burt said. "I was making a joke."

"I know all about your jokes," Wanda said. "Don't you people read his books? Don't you listen to what he says? Don't you care what he stands for?"

"Calm down," Burt said.

He began to stammer an elaborate apology. Wanda heard only part of it because of the blood roaring in her head. Then the blood drained swiftly away. Her thoughts whirled faster and faster and abruptly vanished. Her head fell like a rock and banged hard against the top of the table.

She smelled ammonia. Burt was standing over her, holding a broken capsule next to her nose. Floyd stood beside him. Other people were milling around, but she didn't see Robert.

"She fainted," Burt said. "Apparently I offended her. I was trying to apologize."

"Don't give me that crap," Floyd said. "Is this guy bothering you?" he asked Wanda.

Wanda sat up. Before she could answer, Floyd told Burt to shove off.

"If she'll tell me what's wrong—" Burt said.

"Beat it," Floyd said. Burt shrugged and moved away. "What did he do?" Floyd asked Wanda. "Make a pass?"

"I don't remember."

"He probably did. That's a doctor for you. I wouldn't trust one as far as I could throw him. We'd better not tell Robert about this. He'd break the guy's jaw for sure."

"Would he really?"

"You think he can dance," Floyd said, "you ought to see him fight . . . There he is now. He wants you to go over there."

Wanda looked out at the dance floor and saw that people had gathered for the countdown to midnight. They had stopped dancing and were throwing streamers and confetti and bouncing up and down and waving and making noise. Robert was standing with one arm around Marie and motioning for Wanda to join them. Wanda stumbled across the floor, shoving people this way and that. She reached Robert in time for a New Year's kiss under one of the hideous lollipop lights.

9

Jan 2

Dear Mother Other,

From time to time in these letters I've sounded angry. Maybe you wonder why I never did that before, when you were still with me. Do you think it was because I wasn't aware of my anger—especially toward the end of our time together? Don't kid yourself. I first became aware of it when, about a month before you left, I started writing you a long letter of gratitude for helping me so much (I was full of dumb ideas, wasn't I?). I was going to give you the letter on your last day. I worked on it every night, but no matter how firm my desire to say only nice things, I ended up raving and snarling. I finally gave up on the letter and tucked a razor blade into the lining of my shoe—my intention being, when you said goodbye, to cut my throat and wrestle you to the floor and drown you, if possible, in the real thing for a change instead of the symbolic blood that you had systematically drained from me day after humiliating day.

I didn't do it because your goodbye, when it came, stunned me like a hammer. Probably you counted on that, else you'd have been afraid to see me that last day. The razor blade is still where it was then, in the lining of my shoe.

116

I've been stunned ever since. This depression is much worse than the one I had when you met me. I might still kill myself if you weren't sweet enough to let me write to you. Writing the letters, I guess, is the main thing that keeps me going (if you call this going). Sometimes I wish you'd write back, but I know how busy you must be. I used to be busy myself and too tired to write to people, even when I knew how much it might mean to them. A few years ago, one of my closest friends died with me still owing him a letter, and I've never forgiven myself. Maybe it's just as well I no longer have any friends (except, of course, for you). I'd probably let them all down. I'll never let you down, Wanda, have no fear of that. If you should ever need me for anything, I'm as close as the telephone or mailbox. In-person visits could be arranged at the drop of your hat.

There's another reason I don't kill myself. As I discovered when I was visiting them, my family won't tolerate it. According to my mother, it would destroy my father. According to him, it would destroy her. My sister says if I do it, she'll by God do it too. My son says my grand-daughter—you ought to see her, Wanda, she's really something—would never live it down. My brother says I've got to think of the family business, a thing like that could wipe out everybody. Etc. Of all the people I know, only my ex-wife (#2, I'm not sure about #1) thinks the idea has merit. I remember that you once said, when we were discussing the subject, "That would show the bastards, wouldn't it?" The trouble is, Wanda, I don't want to show the bastards (except maybe you). I just want to be dead. Which means, if I do it, I'll have to make it look like an accident. Which in turn means my choices of method are more limited than I would like them to be. Furthermore, accidents aren't certain. I was in a bad car wreck once (car demolished, best friend killed) and survived with only a few scars. I'm always amused when, in the movies—maybe you've been struck by this too—a mere tumble down the stairs does the trick every time.

Still no snow here, but I guess you've got enough up there for both of us. Let me know if you'd like to hear more about weather conditions in Elmerton or for that matter the entire Southwest. I could copy the infor-mation right out of the Little Rock paper.

How was your New Year's Eve? I'll bet you had a blast, didn't you? Here at the Home, Mrs. Bonds made some punch and opened some pretzels and potato chips. The punch was nonalcoholic, but it was obvious that she and the doc were spiking theirs. The rest of us sat around and watched them get drunker and drunker until, right at midnight, in the middle of dancing to Auld Lang Syne, they collapsed on the sofa. The doc passed out and started snoring; Mrs. Bonds got up and weaved her way to the bedroom. Millie was so overcome by the festivities that she went on a crying jag. Jack tried to comfort her, but she told him to go away, he had a dirty mind. Loy looked on a for a while, then went up to bed. Jack, morose and befuddled, followed shortly afterward. I sat there with Millie, who praised me for always being a perfect gentleman. I responded by telling her how attractive she was. And she is attractive, if you go for faded bombshells. Claire Trevor in Key Largo. Or maybe Anne Baxter in something or other. I used to go for that type in a big way, but not any more. I don't go for any type now; I just go for you. You're one of a kind. Anyway, when we finally went upstairs, Millie asked me into her room. I politely refused, and she said she guessed I believed the stories I'd heard and didn't respect her. I assured her that it wasn't so. She grabbed my arm and tried to pull me through her door, but I jerked free. "I'm honored," I said, "but you see I'm—" That's as far as I got. "Tell me about it," she said, "you impotent pansy pervert." And with that she slammed the door in my face. I've told you before, sweetheart, you have nothing to fear from Millie.

I try to tell myself that you had no choice about leaving, that your time was up, etc. I not only tell myself that, I believe it. I not only believe it, I know it. But I know something else too. I know that if I had been worthy of you, you would have found a way to stay or take me with you. If you'll point out all the flaws in my character, I'll do my best to correct them. We could probably shape me up pretty quickly if we put our heads together like two normal people.

I don't see much of Little Tim except at bedtime. Believe me, that's enough. I can't stand the way he hugs his pillow and cries. He spends most of his other time off by himself. Sometimes when I happen to spot him, he's wearing a stricken, brave little look, as if he's swallowed the sorrows of the world and is holding them in by sheer force of will, in order, perhaps, that someone else, someone far away, can go happily about his or her business. Other times, he's having one of his savage but impotent rages. I'm afraid he might hurt himself, the way he kicks at rocks and trees and slams his fist against the wall. I'm glad, for your sake, that you're not here to see him. He might, in spite of your training, break your fucking heart. Either that or your fucking nose. I sure wouldn't want that to happen.

Love,
Tim

P.S. (next day, 1:15 p.m.): I'm feeling better and thought I'd add a note about Nelda. I visited her for a couple of hours this morning. I was eating some mints when I went to her room, and I popped one in her mouth. She gobbled it down. She's not underweight, and I suspect it isn't food she's hungry for. It's probably affection. As I read to her, she kept putting her hand out for more. She ate till the mints were gone; then she pouted. Maybe I can bribe her into taking a bath and washing her hair. She stinks to high heaven. What's the name of that perfume you always wore?

I don't know why I said I'm feeling better. I'm not.

"He's about as low as a guy can get," Robert said. "It's a real problem."

"It's not *my* problem," Wanda said.

"What if he kills himself?"

"What if he does?"

"Well . . . "

"Well what?"

"I don't know," Robert said. He looked around the room as if searching for help.

"Cheer up," Wanda said. "At least you know they haven't had any snow yet."

"I wish you wouldn't laugh," Robert said. "I've got so I like him."

"Wish wish wish," Wanda said in a voice she didn't recognize. The voice was so bitter she could taste it. "You know what *I* wish?" the voice cried. "I wish he *would* kill himself. Then maybe he'd leave me alone."

"Calm down," Robert said.

Wanda bit her lip. "I shouldn't have said that. I didn't mean it. Can we please just drop the subject?"

"Sure," Robert said.

"Did I tell you your father called me?"

Robert looked at her in alarm. "He knows better than that. I've told him to leave you alone. So has Mom."

"He wants me to come over and cut some wood. I said I'd discuss it with you."

"Consider it discussed," Robert said. "You're not going."

"All right," Wanda said. "But I hope that someday I can be friends with both your parents."

"That'll come. Maybe it will."

"When?"

"When Mom learns to accept you and Dad learns to behave around women . . . Anyway, who are you to talk? *Your* father doesn't even know we're married."

"I'll tell him when the time's right."

"Same with my folks," Robert said. "When the time's right you can visit them."

He went back to brooding over Tim's letter. He wanted to discuss it further, but Wanda refused. After dinner she went to her study and typed. She had mailed five chapters to Dr. Campbell on the day before the wedding, and she wanted to keep up the momentum. At eleven o'clock she returned to the living room and watched the news with Robert. He didn't mention the letter again that night or the next day. Wanda assumed that he had put it out of his mind, but she was wrong. When Floyd and Marie stopped by on Saturday afternoon, he pulled the letter from his pocket and asked them to read it.

"Maybe they don't want to," Wanda said.

"Yes we do," Marie said, "but let me get comfortable first." She removed her coat and scarf and peeled off her sweater. Under the sweater she wore a gray tee shirt with "Property of the Brooklyn Dodgers" printed on it. She was not wearing a brassiere, and the tee shirt jiggled.

"Who's this from," she asked, taking the letter from Robert, "your wife's unrequited lover?"

"I've come to like him," Robert said, "and I'm kind of worried."

Marie and Floyd sat on the sofa and read the letter carefully.

"He's pretty screwed up," Floyd said. He appeared to be giving the matter some thought.

"I'd be depressed too," Marie said to Wanda, "if I lived in a place like that. Why don't you tell him to leave that hole and meet some interesting people?"

"I wish you'd get it through your heads," Wanda said, "that I'm not telling him anything. It wouldn't be appropriate."

"If I'd been down there New Year's night," Marie said, "I'd have snapped him right out of it."

"I'll bet," Floyd said.

"I *would*," Marie said. "I'd have got some of that hooch in him. Then I'd have put on some music. I'd have got him to dance."

"I doubt it," Wanda said.

"Sure I would," Marie said, "just the way I did the big fellow." She stood up and stepped to the center of the room. She clapped her hands, stomped her feet, and shook her head. Her long hair swirled around her shoulders and face. She stopped abruptly and stood perfectly still, her arms extended and her eyes closed. Presently her fingers began to shake, then her arms, and then her breasts. When the shaking reached her hips, she pivoted smartly about and began to clap and stomp again. Robert stared at her as if in a trance. When he realized that Wanda was watching him, he grinned and blushed.

"Hey," Floyd said to Marie, "cut it out. I'm trying to think."

Marie turned on him, her eyes blazing. "*You* cut it out. We talked about that, remember? No more clamps." She laughed and sank to the floor and wiped her forehead with her sleeve. "Believe me," she said, "I'd have got him to dance."

"I doubt it," Wanda said again. "Anyway, it wouldn't have made him well."

"It might have," Marie said. "I'd have waltzed him around the room a couple of times and right out the door and into the nearest motel. Maybe that's all he needs."

"Millie tried it," Floyd said, "and it didn't work."

"Millie's not me," Marie said. "She's as depressed as he is. I still say he needs to be with somebody interesting."

"When you're in his mood," Wanda said, "there aren't any interesting people."

"Except you," Robert said.

"If that's true," Marie said, "it must give you a real sense of power."

"It does not," Wanda said.

"It would me," Marie said.

"Then it's a good thing you're not a therapist," Wanda said.

"At least I'm honest about it," Marie said.

"Or just plain ignorant," Wanda said.

"Hey girls," Floyd said. "No quarrels."

"Yeah," Robert said. He went to the kitchen and came back with four cans of beer.

"Thanks," Marie said. "I could sure do with some cooling off." She pressed the can to her head and muttered, "God, I'm restless."

"Let's try a scientific approach," Floyd said.

"Go to it, Einstein," Marie said.

"Has he read *You Be You, I'll Be Me?*" Floyd asked Wanda.

"Probably not," Wanda said. She smiled at the thought of Tim reading a book like that.

"Floyd and his books," Marie said. "He can't screw without *The Joy of Sex* right there on the bed. His idea of romance is to take your blood pressure while you're having an orgasm."

"Lay off," Floyd said angrily. "There's nothing wrong with science. Wanda knows what I mean. She's done things with rats."

"I'm not a rat," Marie said.

"She's done things with people too," Floyd said. "She's just not telling us about it."

"I wish you'd leave me out of this," Wanda said.

"I think we ought to send him a copy of *You Be You*," Floyd said. "It might do the trick."

"It wouldn't," Wanda said.

"Maybe we could send him the quiz part," Floyd said. "He could take the quiz and get a line on himself. Find out what areas he's strong in and what areas could stand some improvement."

"That sounds reasonable," Robert said. "It might even save his life. He asks Wanda, right there in the letter, to send him a list of his flaws."

Floyd produced a ballpoint pen and a small notebook. "Write this down," he said to Marie.

"Do I look like your secretary?" Marie said.

"I'll do it," Robert said, taking the pen and notebook.

"We'll start with the basics," Floyd said. "Does he understand that life equals growth, and that when you stop growing you start dying?"

"Oh God," Marie said.

"This is pointless," Wanda said.

"Let's give it a try," Floyd said.

"I don't want to," Wanda said. "I'm tired of discussing Tim. I want to do something else."

"The answer to the question is no," Marie said. "That's pretty obvious."

"Does not understand that life equals growth," Robert said, scribbling in the notebook.

"Ability to read people," Floyd said.

"Piss poor," Marie said.

"Why do you say that?" Robert asked.

"Never mind," Marie said with a quick look at Wanda.

"Can't read people," Robert said.

Floyd ran through self-acceptance, sense of identity as a unique being in his own right, best foot forward, ability to distinguish the real from the unreal, assertiveness, ability to tolerate frustration, and capacity to develop new interests. Marie gave Tim a "poor" in each category, and Robert wrote it all down.

"Time," Floyd said. "How does he use time? Does he proceed from one thing to another in an orderly manner?"

"Hell no," Marie said, "and neither do I. That's why we're existentialists. That's a pretty square book, if you ask me."

"Nobody did," Floyd said. "Space. How does he use—"

"I'm still on time," Robert said.

"Put down that he hates it," Marie said. "When you get to be his age, time becomes a burden."

"Hates time," Robert said.

"He hates space too," Marie said.

"How do you know?" Floyd asked.

"Why else would he stay holed up in that depressing house?"

"Hates space," Robert said. "He's not doing too hot."

"You might as well put down that he hates everything," Wanda said.

"Except Wanda," Marie said.

"Hates everything except Wanda," Robert said.

"Half the time," Wanda said, "he hates her too." She and Marie looked at each other and laughed.

"I am so restless," Marie said.

"If we're not going to do this right," Floyd said, "we might as well not do it."

"Now you're talking," Marie said.

"I can't think of any more questions anyway," Floyd said. "But the book's in the car. I could go down and get it."

"I'll go," Robert said.

"No you won't," Wanda said firmly. "We're going to do something else."

"It was written by a psychoanalyst," Floyd said. "I don't know what you've got against it."

"Nothing," Wanda said, "if you're talking about people who are more or less normal." She went on to explain, in some detail, that although the qualities Floyd had mentioned were desirable ones, it did no good to simply *tell* them to a person like Tim. If it were that easy, there'd be no need for therapy. A disturbed person, she said,

124

learned those things, not by being handed a list, but in the progressive stages of his relationship with a therapist.

"Unless the therapist takes a powder on him," Marie said. "Then it's suicide city."

"Shut up," Floyd said.

"Here come the clamps," Marie said.

"Wanda was telling me something," Floyd said.

"Ask Marie to tell you," Wanda said. "She's the expert on everything. I'm not saying another word."

"I'm restless," Marie said. She leaned back on her hands and stretched her legs out and pounded her heels against the floor. Her breasts jiggled. "I want to do something besides talk."

"Me too," Wanda said. She wished she could tell Marie to put on a brassiere, but of course she couldn't. It might sound anti-feminist.

"I'd like to discuss Tim some more," Robert said. "I've learned a lot about him."

"We're going for a snowmobile ride," Wanda said. "I just decided."

"Sounds good," Floyd said.

"You hate those things," Robert said.

"Not today I don't," Wanda said. "I'm in a crazy mood." It had occurred to her that if they went outdoors, Marie would have to wear more than a tee shirt.

They put on their boots and coats. Then they all went in Floyd's car to get the snowmobile. The day was clear and bright, but with a bitter wind; gusts of powdery snow, sparkling in the sun, whipped across the freshly plowed streets. Floyd, undaunted by poor visibility and occasional slick patches, sped along, bragging that he had never had an accident. Of all the people Wanda knew, only her father drove with the same disregard. When they reached Floyd's house, Robert helped him hook the snowmobile to the car. They headed for the trails north of town. Robert tried to get back to the subject of Tim, but Wanda cut him off with a steady stream of questions about other bad winters in the area. Floyd had the information on the tip of his tongue and didn't mind sharing it. Marie yawned a lot. It turned out that the trails were crowded, but Wanda didn't care—the noise would rule out any attempt at sustained conversation.

After a brief discussion, conducted in shouts, of what he called "procedures," Floyd took Wanda for a ride. Although it was exciting, ten minutes was all she could stand because of the blowing snow. Marie and Robert went on a longer ride, and then Floyd and Wanda went out again. Wanda was ready to go home, but Marie insisted on a second turn too. She and Robert got on the machine and roared off. When they didn't return in fifteen minutes, Floyd and Wanda went to the car and sat with the motor running and the heater on. Floyd asked her if she had heard from Burt Epperson.

"He called and apologized," Wanda said.

"What an asshole," Floyd said.

"It was all a misunderstanding. I was as much to blame as he was. What bothers me is the bowling." She explained Burt's ideas about bowling therapy to Floyd.

"Bowling," Floyd said.

"I just don't know whether I can work with patients if I've got to go bowling with them . . . Well, it's not your problem. I shouldn't be bothering you with it."

It's no bother. I might just look into this bowling."

"There's no need for that," Wanda said. She stared off at the snowmobile trails.

Floyd reached over and opened the glove compartment and took out a paperback copy of *You Be You, I'll Be Me*. He read some passages to Wanda.

"Maybe it wouldn't help a sick guy," he said, "but this book has turned my life around. I'm reading one now on how to develop my ESP skills." He began to describe the ESP book.

Wanda put her head against the window and closed her eyes.

"You're the only person I know that I can discuss these things with," Floyd said. "You're the only one who really understands me."

Wanda was dozing when Robert and Marie finally showed up.

"We ran out of gas," Marie said.

"That's impossible," Floyd said.

"The tank probably has a leak," Robert said. "We had to walk up to the old Johnson place and borrow some."

"It must have been a mile," Marie said. "My feet are like two chunks of ice."

On the way back to town she apologized to Wanda for the things she had said earlier. "Sometimes I take potshots," she said. "I don't know why."

Wanda could have told her that insecurity had a lot to do with it, but she decided not to. "It's all right," she said.

"I was tense," Marie said. "Now I'm relaxed."

"Thank God," Floyd said.

"I didn't mean to laugh at Tim," Marie said. "The poor guy's really suffering. But I shouldn't have made that crack about suicide city."

"There's something all of you ought to understand," Wanda said. "Therapy doesn't take on everybody. Some people never learn what's good for them."

"Really?" Marie said.

"Tim's that way," Wanda said. "He's like a little kitten that doesn't want to be weaned. If I'd let him, he'd suck at my breast till the day he died."

"That's cute," Marie said.

"She got it out of one of Tim's letters," Robert said.

"I've got clients who are the same way," Marie said. "They pretend they want jobs, but they really want to stay on welfare."

"It's not quite the same thing," Wanda said.

"You're right," Marie said. "It's not *my* tit they're sucking, it's the state's."

They laughed together, and Wanda felt they were friends again.

"It's odd to think," Robert said glumly, "that while we're riding along like this, without a care in the world, old Tim might be lying dead somewhere."

10

Jan 9

Precious Wanda,

The last three days have been hell—the worst I've had for a while. I did not, till just now when I started this letter, budge from my bed the entire time. (I must have, though, to piss. Otherwise the bed would be soaked, wouldn't it? Hell, I don't know.) The whole thing started Saturday morning when I had what I think is called a hypnagogic hallucination (correct me on that if I'm wrong). I woke up with the strongest possible feeling that you were sitting on the edge of the bed, waiting to surprise me. When I finally mustered the courage to open my eyes, you were there, bless you, real as could be, favoring me with the little smile that draws a guy in, your hands folded in your lap. It was only when I reached out to touch you that you vanished.

Immediately after the hallucination the fantasies started. Like the suicide fantasies I had in the hospital—maybe you remember—they were completely out of my control. I could not stop them; I could not keep them from starting. There were four of them, running consecutively and always in the same order. In the first, I had finally come to Windward to confront you in person. (This is a definite possibility, I hope you realize that.) I called you on the phone and talked you into seeing me at a cafeteria. We met at the door; you did not speak. You continued your silence

128

as we waited in line for coffee. We carried the coffee to an isolated table and sat across from one another. I began to berate you in a loud voice. You listened for a few minutes, then clasped one of my hands between the two of yours and said, so softly as to be merely mouthing the words, "I love you, Tim." (Is that a definite possibility?)

The second fantasy was the same as the first except for the end. In this one, you did not respond to me at all. After berating you, I pulled a revolver from my coat pocket and—as a chubby busboy dropped a tray and hollered—blew your fucking brains out.

In the third fantasy, we were in our little therapy room, which had been outfitted with a narrow bed. The covers were turned back, the sheets were snow white. I lay shivering on the bed, facing the wall. I was a child, I was Little Tim, but as emaciated as the poor children you sometimes see in ads for good causes. You were standing beside the bed, naked, your skin as white as the sheets. (What a generous bush you have, and darling little tits!) You stretched and yawned, then got into bed, all in slow motion. You wrapped me in your heavy arms and clutched me to you. I melted in your marvelous warmth.

Finally, I was in my apartment in Miami—the one I had before I came to the hospital. There was a knock at the door. I answered it, you walked in. You were eight feet tall. You embraced me, lifted me off the floor, and kissed me so hard my teeth caved in. I didn't mind a bit, even when the blood gushed from my mouth to yours and I passed out. It was a good way to die.

Last night the fantasies, which had run almost nonstop for three days, abruptly shut off, and I slid into a bleak but not unpleasant state beyond thought or feeling and not a bit frightening. I wish I could have stayed there, but I must have slept instead. Immediately upon waking, I started writing this letter.

I gave Nelda some candy again yesterday. Chocolates this time, and gooey. She's a mess. I spoke to her about cleaning herself up, but she ignored me as usual. I'm tempted to march her into the bathroom and bathe her myself.

I do my reading to her in a sing-song voice, pretending English is a language whose sounds I know but whose sense escapes me. But the sense seeps in, or part of it, and the part that does pertains to you. You and me and Little Tim. One day, instead of a book, I read—or sang—the entire sports section of the Arkansas Gazette. The sense seeped in. It wasn't about ball games or golf matches. It was about us.

I still haven't seen Loy in the woods, but I did hear a gun blast while I was running a couple of days ago. Later, when I returned to the house, there was a bony old hound lying in the front yard, its head blown off. I went to my room and cried for an hour. Next day I saw Loy and Doc Bonds burying the dog. When I got a chance to speak to the doc alone, he told me the dog had taken to killing chickens and had to be destroyed. If Loy hadn't done it, someone else would have had to. I'm glad there was a reason.

When you were kissing me and my teeth caved in, did you like the taste of my blood? I hope so; I want you like everything about me.

Love,
Tim

P.S. Two inches of snow yesterday. Our first of the year.

P.P.S. I'm giving a lot of thought to phoning you. If I do it, please be kind.

P.P.P.S. I've just now burned myself again. I've been meaning to talk to you about that habit. It's not the doing it that's bad, it's the wanting to do it. The same is true of killing yourself. Once you want to do it, once you're in that grip, you're already a goner. I've been a goner for years. But with you I could feel things beginning to change. Sure, I continued to talk about death—old habits are hard to break—but I was talking with less and less conviction. If we had continued, maybe I'd have changed my whole way of seeing. Maybe I'd have ended up in the grip of life. Who knows? I am so tired of thinking about death and saying wisdom. Of holding a gun to my head and saying authentic. Of saying shit and calling it Kierkegaard.

Robert had spent the week at home with a bad cold, watching television and shuffling back and forth between the sofa and the bed. He had little appetite and no taste for beer, but he consumed a good deal of warm lemonade with gin in it. He read sports magazines and studied basketball scores and standings in the paper. The Super Bowl was coming up, and he read articles about that. Every night, after the eleven o'clock news, he returned to the sports page and read the golf and tennis stories and the bowling results. Although he was not an outdoorsman, he read columns on ice-fishing and trapping; although he couldn't care less about skiing, he developed an interest in slope conditions. As the days passed, he became increasingly moody and preoccupied, and he spent a lot of time gazing out the window. He was, Wanda supposed, worried about business.

One night he handed the sports page to Wanda and told her to look at a picture. She looked and saw a short man in a hunting outfit standing beside a freshly killed deer. The deer, bleeding from a wound in its left side, was hanging head down from a contraption on the back of a pickup truck. The man was holding a shotgun in the crook of one arm and smiling into the camera. His other arm was flung around the deer. You might have thought he was posing with an old friend. The man looked vaguely familiar. Wanda glanced at the caption under the picture and read: "Mayor Kills Deer."

She handed the paper back to Robert. "What about it?"

"You didn't see who took the picture?"

Wanda shook her head.

"Floyd," Robert said.

"I didn't know he took pictures."

"He does a little bit of everything. He also killed the deer."

"The paper says the mayor killed it."

"He's letting the mayor take the credit. He called me and told me about it. The way Floyd's going, he'll be mayor himself someday." Robert shook his head and gave a brief chuckle. Then he went back to being sad and restless.

Tim's letter, which he had looked forward to, did not improve his disposition.

"I'm glad to know he's alive," Robert said, "but now he's having fantasies. He must have gone over the edge."

"Everyone has fantasies sometimes."

"Not like his, do they? He says he couldn't control them. Couldn't eat. Couldn't sleep . . . It's kind of scary."

"You haven't been eating or sleeping too well yourself," Wanda said.

"I've got a bad cold. That's not the same as an obsession."

"Maybe you've got both."

Robert gave her a quick look of surprise.

"I'm exaggerating," Wanda said, "but you do think about Tim a lot."

Robert grinned sheepishly and said he guessed he did.

The phone rang. Wanda, knowing it was Mrs. Martin, let Robert answer it. She had called every day during his illness. Twice she had stayed on the line for an hour while Robert assured her, over and over, that Wanda was taking good care of him. The present call promised to be another long one. Wanda went to her study and closed the door and tried to read, but the sound of Robert's voice interfered with her concentration. After a while she gave up and took a leisurely shower.

As she was drying off, she caught a glimpse of herself in the medicine-cabinet mirror. She dropped the towel to her side and took a good look at herself. She did have darling breasts, and they weren't so little either. If they seemed little, it was only because she was a large woman. She finished drying and stepped into the bedroom and stood in front of the full-length mirror. She did have clear white skin and a dark generous bush. Although she was heavy around the waist and hips, she had those marvelous long legs. She remembered a time when she had thought of herself as a great white slug, but Sarah Pitkin had taught her to appreciate her good points. She squared her shoulders and cocked her head and smiled . . .

On an impulse she went naked into the living room. Robert, no longer on the phone, was standing at the window. Wanda strolled past him and into the kitchen. She got a sponge mop from the broom closet and headed back to the bathroom.

"I left the shower curtain on the outside of the tub," she said by way of explanation. "I've got to do some mopping."

Robert turned slowly, his face blank. "You'd better put on your shoes," he said, "or you'll have a cold too."

Wanda sighed and returned to the bedroom and dressed. She knew that being self-absorbed went with being sick, but Robert was surely overdoing it. Well, maybe her nude trip through the apartment would have a delayed effect. Maybe it would suggest to Robert that it was okay for him to take his own clothes off once in a while. At the rate things were going, she guessed she would have to wait till he was dead to get a glimpse of his penis. For some reason this thought amused her.

At dinner Robert was silent and ate very little. Afterward he lay on the bed and gazed at the ceiling. Wanda reminded him that colds affected not only your body but your mind as well, and that he would feel better in a couple of days.

"Maybe so," Robert said listlessly. "What's on the nine o'clock movie?"

"I don't know," Wanda said, "but I'll watch it with you."

It was a made-for-TV movie about a detective lieutenant who, obsessed ("just like Tim," Robert said) with a murder case he couldn't solve, took a leave of absence. After spending a couple of weeks in an alcoholic stupor, listening to his beautiful but neurotic wife whine about his low salary and her lousy wardrobe and how they never *did* anything anymore, he went, on the advice of a kindly older detective, to a psychiatric clinic. His doctor turned out to be an attractive woman. ("The plot happened to require that, didn't it?" Wanda said.) By the end of one session, the doctor had decided that the only way to help the detective was by solving the murder. ("How stupid," Wanda said.) Before long they were prowling bars together, getting shot at, and being hit over the head in the halls of rundown tenements. About a third of the way through, the detective saved the doctor's life by taking a slug in the shoulder. As they waited for the ambulance, the doctor held the detective's hand. He looked at her in a way that suggested he was seeing her, for the first time, as a woman and not merely as a doctor. To Wanda's vast amusement, the doctor made snap diagnoses of suspects and possible witnesses. She pegged a go-go dancer as having a father fixation, whereupon the dancer quit her job and caught a bus back to her husband and baby in Shreveport. Later, on the basis of a thirty-second conversation, the doctor helped a fat bartender come to terms with his Oedipus complex. Still later, she cured a cub reporter of his feelings of inadequacy by encouraging him to approach a wistful young art student in Central Park. Despite these therapeutic miracles, the murder remained unsolved, and the detective ("just like Tim,"

Robert said) became hellbent for suicide. He was about to throw himself off a building when the doctor, suddenly possessed of tremendous strength, floored him with a right to the jaw. They spent the night huddled on the roof; at dawn, after swapping life stories, they kissed. If the detective hadn't reminded the doctor that he was a happily married man, they might have made love then and there.

At this point, Wanda threw up her hands and retired to her study. She intended to type, but as soon as she sat down she started thinking about Sarah Pitkin. Because Sarah had been trained as an analyst, most people who knew anything about it assumed that Wanda had been psychoanalyzed by Sarah. This idea—that Wanda had been analyzed by the legendary Sarah Pitkin, who soon afterward abandoned her career to take up with a jazz musician—so impressed her professors and fellow graduate students that Wanda would have been embarrassed to try to set the record straight . . .

* * *

Sarah was a tall woman, both voluptuous and motherly, who had completed her training analysis under Dr. North a couple of years before Wanda met her. Wanda had seen her in the house many times but had never spoken to her.

After her father introduced them and left the room, Wanda asked, in a small shy voice, if she and Sarah were going to do psychoanalysis together.

Sarah smiled and shook her head. "We're going to make a young lady out of a sadly neglected little girl. I'm going to teach you *about* psychoanalysis, so you'll understand your father better and respect his work, but we're not going to *do* psychoanalysis."

"Why not?" Wanda asked.

Sarah tossed her head and laughed softly. "I don't think your daddy would like that, and I wouldn't like it either."

"Why not?"

Sarah became very serious. "It's not what you need. You need too much of everything else to need psychoanalysis. One woman already died of neglect around here."

"If you mean my mother," Wanda said, "she died of cancer."

"Only her body. Her soul died of neglect."

134

That was the first time Wanda heard Sarah use the word "soul." Later she would use it more and more often. When she ran off with the jazz musician, Dr. North said that Sarah had been corrupted by "that bastard Jung," who also talked about the soul, and that this had made her easy pickings for the first "nigger ragtimer" to come her way.

"I won't have to lie on a couch?" Wanda asked Sarah.

Sarah shook her head, and Wanda, remembering Mrs. Winslow's agitation, as well as her shiny pink underwear, felt a surge of relief. It was going to be all right, she decided, to put her trust in Sarah Pitkin.

For three years, Sarah was Wanda's dietician, teacher, and all-round role model. She taught Wanda how to sit, how to stand, how to walk, and how to lie on a couch without looking like a slob. She taught Wanda how tall, large-boned women ought to dress. Most important, perhaps, she helped Wanda to a basic understanding of psychoanalysis. She did this by going through some of Dr. North's books with Wanda and some of Freud's papers on analytic method. She talked to Wanda about the harsh self-discipline imposed by the analytic calling—the austere setting, the long periods of silence, and the need to be alert for countertransference feelings. She explained to Wanda the basic rules—the rule of free association and the rule of abstinence—by which Dr. North conducted his patients through their private hells and into a state of acceptance, as Sarah put it, of things as they were. It was during this period that Wanda decided to become a therapist.

Often, at the end of the day, Dr. North and Dr. Pitkin left the house together. Sometimes Dr. North would return; other times he would stay out all night. Occasionally he and Dr. Pitkin came in together the next morning. Although Wanda was often lonely, she drew comfort from the knowledge that her father and her private doctor were spending so much time together, presumably discussing her case. Then, after a couple of years had gone by, it dawned on Wanda that Sarah and Dr. North shared more than an interest in Wanda's growth and development—that they were, in fact, having an affair. Wanda was so devastated that she allowed herself to be seduced by her old classmate Leon.

She and Leon had two main things in common. They were both ugly ducklings and their fathers were doctors—Leon's father being not a psychiatrist but a brain surgeon. Thrown together at the senior prom by their loneliness, they discovered that they had a third thing in common—a sense of being duped and used. They sat at a corner table and talked bitterly about their fathers. As they talked, Leon spiked each new glass of punch with Vodka from a bottle concealed under his coat. Eventually, without knowing how she got there, Wanda found herself lying on the back seat of Leon's Buick with her blue formal up around her waist. Leon was thrusting himself into her and telling her to wake up, for Christ's sake, didn't she know she was getting laid? Wanda, who had felt no pain but realized she was bleeding, moved around and caused Leon to bump his head. Leon said shit, forget about it and lie still, he was already coming. After he finished coming, he sat up and turned on the dome light and said God damn it to hell, the rubber had broken and Wanda was pregnant and his father would kill him. Then he saw the blood on Wanda's formal and said God damn it, wouldn't you know she was a virgin on top of everything else and how did he ever get mixed up with such a klutz in the first place? He pulled his pants up and buckled his belt and cried and cursed and pounded on the seat of the car and said, over and over again, that his life was ruined. All Wanda could think about was that he was as bad at doing sex as he had been, years ago, at describing it. He vaulted over the seat and drove Wanda home at break-neck speed. As she got out of the car, he said he'd kill her if she ever breathed a word of this to anybody.

Wanda entered the house, which was dark, and went to the kitchen. She found a half-gallon of ice cream in the freezer and sat down and started eating it directly out of the container. She had eaten perhaps a third of the ice cream when Sarah came in. She was wearing a light gown over a pair of pajamas. "I heard a noise," she said. She picked up the container of ice cream and threw it across the room and into the sink.

Wanda stood up and started to leave, but Sarah grabbed her wrist. Sarah saw the blood and realized what had happened. "Did he use anything?" she asked.

"It broke," Wanda said.

Sarah led Wanda into the bathroom and undressed her and put her in a tub of hot water. Then she went upstairs and came back with a douche bag and helped Wanda douche. She dried Wanda off, helped her into a flannel gown, and took her into the living room and sat her on the sofa.

Before Sarah could speak, Wanda burst into tears and called Sarah a whore and a slut and accused her of betraying Wanda's trust. Then she threw her arms around Sarah's neck and cried on her shoulder.

When Wanda finished crying, Sarah explained that she had been Dr. North's lover before she became Wanda's companion. Until recently, when Wanda's resentment had begun to show, she had assumed that Wanda was aware of that fact. She had failed to see how naive Wanda was about the ways of the world, and she was sorry for the pain she had caused. She had discussed the matter with Dr. North and from now on she would be living in the house. This was her first night under the new arrangement. She smiled ruefully and said she guessed she was a day late and a dollar short, but wasn't it good to have everything out in the open?

Wanda agreed that it was. She and Sarah hugged and kissed. At that point, Dr. North, who must have been standing in the doorway, came over and squeezed in between them and put his arms over their shoulders. "My two girls," he said. "My two big old girls." He looked handsome in his velvet smoking jacket and silk pajamas. Wanda, snuggling against him, felt more secure than she had ever felt in her life.

The arrangement lasted six months. Despite her pangs of jealousy over her father's devotion to Sarah, it was a satisfying time for Wanda. She felt as if she were part of a normal family. About a month before the big blow-up came, she could sense that something was wrong, but it never occurred to her that the arrangement would come to such an abrupt and shattering end.

The first thing that happened was that Sarah started going out in the evenings by herself. Sometimes she would stay out half the night. Then she started listening to jazz music, either on the radio or the phonograph, for hours at a time. She and Dr. North became cold toward one another, and Wanda could feel her own relationship with Sarah beginning to change. Although Sarah continued to say only good things about Dr. North and his work, her words lacked their former conviction. She tried to get Wanda to listen to jazz with her. She suggested that Wanda get her nose out of therapy books and enjoy some paintings or novels. She tried to get Wanda to read poetry. When Wanda showed little interest in these activities, Sarah sighed and looked sad. Sometimes she seemed on the verge of confiding some great secret to Wanda, but she never did. A few weeks before the blow-up, she terminated her work with the three patients she had been seeing in a small room off the kitchen of the North house. In her conversations with Wanda and Dr. North, she spoke more and more often of the soul.

The blow-up took the form of Dr. North's railing at Sarah for an hour and then kicking her out. Wanda, who was asleep when the row started, might have missed the whole thing if her father had not made so much noise. Hearing his voice, she flipped on the night light and saw that it was three o'clock in the morning. She went out on the second-floor landing and looked down into the living room. Sarah was sitting quietly and without apparent fear; Dr. North was tromping around the room and shouting derisively about the soul. According to him, it wasn't the soul Sarah was interested in but rather some nigger's big prick. Sarah replied wearily that the man's prick was no bigger than Dr. North's. It was his soul that was bigger. Dr. North said not to give him that shit, he knew the score on nigger pricks. Sarah looked at him with pity. "I am so glad to get away from you," she said. "I am so glad you've made it easy." Dr. North said he had not taught Sarah psychoanalysis in order to have her throw it all up and betray everything he stood for. "You don't have to tell *me* what you stand for," Sarah replied. Dr. North said he didn't want to hear any more about *that,* and Sarah said don't worry, she had lost all interest in the subject. Dr. North railed some more about nigger pricks and that bastard Jung and how he wanted Sarah out of his house once and for all. "I'm leaving," Sarah said. "First I want to say goodbye to Wanda." She stood up and started toward the stairs. Wanda moved out of the shadows in which she had been standing and yelled at Sarah not to come near her. "I only wanted to explain some things," Sarah said. Wanda said she didn't want to hear them—she had heard enough already—and for Sarah to leave her alone, she never wanted to see her again. "Goodbye then," Sarah said.

"Goodbye goodbye goodbye goodbye!" Wanda yelled.

For several weeks after Sarah left, Dr. North seldom spoke to

Wanda. When he did, it was to deliver a tirade about women thera-pists and nigger ragtimers and Carl Jung and his God damned soul. Then, with the time for Wanda to leave for college looming up, he started his campaign to send her on an apparently endless world cruise. Wanda stood her ground. Dr. North said the least she could do was forget about psychology and take up art history or com-puter programming or something like that. Wanda told him no, she was going to study psychology and go to graduate school and be-come a therapist. Then she would enter one of the psychoanalytic institutes. "Over my dead body," her father muttered.

Six years later, in her fifth semester as a graduate student, she bumped into Sarah at the Chicago air terminal. Sarah was with a short black man who was carrying a saxophone case. He was being interviewed by a reporter. When he heard Sarah say Wanda's name, he turned and allowed himself to be introduced. His own name was Malcolm. Although he must have been in his fifties, and must have lived a hard life, his face was as smooth and round as a cherub's. He looked, in fact, like a carved black Buddha. His eyes were wide and innocent, his smile sly.

"You the one I heard Sarah talk about," he said.

"She's still fat," Sarah said.

Wanda, fighting back a wave of anger, forced a smile. "I'm thin-ner than I've ever been," she said. "Anyway, look who's talking." Sarah had gained weight in the years since Wanda had last seen her. She was wearing an outlandish red silk gown that made her seem even bigger than she was. A white carnation was fastened to the front of her gown.

"I don't mean fat in the body," Sarah said.

"She jus' need to relax them smile muscles," Malcolm said. He stepped back and looked at Wanda's face. Then he took the carna-tion from Sarah's gown and stuck it in Wanda's hair. He ran a finger along Wanda's mouth. "You relax them muscles," he said. "She got that purty smile," he said to Sarah. "She relax a bit, she look like a white Billie."

"Billie?" Sarah said. She gave a loud laugh.

"You don't worry about a thing," Malcolm said to Wanda. "You got that purty smile. Some dude drag that soul right out of there someday." He turned abruptly back to the reporter, who had watched the episode with a bemused expression, and began to discourse, in a cultured British accent, on what sounded to Wanda like highly technical aspects of the music of Bartók.

"*Billie*," Sarah snorted.

Wanda, totally confused, fled to the restroom. She looked in the mirror and saw that the carnation looked as silly as it felt. She tore it from her hair and threw it in the toilet and flushed it down. Then she marched out of the restroom and, without so much as a glance in Sarah's direction, headed for the departure gate . . .

* * *

She shook her head and settled down to work. When she returned to the living room, after about an hour, Robert was watching the sports news. When it was over, he told Wanda how the movie had ended.

The killer, he said, turned out to be the detective's wife. Her arrest left the way open for an affair between the detective and the doctor. The detective had possessed, all along, the evidence of his wife's guilt, but a mental block kept him from piecing it together. Instead, he had run around in circles and chased after red herrings.

Wanda said it sounded pretty stupid and that she was glad she hadn't watched it.

"The psychiatrist knew from the beginning that it was the wife," Robert said, "but she couldn't tell the detective."

"Why not?"

"He had to work it out for himself," Robert said. "Otherwise he woudn't have been cured."

"Oh God," Wanda said. She went to the kitchen and fixed Robert a cup of gin and lemonade and poured herself some Scotch.

"Did that psychiatrist remind you of anybody?" Robert asked.

"Not of me," Wanda said. "The whole thing was completely unbelievable."

"How about Marie?"

"She didn't look like Marie."

"I don't mean in looks," Robert said. "I mean in the way she plunged in and took matters in her own hands. The way she solved the murder and saved the detective from a loveless marriage. That's the kind of psychiatrist Marie would be."

Wanda remembered what Marie had said about keeping people on welfare. Marie didn't know how to let her clients go. "I see what you mean," she said. "Marie would make a terrible therapist."

Robert seemed not to hear. He picked up Tim's letter and stared at it. "You're right," he said. "I probably worry too much about him. Like you said, everyone has fantasies. That doesn't mean a guy's going over the edge."

When Wanda went to bed, Robert was holding the sports page in his lap but looking at the television set. The station had gone off the air, but he was watching the blank snowy screen with the same interest he had shown in the movie.

11

Jan 16

Dear Wanda,

Have you heard the one about the psychiatrist and the whore?
Goes like this:

PSYCHIATRIST: I'm going to have to drop you as a patient, Miss Seat-man. I'm developing unprofessional feelings for you.

WHORE: Oh yeah? What's that called?

PSYCHIATRIST: Called? Well, it's a countertransference.

WHORE (eyeing the doctor's fly): Jeez, you guys got a fancy name for everything. Where I work, we call it a hard-on.

A real knee-slapper, eh Wanda?

I thought of the joke because I've been having hard-ons galore the last few days—at least a dozen, I'd say, after going for months with scarcely a one. The truth is, after the early erotic stage of therapy—that is, after Little Tim took charge—I found it impossible to fantasize about you. The result was a lack of erections. Then, four or five nights ago, I had the following dream: We were in our little room, engaged in therapy. You were wearing your blue party dress—the one you wore when you entertained that twirpy doctor. Suddenly, I don't know how, you were spilled backward out of your chair and I was on you. At the same time, I was still sitting in my own chair. I was watching myself rape you. You

142

were all blue dress and flailing white legs (I don't know what happened to your pantyhose). I woke with what an old navy buddy used to call a throbber. I merely touched it and was covered with come. I've been having hard-ons, one after the other, ever since, and jacking off as I re-create the dream. Wish you were here; maybe this is what you people call a breakthrough.

In one way the dream was totally unrealistic. I lost so much weight in the hospital that, even though we're the same height, you must have out-weighed me by thirty pounds. I couldn't possibly have raped you. Bet I could now, though—you should see how I've built myself up.

I'm going to have to do something about Nelda, and pretty damned quick. Her face and hands, and her robe as well, are caked with choco-late. She's beginning to turn my stomach. I wasn't up to doing anything about her this week, however. We both ate candy and cried. Her eyes, in case I haven't told you before, are fully intact. They're a deep brown, like yours, and very pretty. The only thing wrong with them is that—except for the crying mechanism—they just don't work.

Why don't you write to me? Excuse me while I burn myself. You bitch. I'll be Little Tim again if that makes me more appealing. Please let me know what you want me to be. Please.

> *Yours,*
> *Tim*

P.S. If you have any pictures of yourself in a bathing suit or shorts, you might send them along.

P.P.S. Speaking of rape, I saw a picture in the paper of some hard hats ogling a woman who was passing by a construction site. The cap-tion said "Psychological rape?" The accompanying story quoted a psy-chologist as saying that the hard hats' behavior could be more damaging than a physical rape. I guess he'd consider this letter an instance of psy-chological rape. If he did to a woman what you did to me—what would he call that? Probably call it therapy, the son of a bitch.

Wanda decided not to show this letter to Robert, who could be counted on to overreact one way or the other. Either he would be angry or he would feel obliged to keep up with Tim in the number of erections he could get. He might even be inspired to enact some kind of rape scene involving the blue dress—which, however, thanks to the twirpy doctor's impatience with zippers, no longer existed.

She glanced at the letter again. It was irritating to think of the hours she had spent with this man, trying to give him a feel for therapy, only to have him write a letter like this one. But she knew that irritation was not an appropriate feeling. The correct thing was to acknowledge that such dreams were a natural product of the transference and then to put Tim from her mind. She wished he could see how sick he was. That was an appropriate feeling. It was also appropriate to hope that he would leave that sleazy rest home and get some decent treatment, but she guessed he wouldn't. It was part of his sickness that he would torture himself. If he wasn't using her as an excuse to do it, he would find another one.

In the same mail she received a letter from Dr. Campbell. He was impressed, he said, with the chapters Wanda had sent him last month. If she could bring the remaining chapters up to the same level, the dissertation would be accepted. He urged her to keep at it. Perhaps, he suggested, she would want to hire a professional typist. The chapters she had sent him were so full of errors and strikeovers that he sometimes had trouble following her argument. The next two pages of the letter described, in scientific terms and great detail, a butterfly Dr. Campbell had caught last week. Wanda skipped over these pages and found a helpful list of misspellings and grammatical errors.

Although she had typed all morning and was looking forward to reading an article on therapeutic technique, she was so encouraged by Dr. Campbell's letter that she decided to return to the typewriter. She tore up the letter from Tim, put the other letter back in its envelope, and went to her study. She was starting to type when someone knocked at the door. By the time she reached the living room, the visitor was pounding on the door and yelling "Let me in! Let me in!"

"Who is it?" Wanda called. Then it struck her that it was Tim. He had said he was coming, now he was here. No doubt he had his gun. No doubt his razor blade. No doubt he was completely insane.

144

One of them, probably both, would be dead in the next few minutes. No telling what he would make her do before he killed her . . . He loved her though, that was the thing to remember. That gave her the upper hand. If she kept her head, she could handle him. If she played it right, he would end up groveling at her feet. Then she would have him put in a nice place where all mail was censored and from which no one escaped . . . That was silly. The thing to do was call the police. The thing to do was go to the window and scream. The thing to do was go to the balcony and jump . . .

The visitor pounded on the door again.

"I said who is it?" But why was she asking? The thing to do was—

"It's me."

"*Who?*"

"Me. Your daddy-in-law."

Wanda leaned against the wall and took a few deep breaths. Then, after putting on the chain lock, she slid back the bolt, opened the door, and peeked out. It was indeed Mr. Martin. He held a six pack of beer in one hand and a chain saw in the other.

"God," Wanda said, "am I glad to see you."

"I hoped you would be," Mr. Martin said. He staggered backward and gave a little bow.

"But I can't let you in. You wait there and I'll call a taxi."

"Why would I want a taxi?" Mr. Martin said in a loud voice.

"I'll call Robert then," Wanda said.

"They try to keep us apart," Mr. Martin said to a woman coming out of the next apartment.

"They'll do that," the woman said, and hurried down the hall.

"This is my daughter-in-law," Mr. Martin shouted after her, "and I aim to see her." He threw himself against the door. The lock snapped and he lurched inside. He reeled across the room and fell heavily into the chair by the window. "Here I am," he said. He put the beer and the saw on the floor and struggled out of his mackinaw.

"You can't stay," Wanda said. "We have to get you home."

"I'm lonesome," Mr. Martin said. He whipped off his hat and ran his fingers through his thick wild hair.

"I'll call Robert," Wanda said.

"You look real good in that track suit," Mr. Martin said. "What's your best time?"

"I only wear it around the house," Wanda said.

"Let's have a beer," Mr. Martin said. He took out two beers and opened them and offered one to Wanda.

She shook her head and sat down on the sofa, trying to think what to do.

"I'll have to drink them both," Mr. Martin said, "but that's okay. I've already had eight." He leaned back and drank from one can and then the other. "They think I'm not welcome here," he said, "but I am." His mouth glistened with beer.

"You catch your breath," Wanda said. "Then we'll see about getting you home."

"I know when I'm welcome," Mr. Martin said.

"Of course you do."

"We'll sit here and chew the fat and then I'll show you the chain saw."

"I'll call Robert right now if you want me to," Wanda said.

"How is old Bob?" Mr. Martin asked.

"He's fine."

"How about the marriage? Is that fine too?"

Wanda nodded.

"Atta girl," Mr. Martin said with a wink. He put the can to his lips, and beer dribbled down his chin. "You sure?"

Wanda nodded again.

"If Bob gives you any trouble," Mr. Martin said, "you let me know." He wiped his mouth with the back of his hand.

"I will," Wanda said.

"How's your father?"

"Okay, I guess."

"Him and his movie stars. I've lived sixty-five years and never met a movie star . . . What do you think of all this snow?"

"I enjoy it," Wanda said.

"I'll bet you didn't have snow like this in Florida."

"It's a change, all right."

"How about inflation? What do you think about that?"

"It's pretty bad, isn't it?"

"Not as bad as the depression," Mr. Martin said. "I'll say that much for it." He polished off one of the beers, set the can down, and attacked the other one. He jerked the can from his mouth and beer foamed over the top and down the side. "They think I don't know how to comport in front of women," he said, "but I do."

"Of course you do."

"Do you think so?" Mr. Martin became aware of the beer on his hand and began to lick it off.

"Definitely," Wanda said.

There was a long pause as Mr. Martin continued to lick his hand. Wanda wondered what he would do if she picked up the phone. She had a feeling he wouldn't like it.

"I always got good marks in comportment," he said. "Or was it conduct?"

"I don't know," Wanda said.

"One or the other," Mr. Martin said. "It's been so long ago . . . " He shut his eyes and looked as if he was trying to visualize an old report card. "It's no use," he said. "The years add up and then you forget."

"I know it," Wanda said.

"Even if you remember, you might remember wrong."

"Isn't that the truth?"

"Right or wrong, no one would know the difference."

"Maybe they would. Can I call Robert now?"

"If they did know the difference, they wouldn't give a damn." Mr. Martin finished his beer and yanked open another one. "They'd say conduct or comportment, who cares? After a while they think you're an old fart and that nothing matters."

"You're down on yourself today," Wanda said.

"All I was ever good for was to carpenter," Mr. Martin said. "I wanted to build houses, but Ma wouldn't let me. 'Get on at the university,' she said. 'Get on at the university. That's where your security is. That's where your benefits are.' So I got on at the university . . . Are you sure I'm comporting myself?"

"You're doing fine," Wanda said.

"Thank you," Mr. Martin said. "I'm feeling a little less nervous. You want to hear a funny story?"

"Actually," Wanda said, "you caught me at a bad time. I was right in the middle of something."

"It's about a psychologist."

"I'm sorry, I don't have time."

147

"It's about a lady psychologist."

"I'm going to call Robert."

"It's about a lady psychologist and a traveling salesman."

"The answer is no," Wanda said. "I've heard enough God damned jokes for one day." She blurted out the words without thinking, then realized that she was being too hard on Mr. Martin. "I'm sorry. I shouldn't have said that."

"Excuse me for living," Mr. Martin said bitterly. He looked as if he might either cry or turn vicious. "I don't know any such story anyway," he mumbled. "I don't think there even is one."

"I'll tell you what," Wanda said. "Let's have a look at the chain saw, and then we'll send you home."

Mr. Martin perked up. "I might have known. The ladies are crazy about chain saws." He picked up the saw and set it on his knees. "It's pretty heavy," he said, "but I can handle it." He held the saw up for Wanda's inspection.

"It's beautiful," Wanda said. It was much bigger than she remembered. It looked as if it belonged outdoors. In a small apartment it took on a menacing look.

"You'll have to come over here if you want the full impact," Mr. Martin said.

"I can see from here."

"No you can't." Mr. Martin set the machine on the floor. He dropped to his hands and knees and began to crawl around, grunting like a pig.

"If you're looking for an electrical outlet," Wanda said, "there's one over there by the desk. We're not going to start it up though, are we?"

"You betcha," Mr. Martin said. He crawled toward the desk; then he stopped and raised up on his knees. "What am I thinking of? This isn't the little old electrical model you saw at my house. This is the one the ladies like. It's a sixteen-incher and it runs on gas." He shook his head and grinned foolishly. "I must be getting old-timer's disease. Or maybe I've had a few too many." Carrying the saw in front of him, he walked on his knees over to Wanda.

"Isn't it dangerous?" Wanda said.

"It would be with some people," Mr. Martin said, "but with me you don't have to worry." Still on his knees, he rocked backward

148

and almost fell over. "First you flip this little switch." He swayed from side to side. Although it was not especially warm in the room, he was sweating heavily.

"I don't think we ought to be doing this," Wanda said. "Why don't I call Robert?"

"And then," Mr. Martin said, "you just pull this cord." He jerked on the cord and the machine roared to life. A puff of smoke drifted toward the ceiling. The room filled with the sharp smell of gasoline.

"It's really beautiful," Wanda shouted. "Please turn it off."

Sweat poured down Mr. Martin's face. "If you wanted to saw something," he shouted back, "you'd hold it like this." He demonstrated the proper grip. "Let's say you wanted to saw this coffee table. You'd bring the saw down like this—"

He accidentally tipped forward. The teeth of the saw touched the table, and the machine bucked in his hands. The teeth hit the table again. The blade flew backward and struck Mr. Martin in the face and knocked him over. From the amount of blood that suddenly appeared, Wanda was sure he was dead.

* * *

"Look at this mess," Robert said when he got home from the hospital. "The carpet's ruined."

"Is your father all right?" Wanda asked.

"The table's shot. That's for sure."

"We'll get a new one. How about your father?"

"He's okay. They put a bunch of stitches in his nose and forehead, and then I took him home . . . What was he doing here?"

"He's lonely."

"Crap. Mom's right there with him."

"People get lonely when they retire."

"He won't bother you again," Robert said. "I gave him a good talking to in the emergency room."

He went to the bathroom and took a shower, and they went out for a sandwich. When they returned to the apartment, Robert spotted the envelope from Wanda's chairman.

"A letter from Tim," he said. "I forgot about him because of

Dad." He picked up the envelope and looked at the return address. "It's not from Tim."

"It's from my committee chairman," Wanda said. "We didn't get one from Tim."

"Today's Thursday."

"Sometimes they don't come till Friday. You can read the one from my chairman. It's good news."

"You can tell me about it." Robert put the letter down and went to the kitchen for a beer. "I hope to God Tim's okay."

When there was still no letter on Saturday, Robert became seriously worried. "We *always* get a letter," he said. "Every week."

"He's skipping a week," Wanda said. "What's wrong with that?"

* * *

Later, at Denny's, they told Floyd and Marie about Mr. Martin's accident.

"Your poor mother," Marie said to Robert. "I'll stop by and see her."

"She'd appreciate it," Robert said.

"We've become friends," Marie said to Wanda.

"You're ahead of me," Wanda said.

"It's a tragedy," Marie said, "the way you've alienated her."

"It's all in her head," Wanda said.

"That's not fair," Robert said.

"I've only heard one side of the story," Marie said. "I think I'd better stay out of it."

"Mr. Martin's the one that's hurt," Wanda said.

"It's his own fault," Robert said.

"He's kind of an elemental chauvinist," Marie said. "Isn't he?"

"He needs therapy," Wanda said.

"I don't think Mom would go for that," Robert said.

"She needs therapy too," Wanda said.

"Don't be dumb," Robert said.

"He's pretty old for therapy," Marie said.

"You can do wonders with old people nowadays," Wanda said.

"There's a section on old people in *You Be You*," Floyd said.

150

"He's been an embarrassment to Mom for forty years," Robert said.

"He used to beat on her, didn't he?" Marie asked. "She told me he did."

"Yeah," Robert said, "till I put a stop to it." He held up his fist.

"Does he understand the value of short-term goals?" Floyd asked. "Does he appreciate the beauty of endings?"

"How would I know?" Robert said.

"The acceptance of life as a finite process," Floyd said. "That's the key."

"He makes me sick," Robert said. "I don't even want to talk about him."

"Doreen called me again," Floyd said. "She still wants to see Wanda. I told her no, of course."

"I don't want to talk about her," Robert said. He struck the top of the table with the flat of his hand, causing the glasses to rattle. There was a long pause; they all looked off in different directions. The couple at the next table got up and left. Robert caught the waitress's eye and ordered a round of drinks. Then he announced to Floyd and Marie that Tim's weekly letter had not arrived. The three of them speculated on what this meant.

Robert took the view that Tim was dead and they might as well forget about him. "He was over the edge a week ago," he said. "If he's not already dead, he soon will be." Marie, on the other hand, was sure he had finally wised up and found himself a girl—not that bag Millie, and not the blind woman either—and forgotten all about Wanda. From her description of the imaginary girl, it was obvious that Marie had someone like herself in mind. Floyd's contention, based on the book he was reading, was that psychotherapy was a disguised form of mental telepathy. If Wanda would lay herself open to all the Tim vibes that were coming her way, she could tell them not only whether Tim was alive or dead but also what he was thinking and feeling at any given moment.

Wanda smiled and said she didn't believe in mental telepathy.

"That's why you're not getting the vibes," Floyd said. "You've got to believe." He told her about the vibes he had been getting from his mother, who had been dead for twenty-two years. "I can't make out words yet," he said, "but the vibes are there."

Wanda was glad when a basketball game appeared on television and the talk turned to sports.

* * *

As they were getting ready for bed that night, Robert handed Wanda the envelope from her committee chairman. "I found this in the bathroom," he said.

"Thanks," Wanda said. "Did you read it?"

Robert shook his head. "You already told me about it. I think you must be trying to lose it."

"Why's that?"

"Every time I turn around, I find it someplace else."

"I'll put it in my desk," Wanda said. On the way to the study she decided to read the letter again. She removed it from the envelope and discovered that she had torn up the wrong letter. Instead of Professor Campbell's words, she was reading Tim's stupid joke. She threw the letter into her desk and slammed the drawer shut. Now she would have to find all those misspelled words herself, and correct all that grammar.

12

Dear Wanda,

A few days after you left me, I went to the hospital library and checked out some books on therapeutic technique. Since my own therapy had turned out so badly—it was, if you can stand the truth, the most humiliating experience of my life—I wanted to find out how the damned thing might have ended if we had been able to finish it. So I read up on such things as the therapeutic alliance, working through the trans-ference, and finally termination. The more I read, the better I felt. We could have done that, I kept telling myself. We'd have by God made it. Under the spell of those books, and in a blaze of good feeling, I con-structed a vision of what our parting should have been like. The vision was this:

Our last session completed, we walk back on the ward together. You're stunning in a soft gray suit, white blouse, and little black tie; I'm slicked up too, in a fresh tee shirt and brand-new khakis. We chat amia-bly till we reach the nurses' station. We stop there, turn to face each other, shake hands solemnly. Overcome by mutual admiration and affection, we embrace. We hold each other at arms' length for a last good look. Those kindly folk in the nurses' station beam their approval. I give you a chaste kiss on the cheek. You turn and walk slowly but pur-

posefully down the hall, headed for new patients and new triumphs, enriched by your encounter with a tough old nut like me. At the end of the hall you look back and give a wave farewell, then disappear. I stand there, completely cured, grinning modestly as the nursing staff shower me with congratulations. Soon, maybe next week, I too will walk down that hall, a reborn man with a bright future, ready at long last to accept his share of the goods of life. That's how the books made it sound.

The vision sustained me for about a week. Then one night I found myself casually burning my legs. We hadn't, after all, really done those things, all that working through, and nothing had changed except for the worse. Instead of being something different, you had revealed yourself as an extra big helping of the same old shit. Another woman who walked away. Still, it was a nice vision while it lasted. I tried to recreate it today and got the following:

Our last session completed, we walk back on the ward together. You're wearing nothing but a pair of white underpants; I'm completely naked. You're scowling, I look defeated. We turn to face each other. Suddenly you embrace me, nuzzle my ear. My prick stirs; I'm going to get something out of this after all. You step back, leer, and give the nursing staff a wink. They produce a piano, trombone, and two B-flat tenor saxes, and break into a barrelhouse version of "Moon River." You reach down and tweak my swollen cock as you might tweak a small boy's chin. You give a cruel laugh and walk down the hall, pausing at the door for a lewd little number with your behind. Old-time burlesque, Wanda, performed with a flourish. The music blares, the nurses sing. The only words I can make out are "cock teaser," which appear in place of the words of the title. The nurses point at me, whooping and hollering. I stand there, a shit-eating grin on my face, my cock in my hand . . .

. . . Even as I sit here now, my cock in my hand. I don't know why you have to drag sex into everything, but obviously you do.

It would have been pointless—I think you'll agree—to wash Nelda if I didn't also change her clothes. After checking her closet and bureau and finding them empty, I rode the bus to Little Rock last Friday and went to Woolworth's and bought three cheap housedresses, several pairs of underwear, and a pair of slippers, along with some shampoo, soap, washcloths, etc. Next day I washed her face and hands. Then I asked her to step into the bathroom and put on one of the dresses. She gave no indication that she understood me, so I pulled her to her feet, removed her robe, and helped her into the dress. I tried to comb her hair, but I couldn't because of the tangles. Furthermore, in spite of the fresh dress, she still smelled very bad. I had no choice but to drag her to the bathroom and give her a shower and a shampoo. I won't bother you with the details, some of which are embarrassing and even disgusting. Let's leave it that I got the job done. For a while, anyway, Nelda will be presentable; for a while, she won't stink up the room. If I'm patient with her, perhaps she'll start doing some things for herself. Until she does, she's not getting another God damned chocolate.

To get back to you and me. The horrible thing is that I understand, from things you said and from my reading, the explanation for my feelings for you—that they're transference feelings, a way of reliving the past, etc. I understand fully; I'm even, in some sense, willing to accept the explanation. I tell myself everyday, in a half-humorous, civilized tone: "Be sensible there, fellow—it isn't her you have these feelings for," and I quote old Freud to myself, and old whoever-else-it-was I read, and I pat myself on the back for being superior to those pathetic housewives you hear about who, not understanding a thing about transference, imagine themselves to be in love with their doctors. Doesn't do a bit of good, Wanda. In my heart I am those housewives.

And who's to say we aren't right, we housewives? Who's to say I don't, or don't "really," love that sympathetic, quietly attentive young woman with the soulful eyes and the dandy legs. However you try to account for it, it's you I love. No reason I couldn't, no reason I shouldn't. Except that maybe you don't love me—but what kind of reason is that? And if you don't, why won't you come right out and say so? Then I'd know where I stood. Then I'd know what I was up against. Then I could go about making myself absolutely irresistible. All I want is the same chance you'd give any one of a hundred other men.

So fuck transference. Transference is the story you tell yourself to make a dirty business sound clean. Transference is your way of distorting my feelings. It's your way of avoiding me. Of pretending I don't exist. Worse yet, of pretending you don't exist. It's your way of living with what you do in case something goes wrong. Let me tell you what happened.

Somewhere in the middle of that elaborate pas de deux called therapy— in response to a hundred invitations and a thousand signals that it was safe to do so—I handed you my fucking heart. I didn't hand it to the ghost of my God damned mother or my God damned female sibling or one of my God damned spouses or some other significant other in my insignificant past. Nor did I hand it to an anonymous, readily exchangeable therapeutic presence. I handed it to you, to the little bit of you that was palpably and blessedly there, in person, day after day. Don't you understand anything? Despite all the distortions I brought to that little room—desperate fellow that I am, I brought a lot—I didn't mistake the nature or meaning of that particular gift. You did the mistaking. Fuck transference.

I'll tell you one thing Freud was definitely right about. He said that when a patient felt rejected by a therapist, all the gains he had made would be blown away like chaff in the wind. I guess you never read that part, huh? You miserable fucking piece of asshole shit.

Sincerely,
Tim

P.S. A bad joke was played on Little Tim a couple of nights ago. Early in the morning, while he was half awake after a series of sinister dreams, a woman crawled into bed and put a heavy arm across his body. His back was to her and he didn't bother to look around. He simply assumed it was you. He snuggled against her—secure in the warmth of her body, reassured by the warmth of her breath against his neck—and fell into an untroubled sleep. An hour or so later he awoke with a feeling of being suffocated. The arm, flabby and moist, lay across his face; the warm breath had become an ugly snore; the soft body had become a lumpy mass that threatened to crush him. The air smelled of wine, sweat, and urine. Little Tim pulled himself free, sat up in bed, and started screaming. He kicked at the woman—who was, of course, Mrs. Bonds—until she rolled off the bed. She didn't show up for lunch, but at supper she looked at me with contempt. Needless to say, she didn't apologize. Once they've defined you as a mental case, they don't bother much with the amenities. Either that or they bother you to death. What the hell are you people so afraid of?

Wanda was touched by the paragraph about how the therapy should have ended. She read it several times. She wasn't sure about the hugging and kissing—she would probably have discouraged it—but the good feelings would have been appropriate. They were the rewards of a job well done. Reading the paragraph, she was more anxious than ever to get on with the real business of her life . . . She shut her eyes and was caught up in Tim's vision. There she was, striding down that corridor, headed for new patients and new triumphs. Her father, proud as could be, was waiting at the door. They took the elevator downstairs. They walked across the long green hospital lawn. Dr. North listened with admiration as Wanda described the ins and outs of the case. They talked far into the night, close now in a way they had never been. Dr. North was asking Wanda's opinion on a difficult case of his own when the phone rang. Wanda opened her eyes and went to answer it.

"Daddy?" she said.

"Wanda?"

"Yes. Is that you?"

"Who?"

"Daddy."

"No," Robert said. "It's me."

"Robert? I didn't recognize your voice."

"I didn't recognize yours," Robert said. "Why were you talking that way?"

"What way?" Wanda looked around the room to get her bearings.

"Like a little girl."

"I was thinking about Daddy," Wanda said. "I must have dozed off. Then when the phone rang, I thought—"

"Yeah well," Robert said. "Listen, I've got to work late."

"Again?" It was the third night in a row. He had fallen far behind, apparently, the week he had the cold.

"That's okay, isn't it?" Robert said.

"I guess so. I need to type anyway."

"I almost forgot to ask, did we hear from Tim?"

"Not only that, but it's a really nice letter."

"I'm just glad to get one," Robert said.

After they hung up, Wanda reread the paragraph about how the therapy should have ended. Then she went to her study. A book about the psychology of fat women had just come out. Although it was written for a popular audience, it contained material that was pertinent to Wanda's own research. In a way, she was glad that Robert was working late again. She could start rewriting her introduction.

Robert came home about ten o'clock. Wanda, who had forgotten to go to the grocery store, was glad to see that he had brought several cartons of Chinese food. Except for beer, the refrigerator was empty. She dished up the Chinese food while Robert read Tim's letter.

"Why do you say it's nice?" he said. "He seems pretty mad to me."

"The one paragraph's nice," Wanda said. "The rest of it's the usual junk."

"He's got sex on the brain again."

"Why do you say that?"

"The part about sitting there with his thing in his hand."

"Oh yeah," Wanda said.

"You know what I want?"

"What's that?" Wanda took a bite of food and looked at Robert out of the corner of her eye.

Robert lifted both arms, and Wanda thought he was going to embrace her. It turned out, though, that he was stretching.

"I want to get a good night's sleep," he said with a yawn. "I've never been so tired in my life."

* * *

The next morning Wanda went to the university library to check some references. When she finished, she drove downtown and bought Robert a shirt. She had bought him something every week since they had been married, with the aim of renewing his wardrobe. She was pleased with the way he was responding. Although he still wore his old clothes to work, he had started dressing up a bit when they went out. He had lost a few pounds and was taking pride in his appearance. Wanda had not said so to Robert—she did not want to make him self-conscious—but she was beginning to think of them as a sharp-looking couple.

As she stepped out of the men's store, she heard someone call her name. She turned and saw Marie hurrying toward her through a cloud of blowing snow. Marie slid on the ice and bumped into Wanda. They clutched at each other to keep from falling.

"Could we have lunch?" Marie said. "There are some things I need to tell you." She sounded so urgent that Wanda gave in.

They walked across the street to a vegetarian restaurant that specialized in soups. The restaurant was crowded and steamy. After standing in line for a few minutes, they started to leave. Then a waitress, ignoring the people in front of them, motioned them to a table that was being vacated.

"That's Janet Plum," Marie said as they made their way to the table. "She's in my CR group. I didn't know she was working today."

They sat down and looked at the menu. Marie recommended the chili.

"What was it you wanted to tell me?" Wanda asked.

Marie fidgeted and said it was nothing specific, she just wanted to talk. They were friends, weren't they? "Have you heard from Doreen yet?" she asked.

Wanda shook her head.

"She called Floyd again," Marie said. "Aren't you dying to know what it's about?"

"I'm curious, but I'm not exactly dying."

"I would be."

Wanda smiled. It didn't take a psychologist to see that Marie was big on instant gratification.

"You're such a patient person," Marie said.

"If I'm going to help others endure frustration," Wanda said, "I have to be able to endure it in myself."

"Nothing seems to faze you. I admire you for it."

"It's partly my training," Wanda said. She wondered why Marie was laying it on so thick. At the same time, she was pleased that Marie had recognized these qualities in her. It was important to be able to accept a justified compliment.

"You're lucky to be that way," Marie said. "The world could come crashing down and you wouldn't even notice."

"I don't know about *that*," Wanda said.

Janet Plum came back to take their order. She was a stocky girl—no more than twenty, Wanda thought—with sandy hair and a pleasant face.

"That was a good session we had the other night," she said to Marie. "I'm glad you brought Mrs. Martin."

Wanda thought for a moment that Janet was referring to her. Then she realized that the girl meant Robert's mother.

"I'd better get on the stick," Janet said, and headed for the kitchen.

"I took Mrs. Martin to a CR meeting," Marie said. "I thought it might do her good to meet some younger women."

"Did it?"

"I think so. She gave us her usual routine about how nasty men are and how dirty and smelly and sweaty and stupid. Stuff like that. Janet laps it up."

"You don't, do you?"

"Lord no, but it's fun to hear sometimes. Mrs. Martin can be so comical. Besides, it gives me ammunition when I get mad at Floyd. Which is pretty often; I'm beginning to realize that I don't much like him."

Wanda, who had no trouble relating to this sentiment, smiled sympathetically.

"He's dynamite in bed," Marie said, "but basically he's very cold."

Wanda continued to smile. The idea of Floyd being dynamite in bed amused her.

"The other night," Marie said, "I woke up and found him under the covers with a flashlight and a thermometer. Do you know what he was doing?"

Wanda shook her head.

"He was taking the temperature of my vagina. Isn't that the dumbest thing you ever heard of?"

They laughed.

"Another time when I was asleep," Marie said, "he greased my entire body with Crisco."

"You're kidding."

"Actually, that turned out to be fun. You can't imagine what it's like to be completely slippery."

"I think I'll pass," Wanda said.

Marie became serious again. "That's the cute and lovable side of Floyd. Floyd the scientist. Floyd the sex maniac. But there's another side too. There's a side that's as dark as night and as cold as ice."

"I don't know," Wanda said. "He just seems so harmless to me."

"He's not," Marie said. "He's a real son of a bitch, if you want to know the truth . . . But listen, I didn't bring you here to talk about Floyd. What was I saying before we got off on this unpleasant subject?"

"You were telling me about Mrs. Martin and your CR group."

"Oh yeah," Marie said. "She gave us her big spiel about men, and Janet lapped it up. But then Mrs. Martin started bragging on Robert and saying how she worshipped the ground that boy walked on. Janet accused her of being inconsistent. They went back and forth about it. And then"—Marie put her napkin to her mouth and giggled—"and then they got into a really bad argument. They finally made up, but for a minute or two I was pretty worried. They're both so hard-nosed."

"What was the argument about?"

Marie giggled again. "It's pathetic really. They argued about whether it was better to make one man miserable for forty years or forty men miserable for one year each."

"You're kidding."

"I swear I'm not. I told you it was pathetic. They finally decided their differences reflected the generation gap, and that's when they made up."

"I don't understand," Wanda said.

"Well," Marie said, "in Mrs. Martin's day it wasn't culturally accepted to switch men all the time."

"If Janet does that, I'd say she's the one who's miserable."

"They both are. They admit it. They say it's the price you pay in the battle between the sexes. Anyway, they ended up pretty good friends. Janet got a kick out of hearing about Mr. Martin and the saw."

Wanda winced. "I don't think you ought to laugh about it."

"I guess not, but it is pretty funny."

"You wouldn't think so if you'd seen it," Wanda said. She had a sudden vivid image of the saw hitting Mr. Martin's face. The blood flew. Then she saw Tim carving the poetry on his arm. He had done it in the shower so the blood would wash away and he could see what he was doing. It was important, he said, that the printing be legible. She had not, of course, witnessed the incident, but her image of it was if anything more vivid than her memory of Mr. Martin and the saw. The blood ran down his arm and his body. He was covered with blood. He was up to his ankles in it, but he just kept carving . . .

Marie reached across the table and took Wanda's hand. Wanda shook her head and the images went away.

"You all right?" Marie asked.

Wanda nodded. "I felt dizzy, but I'm okay now."

"It's probably the heat in here. Either that or the smell. I love cooked cabbage, but I could do without the odor . . . Are you sure you're okay? You look awful."

"I need to get up and walk. Where's the women's room?"

Marie pointed to a narrow, dimly lit hall about twenty feet away. "It's in there. First door to the right, I think. I'll go with you."

"There's no need," Wanda said.

She walked slowly, touching the backs of chairs for support. She stepped into the hall, opened the first door on the right, and found herself in a dank cubicle, face to face with a hairy fat man in a dirty tee shirt. He was sharpening a small cleaver. A cigarette dangled from his mouth. He was surrounded by great piles of potatoes, cabbage, carrots, and corn. The smell of rot was overpowering. On the table in front of the man was a small mountain of cut beets. Juice from the beets dripped like blood off the edge of the table. Wanda's head swam. The man regarded her with a fathomless, speechless, unforgiving rage and contempt. Stammering an apology, she stepped back through the door. In the women's room, which was directly across the hall, she splashed water on her face and combed her hair.

"You gave me the wrong directions," she said when she returned to the table. "I ended up in a room with the butcher."

"There's no butcher here," Marie said. "It's all vegetarian."

"He was a vegetable butcher then," Wanda said.

Marie laughed. "You must mean Ralph. He owns the place. His bark's worse than his bite."

Janet appeared with a tray of food. "I didn't catch your name," she said to Wanda.

"I forgot to introduce you," Marie said. "This is my friend Wanda."

"Wanda what?"

"Martin," Wanda said.

"Hey," Janet said, "you're the Shadow." She set the tray on the table. "I don't care if we are busy. I've got to shake your hand." She gave Wanda a vigorous handshake and then twisted her fingers around and grasped Wanda's thumb. "I really admire the work you're doing."

"I don't know what you mean," Wanda said. "I'm not even working."

"I mean your past work. Marie told us all about it. I think you're off to a good start."

Marie had taken a sudden deep interest in arranging her silverware.

Janet released Wanda's thumb and picked up the tray. "I also admire your mother-in-law, even if she does have a blind spot about her son."

Wanda laughed. "I probably have a blind spot about him too. He's my husband."

"Oh yeah," Janet said. "I didn't even think about that. Anyway, I admire your work with that guy in Arkansas . . . Christ, there's that fucker Ralph. I'd better get my ass in gear." She hurried away.

Wanda looked up and saw the vegetable butcher standing at the entrance to the hall. He was staring in their direction. Wanda turned quickly back to Marie, who was making a production out of tasting her chili.

"Boy, this is good," she said. "Have you ever tried it?"

Wanda shook her head.

"You're going to love it," Marie said.

"Why did she call me the Shadow?"

Marie squirmed and said it was a long story.

"I'd like to hear it," Wanda said.

"I don't know whether you would or not. It was a joke, but Janet doesn't have a sense of humor. She took it seriously."

"Tell me the story."

"Taste your chili first."

Wanda tasted it and said it was delicious.

"I have it a couple of times a week," Marie said. "It's not as fattening, I don't think, as regular chili . . . You're sure you want to hear this?"

"Yes," Wanda said.

"Well, let's see. Janet dropped out of college for a year because she didn't know what she wanted to study. She plans to start back in September, but she's still not sure about a career."

"Does this have anything to do with me?" Wanda asked.

"I'm afraid so," Marie said. "All she knows is that she wants to do something that will give her power over men. She's always asking our advice at the meetings. So I said—don't forget, it was more or less as a joke—that maybe she ought to consider becoming a therapist. She said the purpose of therapy was to help people, wasn't it? I said sure, but you could use it to hurt them too. She asked how and I told her about Tim and how miserable *he* is. Janet thought it was great. She figured out that if she worked with ten men a year for twenty years, she could—"

"That's sick," Wanda said. She put her spoon down and looked hard at Marie.

"Damn it all," Marie cried. "He *is* miserable."

The people at the other tables turned and stared at them.

Marie hung her head. "I shouldn't have said it though," she said softly. "It was a terrible thing to say."

"At least you can see it was terrible," Wanda said. "Tell me something. Does Janet intend to become a therapist?"

"No," Marie said. "She gave it up."

"Thank goodness. If you ask me, she needs to *see* a therapist."

"She does see one. She sees a feminist. That's where she gets most of her ideas."

"That's not therapy," Wanda said. "That's brainwashing." She was deeply shocked. She hoped that Janet's therapist, whoever she was, would not be connected with the mental health clinic. Wanda was not sure she could work effectively with such a person.

"It was her therapist," Marie said, "who talked Janet out of becoming a therapist."

"I wonder why," Wanda said. Maybe the woman had some sense after all.

"Janet's therapist won't even work with men. She tried it and ended up feeling sorry for them. That's what she told Janet. That's why Janet gave up on the idea of becoming a therapist. If there's one thing in the world she doesn't want, it's to end up feeling sorry for some damned man."

"Let's forget it," Wanda said. "The whole thing's insane."

"They both admire you," Marie said. "They admire you for being able to destroy men without feeling sorry for them. According to Janet's therapist, the entire history of psychiatry has been the history of men abusing women. She's glad that people like you have started getting even. She wishes she could do it herself."

"I said forget it." Wanda was becoming dizzy again.

"Now you're the one who's shouting."

Sure enough, people were staring at them.

"Do you want to hear the rest of the story?" Marie asked.

"You mean there's more?"

"The worst is yet to come," Marie said.

"I guess you'd better tell me," Wanda said. Having no more appetite, she pushed her bowl to the center of the table.

"The worst of it," Marie said, "is that I hurt you even more with Mrs. Martin. Your chances of being her friend, I mean. When she heard about you and Tim, she jumped in and said she knew you were a devil."

"A devil?" Wanda smiled in spite of herself.

"She said you'd hypnotized Robert into marrying you and that you planned to do to him what you did to Tim. Janet said she hoped so, the more the merrier. Mrs. Martin ran over and took a swing at her but missed. They both gave you credit for Mr. Martin's accident and made up again . . . God, I'm an awful person."

"I'm glad you told me about it," Wanda said, "in case Mrs. Martin says something to Robert."

Marie finished her chili and ate some salad. She wiped her mouth with her napkin. "You have to understand," she said, "that I sometimes say things at those meetings that I don't mean. The other women are more radical than I am, and they're always dumping on me about it. Sometimes I say things to impress them."

"I wish you'd left me out of it," Wanda said.

"They accuse me of not really being a feminist. They say I like men too well. They say I don't respect women enough. They say I'm romantic and self-centered. They say I compete with other women for the attention of men. They say I want to be put on a pedestal."

"It's all true, isn't it?" Wanda asked gently.

"Every damn bit of it. And look at you. You're none of those things, and you don't even pretend to be a feminist. You're more of a feminist than I'll ever be."

Wanda managed another smile. "I'm not political," she said,

"and I don't like to think in labels. But if you look at it in a certain way, I guess that's true. It's true in the sense of my being my own person."

"You're so strong," Marie said. "Strong and independent and generous. And then look at me. I'm a terrible person. I made fun of you to other people and hurt your chances with Mrs. Martin."

"They were already pretty slim."

"I'm glad you can see it that way. I really admire you."

"Please," Wanda said.

They sat for a few minutes without talking. Marie finished her salad and then ate Wanda's chili. Janet came over and asked if they wanted dessert. Wanda shook her head. Janet tore off the check and put it on the table.

"It was a privilege to meet you," she told Wanda. "Keep up the good work."

"Oh go to hell," Wanda snapped.

Janet looked as if she had been hit in the face. She stood there for a moment, her lip trembling, and then she turned and fled to the kitchen.

"That's my fault too," Marie said. "She's so high strung she'll be wiped out for a week, and it's all my fault."

"Let's get out of here," Wanda said. Although he was nowhere about, she was sure that Ralph was watching her.

They put on their coats. Marie, saying it was the least she could do, picked up the check and paid it.

"There's one thing you didn't tell me," Wanda said when they reached the sidewalk. "Why did Janet call me the Shadow?"

Marie laughed. "It's a joke. She calls you the Shadow because you have the power to cloud men's minds."

"That's absurd," Wanda said, but she laughed too.

Marie became serious again. "There's something you've got to understand about me. I need to be loved."

"I do understand," Wanda said. "That's a universal need, isn't it?"

"I mean really loved," Marie said desperately. "I mean worshipped. That's why I do some of the awful things I do."

"They weren't all that awful," Wanda said.

"I mean worshipped the way *you* are," Marie said.

"Robert doesn't worship me. That's not the kind of relationship we have."

"I don't mean Robert. I mean Tim. I want somebody to love me the way Tim loves you."

"It's not really me he loves," Wanda said.

"Oh God," Marie said. "Let's not talk about it." She wrapped her scarf more tightly around her neck and pulled her collar up to her ears. "It's so damned cold," she said. "No matter how long I live here, I never get used to these winters."

"I know what you mean," Wanda said. "I'm beginning to miss Florida."

They walked in silence until they reached Marie's office. Wanda turned to say goodbye and saw that Marie was crying.

"I'm sorry," Marie said. She stood on tiptoes and pressed her cold wet cheek against Wanda's. "Oh, Wanda," she sobbed, "I am so damned sorry."

"It's all right," Wanda said. "You're going through a bad time with Floyd. It's natural that you'd be anxious."

"Do you really think that's it?"

"Part of it, anyway."

"That makes me feel better," Marie said. She gave Wanda a quick peck on the cheek and darted into her office.

13

Wanda—

If you don't write to me, I'm going to do something drastic. To put my cards on the table, I'm thinking of circulating some stories. About you and me. About the things we did when I was too confused to resist. Don't think I won't do it, if I have to. I'm sick of your stuck-up ways. Here's how I'll go about it. I'll start with the truth—the leg show, the peekaboo blouses, the sexy smiles—and move by degrees into the plausibly false and from there to the outrageous. To give an example, it's a short step from the legs (truth) to how you once forgot to wear a brassiere (plausibly false, might happen to anybody) and from there to how your feet once ached so badly that you asked me to rub them (not quite so plausibly false). From there—you can surely see this, can't you—it's a hop, skip, and a jump to the blow-job you gave me one afternoon about three o'clock (outrageously false, unless I've repressed the incident). Maybe you'd better sit right down and dash off a letter, Wanda.

I'm joking, of course. If I were going to do such a thing, I wouldn't tell you about it in writing, would I? Why do I go on like this? Is it my name you don't like? A lot of people think Jinks is a comical name. You get used to it though, I can tell you from experience. Anyway, there'd be no trouble to having it changed. Why don't you send me a list of names that you'd find acceptable. I'm confident we could come up with something we'd both be proud of. This sounds like a fun project, Wanda, and I'm looking forward to hearing from you. I once thought of changing my name to Sorry. Then I could introduce myself, describe myself, and apologize for being alive all in one whack.

Nelda's mood has improved. She actively listens when I read, and she doesn't cry as much as she used to. When I gave her some candy this morning, I noticed that she was careful not to soil herself with it.

At lunch yesterday, Millie said that a new story about her was making the rounds. (That's where I got the idea for my opening paragraph.) I didn't know what she was talking about till I glanced at Loy, who was smirking. Poor Jack turned pale and began to tremble. You see, Wanda, even in a place like this, with such shabby players as these, the human drama folds and unfolds. Later, as Jack and I sat at the big window, taking in the afternoon sun, we saw Loy and Millie ambling hand in hand across the lawn, in the direction of town. This is the first time that Millie has allowed herself to be courted openly, and I wonder if maybe it's not the real thing. Maybe she is indeed getting better. When they had moved out of sight, Jack, struggling to stay afloat in the slough of despond, said that Loy was nowhere near good enough for Millie. He seemed unaware of the tears that welled in his eyes, that streamed down his cheeks, that dropped from his chin.

Forgive me again my miserable joke. You've got to keep in mind that you're not dealing here with just anyone. You're dealing with a desperate, despicable man. Please write.

Tim

P.S. I keep wondering about your pantyhose. You know, in the rape dream. Is that them? Hanging neatly over the back of that chair? Completely intact? Good as new? If so, you must have slipped them off yourself. Either that or let me do it . . . God damn it, I won't be cheated out of my rape by your timely compliance. I don't care what you say, it was rape, pure and simple. You've got to give me that much.

"He's trying to drag me down," Wanda said. "He's trying to cheapen the whole therapeutic experience."

"He says it's a joke," Robert said.

"He also says he's desperate and despicable."

"What's this about a rape dream?"

"Beats me."

Robert got up and went to the window and looked out.

"I guess you're going to visit your mother again," Wanda said.

"If you don't care."

Wanda shrugged. "I can always work. Unless you want me to go with you."

"It wouldn't be a good idea. Mom's still torn up about the marriage."

Robert had removed his shoes when he came in from work. Now he sat down and put them on again. Although she had offered to go with him, Wanda was glad he didn't want her to. With him working late a couple of times a week and visiting his parents so often, she was making real progress on her dissertation. She had been working so hard, in fact, that she sometimes lost track of days and was barely aware of the world around her. She knew she had to make peace with Mrs. Martin, but there would be time for that when she finished her manuscript.

"Tell your father hi," she said.

"I probably won't even see him. From what Mom says, he never leaves his room."

"He needs therapy. I've told you before."

I mentioned that to Mom. She said for you to mind your own business."

Wanda laughed. "That *is* my business."

"Yeah, but I think Mom's right in this case. Dad's an old goat with funny ideas. He'd embarrass us all if he went to a doctor."

"It would be confidential," Wanda said. "It would be strictly between him and the doctor."

"That'd be even worse." Robert finished tying his shoes and stood up. "If he knew it wouldn't get back to Mom, there's no telling what he'd say." He went to the bedroom and came back with his coat. "What do you think of all this stuff with Nelda? It's kind of creepy, isn't it?"

"You mean like giving her a bath?"

Robert nodded. "But at least he's getting involved with someone."

Wanda made a face.

"You don't seem too pleased," Robert said.

"It's a mistake," Wanda said. "If he starts up with this silly blind girl, he won't solve his problems at all. I wish he could see that. I wish—"

"Whoa," Robert said. "Don't get carried away."

"I'm not. I'm just telling you what he needs."

"I don't know who needs what anymore," Robert said.

After he left, Wanda read the letter again. She was puzzled that he had not reacted more strongly to some of the things Tim said. It was evidence, she supposed, of Robert's growth as a person. He would be a source of strength to her when she started at the clinic.

* * *

One day Wanda answered the phone and heard a man breathing. The breathing was regular at first, though a little louder than normal. Then it became heavy and labored. When it reached the panting stage, Wanda moved the receiver a few inches from her ear and stood there wondering what to do. She had known a girl in college who received similar calls. The girl had finally suffered a breakdown and left school in the middle of the semester. Wanda had no intention of having a breakdown. Knowing the caller was Tim, she was more angry than frightened. She was also disappointed. It was bad enough that he would write to her when she had expressly forbidden it; this new form of acting out marked a deeper and even more unhealthy regression.

When she told Robert about the call, he refused to believe it was Tim. "It's not like him," he said.

"How do you know what he's like?"

"From the letters."

"They're pretty bad, aren't they?"

"Not really," Robert said.

Wanda remembered that he had not read the one about the rape dream. "It's him," she said. "He's been threatening to phone me, and now he's doing it."

They went to Denny's and saw Floyd and Marie. According to Floyd, the call was a criminal offense. "So are the letters," he said, "if they're obscene."

"Would you say they're obscene?" Marie asked Wanda.

"I don't know," Wanda said. "If he said the same things in therapy, I wouldn't think much about it. I'd point out that it was resistance and go on from there."

"That's an interesting point," Floyd said. "The defense could do a lot with it."

"What if a guy breathed heavy in therapy?" Marie asked. The idea seemed to amuse her.

"That would be resistance too," Wanda said. She remembered reading about a young patient who had masturbated while his therapist, a famous woman analyst, sat passively watching. "Let's forget about it," she said.

It occurred to her that Tim might expect her to go to the police. He might even be hoping that the case would end up in court. It would be a way of re-establishing contact with Wanda. Except that he would not, in a courtroom, be seeing Wanda the therapist. He would be seeing a different Wanda—an ordinary, vulnerable, overweight woman with a perfectly ordinary complaint. The thought made her cringe inside.

"I still don't think it's him," Robert said.

"I don't either," Marie said.

"It's him," Wanda said.

"If it is," Robert said, "he's only doing it because he's gone over the brink. It's a cry for help."

"As a feminist," Marie said, "I'm upset by calls like that. But it seems different if the guy's your patient. If he calls again, why don't you try talking to him?"

"That's an idea," Robert said.

"Absolutely not," Wanda said. "It would be a form of incest gratification."

"You're impossible," Marie said.

"I wish he'd try telepathy," Floyd said.

"I hope he won't," Wanda said with a laugh. "That's all I need, is a lot of telepathic heavy breathing."

"You wouldn't get the breathing," Floyd said. "You'd get the thoughts that went with it."

"I already know the thoughts," Wanda said, and for some reason her eyes brimmed with tears.

14

Dearest Wanda,

A marvelous thing has happened. I woke up this morning and realized that I was completely well. I am as mentally healthy a specimen as you would ever be privileged to meet. Now can I come and court you?

Nelda's mood gets better too. A couple of days ago I got her to smile. It was a nice smile, though not, of course, comparable to yours. Not really. Tomorrow I'll work on her hair, which is stringy and too long and not dark enough, it seems to me, for her pale skin. If I'm going to have to sit and look at her, I want her to be at her best. I've been visiting her more often and staying longer. I think it's doing her a world of good. I don't want you to get the wrong idea about this, Sailboat. You're still my one and only. You say the word and I'll drop Nelda like a hot potato.

Despite my own good spirits, Little Tim remains unbelievably morose. I think he's jealous of the time I spend with Nelda. But when I try to touch him, he draws back. The other day, when he was looking especially blue, I quoted to him from Kierkegaard: "When the child has grown big and must be weaned, the mother virginally hides her breast, the child has no more a mother. Happy the child which did not in another way lose its mother." I knew it wasn't the right thing to say, but it's

174

all I could think of. He turned on me with a look that withered my heart. I guess I'm not much good with kids.

I think I've been wrong about Loy. No thrills from that quarter, I'm afraid, unless I invent them myself. I met him in the woods this morning. I had been running for a long time and had slowed to a walk. I came to a clearing and there he was, sitting in the snow with his back to a stump, the gun propped beside him. We exchanged looks but didn't speak. As I reached the edge of the clearing, the gun went off and I jumped a foot. When I turned around, Loy was standing with his back to me, the gun was pointing upward, and a squirrel was falling from a tree. As he bent to pick it up, he saw me and gave what appeared to be a friendly wave. Maybe he's mellowed because of Millie. Or maybe I've been wrong about him from the start. Maybe I've seen menace where none ever was. But he likes to kill, and his mouth, even in its mellowed-out state, still looks cruel to me. What if I offered him a thousand dollars to shoot me accidentally? Do you think he'd do it? I've got a thousand in cash hidden in my room. What you girls call mad money.

You don't know what a relief it is to be rid of that neurosis. You'll like this new me if you'll give yourself a chance.

Cheerfully yours,
Tim

P.S. You're lovely, you're elegant, you're sweet, you're grand. I miss you more than you might imagine. Sometimes I think that seeing you five hours a week, simply to talk to, would be all the woman I'd ever want. I haven't had much luck with them. I'm sorry you're coming to me now in the form you are. I think I'd prefer the other. But I have to take you any way I can get you, don't I? And I'd rather have a fantasy of you than a real woman—unless the real woman was you. That's how much I love you, Sailboat.

"He's not really well," Wanda said.

"I didn't think he was," Robert said.

"He's only pretending to be well in order to impress me. Patients often do that. It's called a flight into health."

"The P.S. breaks my heart," Robert said.

Wanda laughed.

"I'm serious," Robert said. "The poor guy's pining away."

"What am I supposed to do? Pack up and go down there?"

Robert looked at the letter and then at Wanda. "This might sound silly, but I'd understand if you did."

Wanda laughed again. She was always amused when Robert said outrageous things with a straight face.

"What's this about the way you're coming to him now?" Robert asked. "Is he having sexual fantasies about you?"

"Does it matter?"

"I didn't mean that."

"You're very mature," Wanda said. "It would bother a lot of men."

"Not me," Robert said.

He put the letter down and turned on the television set. They watched the six o'clock news from Syracuse, then had a light dinner. Afterward, Robert said he'd better go to his parents' house, his mother wasn't feeling well. "I can carry in some wood for the fireplace and check on the furnace," he said. "Stuff like that. This weather's pretty bad."

"That's true," Wanda said. For the last week, the temperature had not risen above ten degrees. January had left forty inches of snow, which stood now in huge frozen piles along the sides of the streets.

"Dad's still sulking," Robert said, "and won't lift a finger."

He was gone about three hours. When he came back, he had Marie with him.

"God, is it cold," she said, blowing into her mittens. She put her hands on her shoulders and hugged herself and wriggled and stomped.

"Marie was visiting Mom too," Robert said. "I asked her over for a drink."

Robert helped her off with her coat and they sat down on the sofa. Wanda went to the kitchen and made drinks. When she returned to the living room, Marie was reading Tim's letter.

"Robert told me about this," Marie said. "I don't know how you can resist the guy. Talk about sweet."

"Not always," Wanda said. "You've seen some of the other letters."

"Yeah," Marie said, "but when he's nice, he's really nice. Maybe he's going to be nothing but nice from now on."

"I don't think so," Wanda said. "I got another phone call today."

"I've been thinking about those calls," Marie said. "Maybe they're not heavy-breather calls at all. Maybe he wants to tell you he loves you. Then when he gets on the phone, he becomes bashful."

"That makes sense," Robert said.

"They're heavy-breather calls," Wanda said. She wished she had shown them the rape-dream letter. Then maybe they'd believe her.

"Let's not fight about it," Robert said.

"I'm not fighting. I know Tim and you people don't. He's perfectly capable of trying to terrorize me with God damned phone calls. He's a very sick man."

There was an awkward silence, and then they talked about the weather. After a while, Marie finished her drink and left.

"I'm glad she's gone," Wanda said. "She can be so dumb sometimes."

"She's not dumb," Robert said.

"She's dumb about Tim."

"Maybe so," Robert said, "but you could make more of an effort."

"To do what?"

"Act more gracious. You won't let anybody else even have an opinion."

* * *

On Monday afternoon, Wanda answered a knock at the door and saw a young woman with long blond hair and a hard pretty face. She was wearing a suede coat, a short maroon dress, and high-heeled boots.

"Are you Bob Martin's wife?" she asked.

Wanda nodded.

"I'm Doreen."

"I thought you were," Wanda said.

Doreen walked to the center of the room, whirled around, and stood with her hands on her hips. "I don't want to sit down," she said belligerently. "I won't be but a minute. I'll have my say and get out."

"That's fine," Wanda said. "I'll stand up too." She would have preferred to sit. Like Marie, Doreen had a body that made Wanda feel bulky and awkward. Floyd had said she looked like death warmed over, and it was true she was a little pale, but Wanda didn't see how she could look much better than she did right now.

"All I have to say," Doreen said, "is that I want it off of there."

"I'm sorry," Wanda said, "but I don't know what you mean."

Doreen looked skeptical. "You haven't seen it?"

"I don't know. You haven't told me what it is."

"I mean my name. It's on his butt." Doreen lit a cigarette and glared at Wanda through a thick curtain of smoke. When Wanda did not respond, she burst out: "Jesus Christ, the fucker's got my name on his ass and his wife doesn't even know about it." She threw her hands up in disgust.

"You're very angry," Wanda said.

"Hell yes I am. I gave him back his lousy diamond. The least he could do is have that tattoo removed. But according to Floyd it's still on there. Floyd sees him in the locker room."

Wanda had wondered why Robert was so shy about being seen naked. Now she knew.

"I shouldn't have said lousy," Doreen said. "It was a beautiful diamond. It ought to be. It cost two thousand dollars." She looked at Wanda's left hand. "You don't have a diamond," she said spitefully.

Wanda touched her wedding band and realized that she too was angry. Although she would not have accepted a diamond from Robert, he might at least have offered her one.

"I can't believe you don't know about the tattoo," Doreen said. "It's on his left cheek. It's like a neon sign. You'd have to be blind not to see it."

"Never mind about me," Wanda said. "Let's focus on your anger."

"I want it off of him," Doreen said. "He had no right to get married with it on there. I'll go to court if I have to."

Wanda wondered whether you could go to court over a thing like that, but she decided not to pursue the matter.

"You act like you don't care," Doreen said. "You ought to be madder than hell."

"Let's stick to you," Wanda said.

"Miss High and Mighty," Doreen said.

Wanda shrugged.

"You listen to me," Doreen said fiercely. "I wouldn't marry a guy with another woman's brand on him. Or if I did I'd know about it. And if I knew about it I'd kick ass till it came off. That's what *I'd* do." She turned abruptly and stood looking out the window. Her shoulders heaved and then sagged. She pulled a kleenex out of her pocket and blew her nose. When she turned back to Wanda, her eyes were red. "We couldn't get together on a place to live," she said. "That's why we're not married. It's because we're not married that I want it off of there. Having your name on someone's body is a very special thing."

"Why don't you sit down?" Wanda said.

"I know you want to kill me," Doreen said. "I'm only here to cause trouble."

"You can sit down if you want to," Wanda said.

"You must be crazy," Doreen said.

She sat down on the sofa, and Wanda took a chair opposite her.

"Why don't you tell me about it?" Wanda said.

"Well," Doreen said, "he got the tattoo in New York City a month before we broke up. We were there for the weekend. He got it done as a surprise. I was never so proud of anything in my life. I was prouder of the tattoo than I was of the diamond. Then, come to find out, we couldn't agree on a God damned place to live." She dabbed at her eyes with the kleenex.

"You didn't want to live in Windward," Wanda said. "Is that it?"

Doreen nodded. "I wanted to live in the City. I've always loved the City. The Bronx maybe, or Brooklyn. Bob said he wouldn't live there in a million years."

Wanda looked sympathetic. "He wouldn't live there," she said, "and you wouldn't live here."

"Live here?" Doreen cried. "Are you kidding? With that mother of his?"

"You didn't get along with his mother?"

"I *did*. I had to. You can't get along with Bob if you don't get

179

along with his mother . . . You're his wife. You know that."

Wanda continued to look sympathetic.

"Don't you?" Doreen asked.

"Let's stick to you," Wanda said.

"I would have lived in Windward if it hadn't been for her. Maybe I wouldn't have liked it, but I would have done it. Maybe it wouldn't have been so bad . . . We could have gone to the City on weekends."

"Did you tell that to Robert?"

"You call him Robert?"

"Never mind me."

"I called him Robert too," Doreen said, "when I was around that bitch of a mother. But in the bedroom—I shouldn't say that, you're his wife."

"It's okay," Wanda said.

"In the bedroom—anyplace private—he was plain old Bob. Do you know what I mean?"

"Let's stick to you," Wanda said. "Did you tell Bob you couldn't stand his bitch of a mother?"

"I told him I couldn't live in Windward," Doreen said. "I didn't tell him why. We had a fight and I left town. I thought he'd come after me."

"But he didn't?"

"You know he didn't!" Doreen shouted. "I'm sorry, I shouldn't yell."

"It's all right."

"It wasn't his mother anyway," Doreen said. "It was more Floyd than it was her. Floyd never lets go. I hope you know that. Floyd—"

"Never mind Floyd," Wanda said. "Let's go back to what you were saying before."

"After a while I took up with this truck driver," Doreen said. "Now I'm married. We owe a lot of money. Jack—that's my husband—might get laid off because of the economy. Plus he's got a bad back and can't lift as much as some of the others. I work in a dime store. It cost me a day's pay to come and talk to you." She dabbed at her eyes with the kleenex. Then she looked maliciously at Wanda and said: "Bob's sure good in bed, isn't he?"

"Maybe you're the one who's good," Wanda said.

"Hell yes I am. Better than you."

"Do you know why that seems so important?"

Doreen looked exasperated. "You know why." She paused to light a cigarette. "Jack's good too," she said. "I wish he was home more often. He's an okay guy, but he's gone a lot . . . Who am I kidding? There's nothing good about him. I wish he was gone all the time. He can't get it up because of the pain in his back. Then he gets drunk and mean." She opened the top of her dress and revealed a ragged purple bruise that ran from her shoulder down into her brassiere. In the center of the bruise was a set of teeth marks.

The bruise gave Doreen's words a sudden weight of reality. Wanda swayed slightly. She resisted an impulse to touch the bruise, or perhaps to cry out. She pulled back to a safer place within herself and put on a look of unconditional acceptance.

"You can shove your phony sympathy you know where," Doreen said. "I know you hate my guts."

"Let's get back to your story." The words merely drifted from Wanda's mouth.

Doreen covered the bruise and sat back and shrugged. "Sure," she said. "Why not? Suits me." She puffed furiously on her cigarette. "Jack knows I still love Bob," she said. "He'd break my neck if he knew I was in Windward." She looked suddenly worried. "I just have to trust you not to tell Floyd or Bob I was here. You know, woman to woman."

Wanda continued to look sympathetic. Her face ached with the effort.

"I just have to trust you," Doreen said again. "Sometimes on a Sunday morning," she went on, "when Jack was on the road, I used to sit and stare out the window and pray that Bob would drive up. I figured as long as he had the tattoo he might do it. Then I heard he was getting married and I quit looking for him. 'I guess he got rid of the tattoo,' I said to Floyd. Floyd said no. That's when I hit the ceiling. I couldn't stand him getting married with my name on his ass. I don't know how you stand it either."

When Wanda didn't answer, Doreen drummed her fingers on the arm of the chair and looked at the wall. "I don't know what I'm doing here," she said. "I don't know why I'm saying all this."

"You were angry," Wanda said.

"I sure was. I was spoiling for a fight. I wanted to kick ass and cause trouble."

"Now you don't?"

"Now it doesn't matter." Doreen blew her nose again. She sat up straight, took a deep breath, and gave Wanda a friendly smile. "Tell me something. Who would you be if you could be anybody else in the whole world?"

"You're changing the subject," Wanda said.

"I know it," Doreen said. "Who would you be?"

"Why are you changing the subject?"

"I asked who you'd rather be. Ann Landers says it's a sure way to start a conversation."

"Why are you bringing in Ann Landers?"

"She says it puts a person at ease and starts them talking."

"Maybe you're seeking advice," Wanda said.

"Why would I want advice? I was just trying something. It worked on a girl at the dime store. She was shy and wouldn't talk. I asked her who she'd rather be and she talked for an hour. Turned out she'd rather be the Pope. I thought it was funny that a girl would want to be the Pope."

"Now it's the Pope," Wanda said.

"Don't you think it's funny?"

"Let's stick to you. Why are you talking about Ann Landers and the Pope?"

"I've got to get out of here," Doreen said, jumping to her feet.

Wanda looked at her watch. "You can stay a few more minutes."

"No thanks," Doreen said.

Wanda followed her to the door. "Maybe you ought to ask yourself," she said, "why you connect me with Ann Landers and the Pope, and why you ask so many questions. You also ought to ask yourself why you're not still angry. Do you have a handle on that?"

Doreen looked embarrassed. "Well . . . "

"It might be important," Wanda said. "Do you have any idea why you're no longer angry?"

"Sure I do." Doreen opened the door and stepped into the hall. "But I don't think I ought to say it."

"It's up to you," Wanda said.

"Well," Doreen said, "it's this way. I just figure Bob's worse off than I am."

She pulled a pair of mirrored sunglasses out of her coat pocket and slipped them on. Wanda could see herself in the mirrors. She was fat and misshapen. One of the mirrors was cracked, and Wanda was cracked too. Finally Doreen shook her head, turned quickly, and walked down the hall, swinging her trim hips with perfect assurance.

* * *

For the next few days, Wanda wondered off and on what to do with the information Doreen had given her. She wanted to tell Robert that she knew about the tattoo and that she didn't mind it. Getting a tattoo was the kind of thing people did and then lived to regret. She wanted to assure him that she understood such things. At the same time, she didn't want to embarrass him or appear to be making a fuss or invading his privacy. If he weren't defensive about the tattoo, he wouldn't become upset at the mention of Doreen's name. After a good deal of thought, she decided to wait for Robert to reveal the secret himself. She only hoped he would do it soon. It occurred to her that the strain of keeping the secret might account, as much as having to work late and having to devote more and more time to his mother, for Robert's recent spells of moodiness. She would give him a couple of weeks. Then, if he didn't confess about the tattoo, she would bring the subject up herself.

15

Dear Wanda,

Are you taking good care of yourself? Please do. When I finally come for you, I want you to look as pretty as ever. I want to look nice for you too, so I've carefully refrained from burning my face, good as that might feel. (It's the old principle of hurting one kind of pain with another.)— I don't figure you'll mind scarred legs, especially if the scars spell your name in attractive letters. I lied, incidentally, when I said I'd built myself up. I'm as skinny as I was when you left. Besides that, I'm old and battered and foul breathed from smoking. My fingers and teeth are stained with nicotine. On the other hand, I can still look pretty good if the light's not bright. I can put on weight if I really try. I'm in great shape for a man who chain smokes. I can have my teeth cleaned. I can even give up cigarettes if you insist on it, and I hope you will. I would not want to kiss me if my breath is as bad as you seem to think it is.

The hard-ons keep coming; maybe we ought to regard them as a plus. I continue to deal with them by thinking of you—thinking of the rape, if that's what it was—and relieving myself by hand. A purely stop-gap measure, of course, till we can be together again. If you've ever had any idea that I was impotent, you can rest easy. My masculinity is no longer a matter of conjecture but a hard, not to say persistent and

inescapable fact, which I'm handling as best I can under the circum-
stances. I hope you're handling your end of it successfully too. These
forced separations are hell on both parties.

Sometimes I can control the fantasy, sometimes not. When I'm in
control, I usually do it only once or twice a day. Sometimes I even skip a
day. When the fantasy's in control, it's a different story. I milk myself dry,
wear myself out, sweat till I stink so bad I can't stand it—and then I do
it a few more times. A typical week might go like this: Mon X, Tue XX,
Wed O, Thu X, Fri XX, Sat O, Sun XXXXXXXXX . . . Would you be-
lieve that I used to think of you as my

> *Lady of silences*
> *Calm and distressed*
> *Torn and most whole*
> *Rose of memory*
> *Rose of forgetfulness*
> *Exhausted and life-giving—*

No need to go on, you know the poem as well as I do. Anyway, I now
renounce that shit. Now you're just the girl I think of when I jack off. The
lousy whore I happen to love.

Speaking of separations, it's all over between Loy and Millie. She
announced on Friday, without naming names, that she was through
wasting time on riff-raff. If she was ever going to put her life in order,
she said, it was imperative that she get to California where she could
make a fresh start. If a man couldn't take her to California, then far as
she was concerned he was riff-raff. Loy has fallen into a bitter silence.

I've cut Nelda's hair and also tinted it. I parted it in the middle like
yours. Foreseeing that I might have trouble with the "sails," I bought
some hairspray. It made the hair stiff to touch, but you can't have every-
thing. From a distance of about ten feet—remember I'm still without
glasses—I could almost swear it was you sitting there. Maybe you'll
agree I've done a remarkable job. When I told Nelda how good she
looked, she favored me with the sweetest smile. I'm going to make a run
into Little Rock tomorrow and get her some nicer clothes. I've taken
careful measurements this time, so as to eliminate guesswork. No point
in buying a pig in a poke, I always say.

I've been thinking about the day we met. How the first therapist hadn't helped much. How sick and ashamed I still was. I remember your firm handshake, the steady regard of your eyes, your reassuring smile; and I remember thinking, *This person can help.* I was already sick and ashamed; why did you have to play the mystery lady and make everything worse? Was an A in Transference 801 all that important? Would your supervisor have known the difference if you'd sat and talked to me like one human being to another? Knowing you in that way, I might have liked you, but I would never have fallen in love. You're dumb if you think otherwise. Oh yes I would; oh no you're not. We'll never know, will we?

Did it give you a thrill—'fess up now—to think that a man who'd mastered Wittgenstein couldn't figure you out for a minute? That's a cheap little thrill, isn't it, if the man is already sick and ashamed? On the other hand, what's to figure out? You remind me of an ostrich, Wanda. You think if you bury your head in Freud, or in some textbook, your ass don't show. Forgive me, that's a cruel way of putting what's meant as a compliment. Forget I said it. What I should have said is that the way one chooses to hide, as well as the fact that one chooses to hide, is itself a revelation of character. You can wear a hat to hide the color of your hair, but in doing so you reveal your style of wearing a hat. It's your style I fell in love with; the rest is mere biography, minor detail—fill me in later, maybe during one of those mellow periods after making love. But I still wish you'd talked to me as one person to another, directly as it were. I wish you'd admit you were there. Then you'd be more inclined to believe I love you. Once you believed that, who's to say you wouldn't love me back?

Tim

P.S. I've told you about my legs, so I might as well give you a progress report. I've so far done the first four letters ("WAND"). Each letter is about three inches high. I wonder if you have any idea what painstaking work it is. If I made a mistake, I don't know how in the world I'd erase it.

The thought of Tim burning her name on his legs made Wanda almost sick. She wanted to get on the phone and scream at him that he had no right to do such a thing, but of course she couldn't. It wouldn't be professional; it might feed his fantasies . . . Now she could understand Doreen's anger about the tattoo. Doreen was right, there was something special—*peculiar* might be a better word—about having your name on someone's body. It made you feel funny to think about it. Not that the two cases were really comparable. Robert's action had no doubt been impulsive and was rather charmingly adolescent; Tim's was pathological. Wanda stuffed the letter back in the envelope and tossed it aside in disgust.

Then she realized that something good might come out of the letter. After reading it, Robert would surely tell her about the tattoo. If he didn't, she would have an excuse to bring the subject up herself. Once the matter was out in the open, once Robert saw that her reaction would be one of mature acceptance and understanding, once they had *talked* about it, they could put it behind them. They might even get a few good laughs out of the whole business. Afterward, they might be closer than they had ever been. At any rate, the marriage, which Wanda had to admit was floundering, would get back on an even keel.

With these thoughts in mind, she worked hard all afternoon. It had occurred to her more than once that her absorption with her manuscript might be one reason for Robert's lack of interest in her. If she could accomplish more in the afternoons, she would not have to spend so much time at the typewriter in the evenings. Then maybe Robert would stop working late at the plant and visiting his parents so often. Maybe he would stop watching television till all hours and falling asleep in his chair. He had not even thought to give her a valentine . . .

When the phone rang at five thirty, she decided it was time to be firm. If it was Robert calling to say he had to work late, she would tell him it was important that he come home at once. She picked up the receiver and heard a long sigh, followed by a slight gurgling sound, and she realized that it was not Robert after all, but Tim. She almost slammed down the receiver but caught herself in time. Her policy had been to listen till he grew tired and hung up, and she knew it was important to be consistent. She put her hand over the mouthpiece and waited for the breathing to start. To her surprise, Tim began to speak in a hoarse muffled whisper.

187

"Wanda," he said. "Wanda, are you there?"

Wanda did not answer. She guessed he was trying to disguise his voice, but she refused to be taken in.

"Listen, Wanda," the voice pleaded, "you've got to help me. They've got me surrounded. I can't talk much longer . . . You've got to—"

At this point, Wanda heard a shout in the background, excited talking by a man and a woman, and the sounds of a struggle. The voice gave a last feeble yelp, which was followed by a crunching noise and a loud clattering sound. Then came a click and the line went dead.

Wanda put down the receiver and wondered what kind of mess Tim had gotten himself into. She recalled that in his days as a drinker, he had often become involved in barroom quarrels and had sometimes tangled with the police. He had, she supposed, returned to the bottle . . . She went back to her study and began to type as fast as she could, with no regard for mistakes of any kind.

After a while she heard the front door open and then slam shut. She finished the paragraph she was typing and went to the living room, where she found Robert pacing around with a beer in his hand. His face was white and he had a wild look in his eyes.

"I told you it wasn't Tim," he said in a loud braying voice. "I told you it wasn't."

"What wasn't Tim?"

"Making the calls," Robert said. "It was my God damned Dad."

"Oh shit," Wanda said, and sat down on the sofa.

Robert, continuing to pace, told her the story. After work he had stopped by to see if his mother needed anything. When she began to complain, for the umpteenth time, that Mr. Martin was not doing his share of the chores, Robert decided to speak to his father. He and Mrs. Martin headed up the stairs. About halfway up, they heard the sound of the phone being dialed. They crept to the top of the stairs and peeked into Mr. Martin's room. He was sitting in his underwear, holding the phone in his lap and making funny noises. Presently he said Wanda's name and then something they didn't catch.

"First he asked if I was there," Wanda broke in. "Then he said, 'They've got me surrounded.'"

"I knew it was something crazy," Robert said. "Anyhow, he looked up and saw us. You never saw such a guilty expression in your life."

"God," Wanda said. Thinking about it, though—remembering the lewd winks, the innuendos, the peeking up her dress, the jokes, the kiss at the wedding, the man's desperate loneliness—she wasn't so much surprised as dismayed for Robert's sake. "Maybe you were right about Tim," she said, "but I was right about something too. I've been telling you for weeks that your father needs help."

Robert stopped pacing and looked at Wanda with an odd grin. "Not any more, he doesn't."

"I don't know what you mean."

"I mean I've already helped him." Robert shook his fist in Wanda's face.

"I still don't—"

"*I mean I broke his God damned jaw!*" Robert yelled.

Before Wanda could reply, he threw his beer can across the room and ran from the apartment. Although she understood the shame he was feeling, she was exasperated to think that, at the time he needed her most, he would run off into the night.

When an hour passed and he hadn't returned, Wanda phoned Denny's. The man who answered said Robert had not been in. She called the hospital and learned that Mr. Martin had indeed been admitted with a fractured jaw but that only his wife was with him. Thinking that Robert might have gone home to wait for his mother, she tried the Martin house but got no answer. She thought a minute, then called Floyd, who, it turned out, had not seen Robert all day. Floyd asked what was up, and Wanda told him about Mr. Martin's jaw.

Floyd whistled and said, "I'll be damned. Why did Robert do it?"

Wanda hesitated, then realized that Floyd would find out soon enough anyway. "Mr. Martin was the caller," she said. "The heavy breather. Robert caught him."

"I'll be damned," Floyd said again. "I guess I'm not too surprised though."

"Me either," Wanda said, "now that I've thought about it."

"I hate to bring up another problem," Floyd said, "but have you seen the paper?"

"It wouldn't be in the paper. It happened too late in the day."

"I don't mean about the jaw. I mean about your boss."

"Dr. Epperson? . . . I haven't seen it."

"I'm glad the bastard's off the City Council," Floyd said, "but it's too bad about the other thing. It might put you in an awkward position, jobwise."

"What other thing?"

"You'd better read it yourself," Floyd said. "I'll call you if I hear from Robert."

The story, which was on page two, said that Dr. Epperson had unexpectedly resigned his position as acting director of mental health. He was also taking a leave of absence from his post at Windward University. He was going to India to study first hand the relationship between Eastern modes of thought and Western psychiatric practices. "Although I leave Windward regretfully," he was quoted as saying, "I do so in pursuit of a lifelong dream." He had no idea when his successor as mental health director would be named. In a related development, Mayor Bill Conroy had announced Epperson's resignation as City Councilman from the 4th Ward.

Wanda's first impulse was to go to her study and type, but instead she lay back on the sofa. It was more important, right now, to think than to type. She tried to think about Dr. Epperson and Robert and the marriage, but her mind kept flashing to Tim. He was sitting naked on a narrow bed with dirty sheets in a shabby, dim little room. His body was childishly frail, but his face looked older than time. He was burning Wanda's name on his calf with cigarettes. The work was agonizingly slow, but Tim was getting it done. Each time the cigarette touched his leg, he threw his head back and gritted his teeth. Wanda winced. Now and then he paused to wipe the sweat from his forehead and the tears from his eyes. A tear fell to his leg. Touched by the cigarette, it hissed like water in a skillet. When he finished the "D," he snuffed out the cigarette—it must have been the fiftieth one—and masturbated. Wanda tried to stop looking but couldn't. He did it slowly, using the thumb and second finger of his right hand, his head thrown back and his face set in a mask of ecstasy or pain. Occasionally he moaned or said "Wanda," and after a while come spurted on his leg. When the spurting stopped, he leaned over the leg and rubbed the come into the wounds as if it were ointment . . .

She hoped Robert wasn't driving around drunk. She wished he would come home.

Tim was burning the "A" on his leg. She wanted to step into the room and knock the cigarette from his hand and tell him—

What? Tell him what?

She thought she knew the answer but she could not say it.

She shook her head violently and sat up straight. She had enough problems without indulging in rescue fantasies about Tim. She tried to think again where Robert might be. Her temples throbbed and she lay back down. She was debating whether to go type or call the police when, overcome by exhaustion, she fell asleep.

She had a dream in which she was trying to explain something to the vegetable butcher. He was wearing Doreen's sunglasses. The glasses kept him from hearing Wanda. The more frantically she talked, the madder he became. A cleaver appeared in his right hand. Wanda ran in big looping circles. The harder she ran the closer she came to the butcher. He seized her neck and pinned her against a wall. She squirmed helplessly. The cleaver fell.

"Cabbage," Wanda murmured as her head split painlessly open.

"I know I'm dumb," Robert said, "but don't call me names."

He was standing over Wanda with his hand on her shoulder. She could smell liquor, but he didn't appear to be drunk.

"I'm not very good with words," he said hoarsely, "but there's something I've got to tell you and I want you to listen for a change. I don't love you and never have. I'm not going to stay here another minute. I love Marie and I want a divorce. If that's not clear, you'll have to figure it out for yourself."

Wanda blinked a few times to be sure she wasn't still dreaming. "It's pretty clear," she said then.

"I'm sorry," Robert said. "I'm really sorry. I didn't mean to do you this way."

He turned and strode out of the apartment, leaving the door open behind him. Wanda could hear him and Marie talking in the hall.

"Did you tell her?" Marie asked.

"I think so," Robert said.

"Oh Bob," Marie squealed.

Then they ran down the stairs.

part three

16

Feb 20

My darling Wanda,

Nelda spoke to me yesterday for the first time. I'm not up to writing about it now—I don't even know how I feel about it—but it was a notable occasion. Did I tell you I quit reading to her a couple of weeks ago? I started talking to her instead, saying whatever came to mind. She'd sit there smiling at me and crossing her legs the way I trained her to do. Then yesterday she spoke. I'm going up to see her as soon as I mail this letter.

I love you, Wanda. Maybe you don't know how much. Please write to me. A letter from you, especially now, would mean more than you can possibly imagine. Better yet, why don't you phone me? This is urgent, Wanda.

Love again,
Tim

P.S. Will you marry me? Please answer.

Two weeks after this letter arrived, Floyd showed up at Wanda's apartment with a bottle of Scotch. He would have come by sooner, he said, but he was ashamed to face her.

"Because you knew about Robert and Marie?"

Floyd nodded. "They told me about it a few weeks after they started. I was pretty damned mad, but I promised to keep it a secret." He handed the bottle to Wanda. "Let's have a drink," he said.

"Sure," Wanda said. Although she had never liked Floyd, she was curious about Robert and Marie. She had intended to call him and get the answers she wanted. Now that he was here, she might as well talk to him. She went to the kitchen for some ice cubes and glasses and came back and joined Floyd on the sofa. Floyd opened the bottle and poured the drinks.

"Here's to the lonely," he said, and they clicked their glasses. "How are you holding up?"

"I've thrown myself into my work," Wanda said. "That's carried me through. I'm almost finished with my dissertation."

"Work's a great healer. I learned that from *You Be You*. Are you going to stay in Windward?"

"I think so. I found out that even with Burt gone I can still have the job. So I'll probably stay for a year. Maybe longer, if Robert decides to come back."

"He was buying up bowling alleys."

"*Robert?*"

"Epperson. I've been trying to get something on him for a long time. When you mentioned his big interest in bowling, I did some digging in that direction. Turns out he and a guy in Toledo had formed a dummy corporation and were buying up all these alleys. I told the mayor about it and he looked into the matter. That's when old Burt decided to take a vacation."

"I'm glad you caught him," Wanda said. "He might have destroyed the whole clinic." She shuddered at the closeness of the call. If she had been implicated, even indirectly, in a bowling therapy scandal, her professional integrity might have been questioned for years to come.

"It's good for him that he left," Floyd said. "I also found out about him and Prince Mysore. That's who he ran off with, was that cock-sucking Indian. Epperson's finished in this town. I'll see to that."

196

"I don't even want to hear about him," Wanda said. If she let herself, she could get pretty angry, and no doubt depressed, about Burt Epperson. Such people brought disgrace to the whole profession. "I want to know about Robert and Marie. When did they start?"

"New Year's Eve." Floyd said.

"God."

"It was while they were dancing at the Country Club. The way they told it to me, they happened to dance into the little storeroom by the bar. Next thing they knew they were going at it. It was one of those impulse deals. You know what I mean?"

"Not really. I'm not much given to impulsive behavior."

"Me either," Floyd said. "I like to plan things out." He was holding his glass in his lap, rubbing the side of it with the fingers of his right hand. "Spontaneous yes, impulsive no. That's what it says in *You Be You*."

Wanda hoped he wouldn't go on about the book. "What hurt the most," she said, "even more than the deceit, is the way they just went through me. How can you just go through a rock?"

"A what?"

"A rock. You told me Robert called me his rock. Like the Rock of Gibraltar."

Floyd, looking slightly embarrassed, ran his hand slowly up the length of his thigh, then abruptly plunged his finger into his glass. "He didn't say Rock of Gibraltar. *You* said Rock of Gibraltar."

"It's what he meant though, isn't it?"

"Not exactly."

"What then?"

"Well," Floyd said, "have you ever heard of a pet rock?"

Wanda stared at him in disbelief, then sat back and looked straight ahead. She squeezed her glass so hard she thought it might break. "Why would he marry me, if that's what he thought?"

"What you have to keep in mind," Floyd said, "is that Robert always chased after the glamour-girl type. Girls like Doreen and Marie. What he called a hot piece of ass. You know what I mean?"

Wanda nodded. Although she found the language offensive, she decided it was important to let Floyd tell the story in his own way. He was probably expressing some of his hostility toward Marie by using such words.

Robert would chase after these hot pieces, Floyd went on, and fall madly in love. He described three of the hot pieces, as well as Robert's frustration at not being able to marry them. "Then he met Doreen, and it looked as if things might finally work out."

"I know all about Robert and Doreen," Wanda said. "She told me."

Floyd, who had been conspicuously eyeing Wanda's feet, looked up in alarm.

"She visited me," Wanda said.

"That bitch," Floyd said in a tone so savage that Wanda recoiled. "I told her to stay away from you." His hands trembled. He seemed about to lose all control. Gripping his knees tightly, he demanded to know exactly what Doreen had said.

Speaking in soothing tones, Wanda told him about Doreen's visit.

"That's all she said about why she left town?" Floyd asked. "She blamed it all on Mrs. Martin?"

"Sure," Wanda said. "She told me the whole thing. It was mainly the tattoo she was concerned about."

"No harm done then," Floyd muttered. "But she's still a miserable bitch. I might fix her good. Her and her stupid truck driver." He grinned suddenly. "I think I will. I told her to stay away from you, and I by God meant it."

Wanda felt a rush of sympathy for Floyd. He couldn't see that his irrational attitude about Doreen's visit was a way of avoiding his feelings about Marie. She hoped he wouldn't go off the deep end and become suicidal.

"We don't have to talk about Robert and Marie," she said. "We can let the matter rest."

"Why wouldn't I want to talk about them?" Floyd said jovially. "Where was I?"

"The pet rock."

"Well," Floyd said, "it about killed Robert when Doreen moved to Albany. I tried to tell him there'd be other girls, but he said he'd had it. I told him if that's how he felt, maybe he ought to give up on women and get himself a pet rock. A couple of weeks later he met you. I asked him if he thought he'd be satisfied with a rock, and he said it beat the hell out of having your heart broken every minute."

"Maybe he was finally learning the difference between infatuation and mature love," Wanda said.

"Naw," Floyd said, "he was playing it safe. He wanted a girl, but he didn't want to get burned again."

Wanda sighed. She poured herself some Scotch and then handed the bottle to Floyd. Holding his glass in his left hand, Floyd rested the bottle between his thighs.

"Go on with the story," Wanda said.

"It was about then that Marie came on the scene," Floyd said. He unscrewed the cap of the bottle; then, apparently forgetting he wanted a drink, he screwed it back on. He did this three or four times and then ran his hand up and down the neck of the bottle. Wanda had never seen him so fidgety. "After I told him what a hot piece she was, he started pining after the glamour-girl type again."

"Then why did he marry *me?*"

"That's where Tim comes in." Floyd quit fooling with the bottle and poured himself a drink. "Tim and his sexy letters."

"Not sexy. Sick. The man's a mental patient."

"They might be sick to you, but they were hot stuff to Robert."

Wanda nodded thoughtfully. "I'm beginning to get the picture."

"Robert looked at it this way," Floyd said. "If an intelligent, sensitive man like Tim, with all his education, found you so all-fired attractive, there must be something there he was missing. Robert was always very respectful of educated people. He took old Tim seriously."

"That's true," Wanda said.

"So," Floyd said, "if Tim felt that way about you, Robert figured Tim was right. Then, after you got married, he realized he couldn't see you the way Tim did and couldn't want you the way Tim did. As far as Robert was concerned, you never got much beyond the rock stage. At first he thought it was his fault, and he got down on himself. If Marie hadn't given him a boost, I don't know what would have become of him. After he fell for Marie, he started resenting you. And then he'd feel guilty, because *he* was the one who wanted to get married."

"You don't have to go on," Wanda said. "I understand it now. I'm sorry he felt that way."

"I want you to know," Floyd said, "that I never bought that frigid stuff."

"That son of a bitch," Wanda said.

They sat in silence. Floyd rubbed his nose with his thumb and index finger for what seemed a very long time.

"Speaking of Tim," he said finally, "I wish you'd tell me how you hooked him."

"I didn't hook him," Wanda said irritably. It occurred to her that she had not received a letter from Tim in exactly two weeks. She guessed he had deserted her too.

"I'll tell you what *I* think it is," Floyd said. "I think it's either ESP or hypnotism. Or maybe you give off some kind of scent that only certain men can pick up. Or maybe it was body language. Body language is a powerful tool."

"It was nothing like that," Wanda said. She wondered if she had ever met such a moron in her life. "I think you're upset about Marie. If you are, you can probably get her back. Robert's infatuation with her won't last."

"It might," Floyd said. "Robert's been wanting to love somebody the way Tim loves you, and Marie's been wanting to be loved in that same way. I think maybe they were made for each other."

He was talking perfectly good sense again, and Wanda had to admit that he could well be right.

"I think it hinges on whether Marie can get him to move out of Windward," Floyd said.

"Why would she want to move? She has a good job and likes it here."

"I don't know." Floyd grinned and shook his head. "I just have this feeling."

"She's also a good friend of Mrs. Martin," Wanda said.

"The problem's not Mrs. Martin. The problem's me. I don't think Marie's going to want to live anywhere near Floyd Robbins."

Wanda looked at him with pity. There was no question but what his ego had been severely bruised by Marie's leaving. "Did you say they were out of town?"

"They went to the City," Floyd said. "Marie's been dying to see *Rock, Rock, Rock.*"

"We saw it on our honeymoon," Wanda said.

"That must make you sad," Floyd said, "to think of *them* seeing it. You can cry if you want to."

"I don't want to," Wanda said.

"Crying's not the only way to show grief. Some people laugh and let their hair down. In some cultures they even have orgies. That's what it says in *You Be You*."

"I haven't felt much grief. I feel some hostility, especially after what you've told me, but I haven't felt much grief."

"Hostility's natural too. You wouldn't be you if you didn't get angry and want revenge."

Wanda smiled. "You know what I'd like? I'd like to be there when Marie discovers that tattoo."

"She already knows about it," Floyd said. "He showed it to her the day we went snowmobiling. When they sneaked up to the old Johnson place. She thought it was the most romantic thing she'd ever heard of. That's another reason they went to the City. He's going to see a doctor and have Doreen's name taken off. Then he's going to have Marie's name tattooed on the other cheek."

"That hurts as much as the rock," Wanda said. "The fact that he showed her and not me."

Floyd smiled and focused on a spot above Wanda's left eye. "He thought you wouldn't understand about the tattoo."

Thinking there must be a smudge there, Wanda rubbed at the spot above her eye. "Of course I understand. I understand everything. I'm a God damned psychologist. Besides, Marie shouldn't feel so honored. I've got my own tattoo."

"Really?" Floyd let his eyes roam over Wanda's entire body. It was as if he had X-ray vision and was looking through her clothes, searching for the tattoo. His eyes came to rest on her right shoulder.

Wanda scratched the shoulder, then realized that Floyd had shifted his gaze to her left breast. "It's not on *me*," she said. She held her glass so that her breast was hidden behind her arm. "It's on a guy I know. My name. It's not a little one either. It's a great big one." She was flustered and spoke very fast.

"You didn't tell Robert?"

Wanda shook her head. "I shouldn't have mentioned it to you either. Tattoos are childish." She decided she was tight; otherwise she would not have told Floyd the story.

"I can see this person was someone very special," Floyd said.

Wanda excused herself and went to the bedroom and sat on the bed and cried for several minutes. Then she stepped into the bathroom and washed her face with cold water. When she returned to the living room, Floyd was at the radio, fiddling with the dials. He found a station he liked—it was the soft rock station that Wanda and Robert had always listened to—and then he turned and looked at Wanda.

"Hey," he said, "have you been crying?"

Wanda nodded and sat down on the sofa.

Floyd came over and patted her hand. "You didn't have to go in there to cry. You could have cried in here."

"I didn't want to. I wanted to cry in there."

"Then you did the right thing. The important thing is that you be you."

Wanda was immensely tired of Floyd. It must have showed on her face, because he glanced at his watch and said he had to be leaving.

"I've got plans," he said.

"That's fine," Wanda said. "Thanks for stopping by."

"I want you to know," Floyd said, "that I kept *your* secret too."

"Secret?"

"You know. You and Lester."

"Oh," Wanda said. "You saw that."

"The whole thing."

Wanda felt herself blushing. "I'd rather not talk about it. I appreciate your keeping it a secret."

"That's okay," Floyd said. "What are friends for?" He went over and got his coat and put it on. Wanda followed him to the door and thanked him for the Scotch.

"My pleasure," Floyd said. He turned and looked intently at the lower half of Wanda's body. "You've sure got those big long legs," he said.

"Please." Wanda hoped he wasn't getting ideas. She didn't want to have to be rude to him.

"You remind me of Thelma. You've both got those big long legs."

"I don't know Thelma," Wanda said coldly.

"She's a girl I went with a couple of years ago," Floyd said. "She was a little bigger than you, but built the same way. She used to call me her little pepperpot. She thought she was frigid too, till the little pepperpot got hold of her."

"Please go," Wanda said. She reached around him and opened the door.

"Sure." Floyd squared his shoulders and straightened his tie. "Wish me luck with Amy."

"I don't know Amy either," Wanda said.

"She's a new waitress at Denny's. We've gone out a couple of times and I think this is the big night. I've been laying the ESP on her for two whole days."

"Be careful driving," Wanda said. She had backed him into the hall, and now she slowly closed the door.

She went to the window and watched as he got in his car and drove away. It was snowing again. As she watched, the street light burned out. For a moment she could see nothing but her own reflection. Then her eyes adjusted and the stark whiteness of the fresh-fallen snow reasserted itself through the image. She shivered and jerked the curtain shut.

Then, ravenously hungry, she picked up the phone and called a fast-food restaurant and ordered a large pizza, a milkshake, French fries, and three packages of M & M's.

17

Dear Wanda,

It has been—maybe you've noticed—more than three weeks since I've written. Fact is, I don't need you any more. Fact is, I've got somebody else. (I'd like to see your smile 'long about now.) As you could easily guess, the somebody is Nelda. Let me go back a way.

When I last wrote, you'll remember, I had made Nelda up to look like you and was talking to her as if she were my therapist (maybe that was sick, but it no longer matters). I did this for a couple of weeks, and suddenly she spoke. That's as much as you know. What she said was: "I don't like this stupid game." Then she started talking about herself. At first I was angry. By intruding her real self into the proceedings, she was destroying the illusion I had worked so hard to create. She was a regular God damned chatterbox. I was mad enough to kill her. But the longer she talked, the more interested I became. She's a marvelous woman, Wanda. First thing I knew, we had a conversation going. Next thing I knew, I was connecting with her, relating to her, I guess falling in love with her. After a few hours, I went to my room and tried to think about you but couldn't. All I could think about was her. When I returned to her room the next day, we made love. We've done it every day since. There is no more you here, Wanda, only Nelda.

What an incredible person she is! After weeks of being a vegetable,
she is suddenly full of life and hope (so am I, if you can imagine that).
Which makes me a pretty good therapist, wouldn't you say? I have
brought a woman back to life, and she has done the same for me. And
guess what. We're going to be wed. Yep, old Nelda and me, we're going
to tie the knot and step out there and be right happy. So, kiddo, the
upshot is—no more letters for you. Hope you're not all shook up about
that (ha ha). God, am I giddy.

Now for the good news. Turns out Nelda was not really blind. What I
mean is that her blindness was psychological in origin. She did have a
bad accident—that much was true—but she was barely scratched in it.
She was rushing to take pictures of a tornado scene when she drove off
the road. Her husband was killed. He was a reporter on the same paper.
She didn't love him—she's never loved anyone but me—and she pun-
ished herself by going blind. She remembers, however, that he was in as
big a hurry that day as she was (she even remembers that the fool was
exhorting her to drive faster, drive faster, when the accident happened).
More important, she realizes that not loving him was no reason to feel
guilty the rest of her life. Presto chango!—from insight to sight restored.
(You'll understand the psychology of this better than I do. I'm sure your
books are full of similar cases.)

She is a radiant woman, Wanda. I bask in her warmth as I once
basked in yours. And her warmth—honesty compels me to say this—is
better than yours, simply because the possibility exists, between Nelda
and me, for a fully realized human relationship. My relationship to you,
I now admit, was severely limited by the ground rules of the therapeutic
situation—rules that I understood and tried to accept, despite your con-
stant signals that they didn't apply.

Which brings me to an important point. I can see now—what you
must have seen all along—that the letters were no more than a con-
tinuation of my therapy in another medium. They were, in your jargon,
a way of working through the transference; thank you for letting me
write them. I would apologize for them, but I know they caused you no
pain. Your "professionalism" will have protected you against the letters
just as it protected you when we were face to face (and knee-cap to

knee-cap, eyeball to thigh (ha ha)) in that little room of ours. Does it feel as good to you as it does to me—after all this time—to terminate properly? No answer required.

Goodbye, Home for the Disappointed. Goodbye, Doc and Mrs. Bonds, you old sots. Goodbye, Loy, Jack, and Millie. As Wittgenstein said, the world of the happy man is a happy world, and—till Nelda and I can get away—you'll have to forgive me if I parade my unseemly joy through your house of despair.

Goodbye, Wanda. Thanks for everything.

Affectionately,
Tim Jinks

Wanda did not pick up the mail until six o'clock. She would not have done it then if her typist, Mrs. Dobson, had not delivered two chapters of the dissertation. Wanda, in turn, handed over another chapter and walked Mrs. Dobson down to her car. On the way back she checked her mailbox. If she had not needed a break from her work, she might not have opened the letter.

She was halfway through it before she realized what Tim was saying. She went back to the beginning and read carefully. By the third reading, she was crying as she had never cried before. This was the real thing, all right; this was what it was all about. The tears poured from her eyes. Tears of joy and sorrow and relief, all mingled together. Relief at the happy ending; sorrow at parting, at long last, with a patient she had come to admire and respect; joy at her own role in helping to ease his pain.

Tim was right, of course: the letters had been his way of working through the transference. Only someone of his intelligence and strong determination could have pulled it off. But Wanda deserved credit too. If her response to the letters had not been precisely right, the recovery would not have occurred. Her silence—cruel as it must at times have seemed—was exactly what was needed. As her father had said in one of his books, "Silence, when you come right down to it, is the sharpest arrow in the analytic quiver." How true that was! Wanda's massive silence had provided Tim with the screen he needed on which to project his love and his hate, his hopes, fears, anxieties, and whatnot. Having projected them there, he could see his problems writ large, sort through them, and correct them. Such had been the power of her silence. Like any good therapist, she had instinctively chosen the right approach; having done so, she had brought about a cure. "Every cure," her father had so movingly written, "is like the dawn of a new morning. Although there is no such thing as a miracle cure—there is only the day-by-day grind of the analytic process—every cure, when it comes, comes with the glory and grandeur of a sunrise. In that sense, every cure is a miracle cure." If that was true, Wanda had pulled off a minor miracle.

She went to the bedroom and lay down and read the letter again and thought about silence and the power of silence. Her silence had been like a rock to Tim. It had been steady, impervious, and seemingly indifferent. Above all, it had been *there*. There for him to use. He had pounded his head against the rock and, in doing so, had made his head well. That was a nice way of putting it, Wanda thought. Beating your head against a rock couldn't help but hurt, but the hurting had a purpose. "Although there is suffering without therapy," her father had written, "there is no therapy without suffering. But the suffering of therapy has a rhyme and a reason. *In* therapy, the purpose of suffering is to end suffering."

Tim's letters, Wanda realized, provided a running record of one man's suffering. She would go back and read them again. If she read them carefully enough, alert to every nuance, she was willing to bet that she could chart not only the course of Tim's suffering but the course of his progress as well . . . She was crying again. Now that it was over, she was permitted to cry. She spread her arms wide, relaxed completely, and let the joy and relief—yes and the sorrow too—flood over her in waves.

It was while she was lying there, caught up in her feelings, that the idea for the book came to her. She had her hospital notes and she had the letters. She would edit them, add a hundred pages of commentary, and turn the whole thing into a book. It would be a moving human document, full of warmth and drama, about how a young woman therapist, working under less than ideal conditions, had helped a high suicide risk regain his sense of balance and resume a normal, happy life. She would call it *Lady of Silences* . . .

She had wondered all week what she would do if Robert grew tired of Marie. She wondered if she would take him back. Now, suddenly, she could see that she did not want him. She did not want a job in Windward either. Windward was the pits. She would go to Chicago and live with her father and write her book. It's what she had always dreamed of. She would write during the day and spend the evenings discussing the manuscript with Dr. North. She would incorporate his ideas into a series of short, pithy "responses" to some of Tim's letters. These responses, designed to show her ability to cut through his defenses, would give the reader a good picture of a skilled therapist at work. They would give the book a certain dramatic effect. It would not do, after all, for the Lady of Silences to be *completely* silent. A reader wouldn't swallow that in a million years.

She went to the phone and dialed the number of her home in Chicago. When she got no answer, she tried her father's office number. A recorded voice told her that the doctor was unavailable. At the sound of the tone, she had thirty seconds in which to record a message . . . Wanda hung up as the tone sounded. It would mean breaking her lease, and it would mean breaking her contract at the clinic, but she could be out of Windward in two or three weeks. If she could not reach her father by then, she would drive to Chicago and wait for him to return.

She had an overwhelming urge to share her good feelings with someone. She thought about calling Eric, or even Lester, but decided against it. They wouldn't appreciate what she had done or the book she was planning. They might even laugh. Lester would start panting after her. She thought of calling Dr. Campbell, but he didn't seem right either. He might try to talk her out of writing a book till she was more experienced. Either that or he would insist that she give the book a behavioristic turn. "You did it with your rats," he would say. "You can do it with Tim as well." She didn't know where any of her old classmates were. She thought of calling the hospital in Miami and talking to Lorna Beane, the head psychiatric nurse, and maybe to her supervisor. But they deserved more than a phone call. She would wait a few weeks, then send a copy of Tim's letter to the director of the psychiatric unit. Across the top of the letter she would write: "In case you've been wondering whatever became of Tim Jinks, I thought you might want to see this." Something offhand like that.

She thought briefly of Robert. She was glad to be rid of him. He would never understand the feelings she was having. Neither would Marie. Anyway, Marie was with Robert . . . She wished Tim was here. Thinking about him made her mouth dry. If he was here, she would give him a hug and a kiss. Well no, she wouldn't. It might reactivate the transference. The most she could give him would be a handshake and a pat on the back. Now that he was well, it would be *proper* to give him a hug and a kiss, and yet she couldn't do it because part of his being well was being over her. She wondered if he would read her book. Now that he was over her, he might not even be interested. She was pondering the ironies of the situation when somebody knocked at the door.

She opened the door and found herself looking at Floyd. He was the one person she hadn't thought of at all. For once she was glad to see him. "I've got the best *news*," she said. She threw her arms around his neck and squeezed him. Then, clasping his face in her hands, she leaned down and kissed him. She was astonished at what happened next.

Floyd stepped forward and pressed his body tightly against hers. His left hand grabbed the back of her head so that she could not pull away. His mouth opened and turned to the side, causing Wanda's mouth to open too. His tongue touched hers. At the same time, his right hand circled her waist, slipped inside her jogging pants, and carressed her buttocks. The hand peeled the pants down over her hips and let them fall at her feet. She was wearing nothing under the pants. The hand moved between her thighs; a finger popped inside her. She shuddered and moaned. Her knees buckled. She thought she might faint. Her head lolled on Floyd's shoulder.

"I knew you'd be ready," he said, "but I didn't know you'd be *this* ready." He withdrew his finger and brought his hand up to Wanda's face. The whole hand was wet. He unzipped the top of her jogging suit and stripped it off. He bent down and removed her sneakers and pulled the pants from around her feet. He stood up and grinned at her, casually fingering her breasts.

* * *

"You didn't know it," Floyd said, "but you were a dead duck from the day we met."

Although they were lying side by side, and Floyd was holding her wrist, his voice seemed to come from far away. Wanda, lost in her own thoughts, hoped it would stay like that.

"I could tell you didn't like me," Floyd said. "You were kind of snooty. That's the reason I decided to nail you. That and the fact that you were Robert's."

Wanda yawned. Even a yawn caused her to tingle.

"Don't feel guilty about it," Floyd said. "You never had a chance. It's all a matter of technique."

"Why should I feel guilty?" Wanda said. She ran her hand along the inside of her thigh and up her belly to her breast.

"I just thought you might," Floyd said. "Me being Robert's best friend."

"He doesn't have anything to do with it," Wanda said. She

started to add that *he* didn't have much to do with it either, but she decided not to. He had helped to turn her on in this marvelous way; the least she could do was listen to him drone.

"At first you were a challenge," Floyd said. "Then, when I realized I could nail you any time I wanted to, I decided to keep you waiting."

"When did you realize that?" Wanda liked the dreamy quality of their voices. It was like overhearing an intimate conversation between two strangers.

"The night your brother was here and you sent Robert home early," Floyd said. "That was the night."

"You thought I wanted *you?*"

"Sure. You may not have known it—this stuff is all subliminal—but *I* sure as hell knew it."

Wanda giggled softly and then yawned.

"When Lester made his big pitch," Floyd said, "I sort of laid back and let things develop."

"I think I'm going to sleep," Wanda said.

"Not yet. I want you to hear this. In terms of planning and waiting, it's probably my masterpiece."

"That's nice." Wanda played with her right nipple and made it hard.

"Even after I saw you were falling for that den-mother line," Floyd said, "I could have moved right in."

"You could, could you?" Wanda giggled again.

"Sure. An old guy like that, with a hokey technique. I could have cut him right out of the running . . . You following all this?"

"I guess so," Wanda said. She was following it in a vague sort of way. It was like hearing a newsbreak on the muzak machine in the supermarket. You were hardly aware you were listening to it at the time, but later in the day you'd remember that there had been a shooting or a plane crash or an important debate in Congress.

"I kept thinking I might wait the old guy out," Floyd said. "I figured he'd have to go to bed some time or other—he looked half dead anyway—and I knew I could outlast him. Then we could have had the couch to ourselves. You and me, I mean. I thought maybe you had the same thing in mind."

"Not quite," Wanda said.

"Not consciously. Then you started that nose-rubbing and kissing. I willed all that. When you put your head in his lap, I started talking about Masters and Johnson. I knew that'd make you hot."

"Good Lord," Wanda said.

"When you went to sleep I closed up shop. I didn't want you in that condition—stoned out of your mind, your dress hiked up to your waist. You were offering it to me in such an obvious way that I decided not to take it. I thought what the hell, let old Lester have it. When Eric went to bed I acted very sleepy and stumbled to the couch and acted like I had passed out. I wanted to see how Lester would carry the ball. I had a ringside seat for the whole show."

"It was pretty dark," Wanda murmured. "Wasn't it?"

"Your eyes soon adjust," Floyd said. "The eye is an amazing organ in that regard. I could see plenty. It put me in a funny position. I mean I'm an attorney. I'm an upholder of the law and all that stuff. And here I was, watching a girl get raped."

"Raped?" The idea had never crossed Wanda's mind.

"I don't know what else you'd call it," Floyd said. "He took you by force, didn't he?"

"I guess he did," Wanda said. "Sort of." She thought of Tim's rape dream and how excited it used to make him. Those days were gone forever. She thought of Little Tim and how he had tried to please her. She thought of his little hard-on. She thought of Tim and Little Tim and she explored her body. "Jesus," she said.

"I don't blame you for being mad," Floyd said. "I was incensed myself."

"I'm not mad."

"I didn't catch that."

Wanda moaned and said the word "Jesus" several more times. She was aware of clenching her teeth and turning her head from side to side on the pillow. For a moment she seemed in danger of being carried off the bed by an incredible wave of sensations. The wave crested and then slowly subsided. Wanda went slack all over. The mellow feeling settled in again.

"What's the matter?" Floyd asked. "You get a cramp?"

Wanda mumbled something that meant no, it wasn't a cramp.

"I didn't think it was," Floyd said.

He chuckled and Wanda felt his breath on her cheek. She opened her eyes and saw his face directly above hers. He was grinning. His face came closer. She was afraid he was going to kiss her, but he didn't. He looked intently into her eyes and then settled back on his pillow. He was holding her wrist again. There was a long silence during which Wanda realized that he was taking her pulse. She almost laughed out loud.

"I wish I'd had you hooked up to a blood pressure machine," Floyd said. "I wish I'd had my thermometers. I wish I'd had my camera."

"Camera?" Wanda said in alarm.

"Sure," Floyd said. "You wouldn't believe the pictures I've got of Doreen and Marie."

"Please," Wanda said. "No cameras."

"I've got one of Marie with her finger up her ass. It's the goofiest thing you ever saw. If I show that picture to the right people, Marie Becker's done in this town."

"You wouldn't do that though," Wanda said.

"The hell I wouldn't."

Floyd's voice was as hard and cold as a rock. Wanda was suddenly afraid. Not wishing to rile him, she lay perfectly still.

"Of course," he said in a lighter tone, "it wasn't really rape."

"What wasn't?"

"The business between you and Lester. You just made it look that way because you knew it would sex me up."

"Why don't we sleep for a while? You sound a little tired."

"Me? I never get tired."

Wanda had heard of people like that—crazy people who could talk for days without stopping.

"After that night," Floyd went on, "I could have nailed you anytime I wanted to. At the dance, for example, or the day we went snowmobiling. I didn't want to though. I'm not opposed to a quickie now and then, but with you I wanted to do it up right. Of all the girls I've ever known, I thought you'd appreciate it the most. You being a psychologist."

Shut up and go to sleep, Wanda commanded him mentally.

"I could have come by any afternoon and done it," Floyd said. "You know, while Robert was at work. Don't think I wasn't tempted, especially after I learned about him and Marie. She's the third one

213

he's swiped out from under me. Doreen, Marie, and before that a girl named Thelma. Doesn't matter though—I always get my revenge. I'm getting my revenge right now."

A heavy fatigue had started at the center of Wanda's body and was spreading outward. When it reached her fingers and toes, she would be paralyzed. She wondered if she could do anything about this and decided she couldn't.

"I was a little worried about making the phone calls," Floyd said. It took a minute for this to sink in.

"The heavy breather calls," Floyd said.

Wanda knew she ought to be surprised, but she wasn't. The fatigue, she supposed, had reached her brain.

"So it was you. Why were you worried?" She felt no real curiosity, but it seemed important to keep talking. There was no telling what Floyd might do if she went to sleep. For all she knew, he had brought a miniature camera with him. He might grease her with Crisco.

"Voice patterns," Floyd said. "They're like fingerprints. They're a dead giveaway to the trained ear."

"I thought it was Tim," Wanda said. In the image that came to her now, Tim and Nelda had stopped making love and were curled up in each other's arms. Seeing them like that, Wanda wanted to cry. Tim Jinks was the sweetest, gentlest man she had ever known. "I thought it was Tim," she said. "Then I thought it was Mr. Martin."

"That was consciously," Floyd said. "Unconsciously you knew it was me."

Wanda wondered if this could possibly be true.

"I don't mind telling you," Floyd said, "I got pretty hot making those calls. I had no idea it would affect me that way. Then I realized you were laying some kind of unconscious reverse subliminal stuff on me. That sexed me up even more. I was always afraid you'd hang up before I could come, but you never did."

"I thought it was Tim," Wanda said. "I was helping him with his transference."

"Then later I'd see you in Denny's," Floyd said, "and you'd wink at me. That always drove me right up the wall."

"I never winked at you," Wanda said.

"You probably thought you were just blinking," Floyd said. "But to someone who can read the unconscious, it was an obvious wink.

Incidentally, I learned something from making those calls. I got some insight into the mind of the pervert. It might come in handy in the courtroom someday."

There was no question about it, Wanda thought. Floyd Robbins was completely insane.

"When I was here before," Floyd said, "I put down enough body language and ESP to seduce a battleship. I could have fucked you then, of course, but I wanted to let you ripen. Also I wanted to see if I could set the exact time."

"Time?"

"Eight oh five p.m. All week long, I've been sending you that message. Fuck Floyd at eight oh five p.m. That's why I wasn't surprised when you threw yourself at me. You started coming when I walked through the door, and it's all because of ESP."

Wanda thought about trying to clear up these misunderstandings, but decided it would not be possible. The fact that she had fallen into Floyd's arms at eight oh five p.m. gave the rest of his ideas, crazy as they were, a plausibility that would be hard to challenge. She was glad she didn't have him as a patient. It might take years to break through such a tightly organized delusional system.

"I just thought of something," she said. It was something she ought to be angry about, but she wasn't capable of anger. "You made those calls and Mr. Martin got blamed for them. The only one he made was the last one. The one Robert caught him making."

"That's about the size of it," Floyd said.

"It was because of the other ones, though, that Robert got so mad. You caused Mr. Martin to get his jaw broken." Wanda was becoming dangerously sleepy. She had a sense of her words leaving her mouth in bubbles. It was not until the bubbles had drifted to the ceiling and burst that the words became audible.

"Robert's been wanting to break his old man's jaw for a long time," Floyd said. "All I did was provide an excuse. Anyway, it was your doing as much as it was mine. Robert told me how you flirted with the old man. I saw for myself that kiss you gave him at the wedding."

"He gave *me*, you mean."

"Kissing's a two-way street. Did you hear what happened yesterday? It was in the paper."

"I've quit reading the paper. I've been too busy."

"Well," Floyd said, "early in the morning, before it was hardly light, Mr. Martin sneaked outside and got a ladder and started painting the house."

"Maybe that's a good sign. Maybe he's getting back some of his interests."

"He was painting it black," Floyd said.

"Oh," Wanda said.

"After two or three hours Mrs. Martin missed him and went out looking for him. When she saw what he was doing, she called the police. They sent a man up the ladder after him, and Mr. Martin dumped the paint on him. The man fell to the ground and broke his leg."

"That's awful," Wanda said. The words, lacking any force or conviction, seemed to come from a record being played at half speed.

"Then Mr. Martin crawled up on the roof and tore off his clothes. He ran around up there calling out 'Wanda, Wanda' at the top of his voice."

"Shit," Wanda said. "I'm glad I'm leaving this town."

"You'll have to speak up," Floyd said. "I couldn't hear you."

"Never mind," Wanda said. The less Floyd knew about her plans the better.

"It was noon before they could get him down," Floyd said. "They committed him to the state hospital."

"This was all in the paper?"

"Not the part about you. I heard about that at the police station. The guys down there were laughing their heads off about this mysterious Wanda, so I told them all about you. They were pretty impressed when I said I'd be fucking you tonight. I've got a good rapport with the guys at the station. Don't be surprised if some of them call you."

"Me?" Wanda said. "Policemen?"

"For dates," Floyd said. "With Robert gone, you'll be wanting to catch some of the local action."

"Don't talk any more," Wanda said. "I can't stand to hear another word."

"Sure," Floyd said. "Whatever you say."

He flipped on a small light by the side of the bed. Wanda pulled the sheet up to her neck and looked at the ceiling and didn't move a muscle. She was sure he was getting his camera. She was relieved when she heard the sound of a bottle cap being unscrewed and then the sound of glass touching glass.

"You want a drink?" Floyd asked.

"No." Wanda remembered that there was a box of chocolates on her bedside table. She reached over and got it and put it on the sheet beside her. She had opened the box early that afternoon. Fumbling in it now, she was surprised to discover that she had already eaten the entire top layer of candy.

"How about another quaalude?" Floyd asked.

"Huh-uh."

"Want me to light a joint?"

"No, thanks."

"What's that you're eating?"

"Cherry chocolates."

"Ugh," Floyd said. "As big as you are, you ought to lay off that stuff."

Shut up and go to sleep, Wanda yelled in her mind. You'd think a hotshot ESPer could pick up that simple message.

Floyd leaned back against the headboard and sipped his drink. "With the old man in the loony bin," he said, "I'm betting Robert'll move back with his mother. Marie'll go the way of Doreen." He sighed heavily. He drained his glass and smacked his lips. "Ah well, I guess that's life."

Wanda made a great effort to pull herself out of her apathy and fatigue. "You're a terrible person," she said. Speaking through the goo in her mouth was like swimming in mud.

Floyd chuckled. "Look who's talking. Anyone who'd drive rats crazy oughtn't to be giving lectures. Marie always said you and I are exactly alike."

Wanda rolled a cherry around in her mouth. She was glad Floyd had the picture of Marie with her finger in her ass. She hoped he showed it to everyone in town. She sucked on the cherry and then bit through it. She thrilled at its sweetness. She stuffed two chocolates into her mouth at once. If Floyd would only go to sleep, she could sneak into the kitchen and eat ice cream and cake. She wondered if she could hypnotize him.

Floyd poured himself another drink. "Damn," he said. "It's after eleven. I hate to fuck and run, but I'm picking Amy up at midnight."

"You're leaving?"

"I don't blame you for being angry," Floyd said. "You have my permission to be as angry as you need to be."

"I'm not angry. I'm happy for you." A pain shot through Wanda's stomach, followed by a faint but ominous burning and gurgling.

"I thought you might be," Floyd said. "You and your scientific mind. I'm not even going to shower. Does it excite you that I'll be fucking Amy with your juices still on me?"

"Well—" The last of the chocolates had melted in Wanda's hand. She wiped the hand on her body and then on the sheets. She put the cherry in her mouth and her stomach groaned.

"I knew it would," Floyd said. "It excites me too. Boy oh boy. Maybe in a couple of weeks the three of us can get together in one bed. I've not done that yet."

The cherry Wanda had just eaten was acting funny. She lay very still with her hands pressed to her belly.

"I won't forget your pulse rates," Floyd said. "I'll put them on the computer first thing tomorrow. When you come to my place, we'll do a complete work-up. You won't believe the stuff I've got over there."

"I'm sick," Wanda said. She put her feet on the floor and sat on the edge of the bed. The bed was warm but the room was chilly.

"I've got dildos and vibrators," Floyd said. "I've got a massager. I've got medical equipment. I've got Marie's ba-wa balls. I've got my Polaroid. I've got books and movies. I've got an electric butt plug that'll drive you out of your mind."

"I have to go to the bathroom," Wanda said. A hot foul liquid with lumps in it bubbled up from her stomach. She swallowed it, but it kept coming back.

"You go right ahead," Floyd said. "I'll just sit here and send Amy messages. What shall I tell her?"

"Anything," Wanda said. "Tell her anything." Her guts were boiling. She looked at the bathroom door and wondered if she could possibly make it.

"I'll tell her to give me a blow-job," Floyd said. "How's that?"

"That's great," Wanda said.

"Or maybe I'll have her suck my toes," Floyd said.

Wanda reached the bathroom in two long strides. She slammed the door and leaned over the stool. The bathroom was freezing cold. Her stomach was suddenly and perversely calm. She sat down and peed. The stool was like ice. A robe hung on the door. When she stood up to get it, her stomach churned and bubbled. She dropped to her knees. Her body heaved but nothing came out. She felt a trickle on her leg and realized she had to do the other instead. By the time she could get back to her feet, a hot brown liquid was running freely down her thighs. Then, as her buttocks touched the stool, the liquid poured out in a long scalding gush that left her clammy, weak, and trembling. She wiped herself as best she could; when Floyd left she would take a shower. She stood up to wash her hands and saw something awful in the mirror.

Her hair was so greasy she could have spiked it. Her face and chest were smeared with chocolate. Her eyes were red, she guessed from crying. Her teeth were chattering uncontrollably. Her lips were swollen from kissing and blue from the cold. An enormous yellow blister—a pimple, a boil—had formed at the corner of her mouth. Her sex flush was a hideous purple blotch. She was covered with goose bumps. Worst of all was the fat. She had gained twenty pounds and all of it showed. Her eyes were getting smaller by the day. Her cheekbones had disappeared. Her nose was a tiny red snout. She had three or four chins and no neck. Her arms had turned to dough. Her breasts sagged and her belly swelled. She was pregnant with pizza. Depression, as gray, cold, and smelly as the bathroom air, settled into her bones. She put the robe on. It helped a little. It covered some of the fat.

She looked in the mirror again and saw Tim and Nelda. They were still curled up together. She thought how happy they looked. How toasty warm. Tim stirred, rubbed his eyes, and sat up and looked at Wanda. For one thrilling moment she was sure he was going to say "I love you." Her beauty would be restored. Then she blinked and looked closer. The face was not Tim's after all; it was the face of a gigantic pig.

She thought about the ice cream in the refrigerator. She thought about the cake in the cupboard. The cake had icing an inch thick. She thought about French fries and fudge. She thought about the volcano in her belly and the shit on her leg. She thought about Tim and Nelda, Robert and Marie, Burt and Mysore. She thought about the God who had paired up all these other people and left her here with Floyd Robbins. Wide awake now, she thought about the hours till dawn. She thought about loneliness and the fickle nature of need. She thought how being an expert in such matters didn't help a bit.

Floyd was the craziest person she was ever likely to meet. He was crazy and mean and dangerous, but he was all she had. She would encourage him to talk. She would share his amusement at running people out of town. She would agree with his ideas. She would give him a thermometer to play with. She would smear him with lard and she would suck his toes. She would do anything but pose for pictures. If nothing else worked, she would tie him to the bed. She would kill him if she had to, but she would not let him leave.

She glared at the pig and the pig glared back.

"Fool," Wanda said. "You fool."

"Fool, you fool," the pig said.

"I hate you," Wanda said, and the pig said it too.

Wanda flipped off the light and the pig disappeared. She opened the door and stepped into the bedroom.

"Floyd?"

He was not on the bed and for a moment she panicked. Then she saw that he was crawling around on the floor. He was wearing his undershorts and one of his socks. His wiry body looked frail and childishly awkward. Wanda towered over him. She could have squashed him like a bug.

"I can't find my other damned sock." His voice was a child's puzzled whine.

Wanda sat down on the edge of the bed and smiled at him. "Poor little Floyd," she said. "He can't find his sock. But that's okay. He don't need that old sock." She reached out and tousled his hair.

Floyd started babbling but Wanda silenced him by putting a finger to his lips.

"Poor little Floyd," she murmured. "Poor little pepperpot. Come here to your mommy."

"Oh," Floyd said, "we're going to play *that* game. I love it."

* * *

Two nights later, on the eleven o'clock news, Wanda learned that her father had married Mona Matson and was honeymooning in Spain. He was writing a book about their therapy together. The book had already been sold to the movies. All of this was revealed in a brief interview, during which a bull was killed in the background. Wanda, who was drinking a Tab, hurled the bottle through the screen.

Then she phoned Sarah. After about twenty rings, the receiver at the other end was picked up.

"This is all your fault," Wanda shouted. "You drove him to this."

"I didn't drive nobody to nothin'," a man said gruffly. "I guess you want Sarah."

By the time Sarah got to the phone, Wanda was crying. "I liked it when *you* were in love with Daddy," she said. "Now look what's happened."

"*I* didn't like it," Sarah said with a laugh. "But I couldn't help it either. Then Mona came along and saved my soul."

"Don't talk in riddles," Wanda said.

"Riddles," Sarah snorted. "To you everything's a riddle. I just mean that when Mona came along I was able to give him up. I could tolerate the Mrs. Winslows and the Mrs. Smythes, but I couldn't tolerate Mona Matson. The combination of her sex appeal and your father's greed was too much for me to contend with."

"You make it sound as if . . . as if . . ."

"You can't even say it," Sarah said. "You can't even think it."

"If he had," Wanda said, "I'd have known about it."

"Honeychild," Sarah drawled, "you *did* know about it. You buried it, but you knew. Why do you think he's so against you being analyzed?"

"God," Wanda said. Her ear—her whole head, in fact—was suddenly filled with the wild honking of a tenor saxophone, accompanied by Sarah's raucous laugh.

"I've got to go now," Sarah said when the honking stopped. "That's Malcolm's mating call. I'll end by telling you what I once told your father. Give it up."

"What?"

"Therapy," Sarah said. "There are better ways of getting the love you need than by being a therapist. Marry a poet or something, but don't be a therapist."

Wanda tried to think of a response but couldn't. Finally she said, "I don't *have* any love," but by then Sarah had clicked down the receiver.

"Except maybe Floyd," Wanda added pointlessly.

18

April 1

Wanda—

The letter I wrote you a couple of weeks ago was a fake from beginning to end. Time for the truth now, and then I really will shut up. I wish I could have pulled off the happy ending, but I can't. I'm bound, don't forget, by my oath as a patient, to tell it all, every last bit of it.

Nelda was never blind and never a photographer. As far as I know, her name was never Nelda. Except when writing to you, I called her Wanda. There were no books, just a pile of old papers and telephone directories. I made that stuff up to impress you, I guess to make you jealous. It is more romantic, after all, to be blind than to be deaf and dumb and have the brain of a three year old. And it's more romantic to cry all the time than to drool. Nelda never spoke to me or anybody else; she has no "real self" to intrude anywhere. She is nothing more than a blank screen, a poor white slug of a thing, on which I could superimpose a crude version of you. The rest of it, God help me, is true—the candy (how the poor thing loved it!), the time I spent in her room, the reading aloud, the clothes I bought her, the whole sick works, including the love making. Except you wouldn't call it making love, would you? It wasn't just once either, it was more times than I can remember, until the air stank with come and sweat and pukedup candy and the pretty blue dress was a wreck. That's how much I love you, Wanda. There was never anyone else but you.

The first time I did it, Little Tim caught me. I heard a noise at the door and looked up and saw him flying across the room. He threw himself on me and pounded my head and shoulders with his tiny fists. I shoved him and he fell down. I yelled at him to get out and stay out, but he came at me again. I let him have it with the back of my hand. Blood gushed from his nose and a tooth flew across the room. He didn't cry though, I'll say that for him. He just looked at me for a minute, his face smeared with blood and snot, and then hightailed it on out. I haven't seen him since.

Goodbye now. I'm supposed to meet Loy in five minutes. At the end, what I'll remember best is how sweetly you smiled. Either that or the look in Nelda's eyes.

Your zever,
Tim

P.S. I finished work on your name a few days ago. Wanda on the left leg, North on the right. I made the "O" in the shape of a heart. I wish you could see it. I wish you could touch it. I wish you could kiss it and make it well.

epilogue

Conclusion
((Rough Draft))

I knew, of course, after the three-week gap in correspondence, followed by the thinly disguised attempt to put a good face on everything by pretending to have completed the tasks of therapy and by professing love for his hippie girl friend, that Tim was abandoning the therapeutic endeavor with its sometimes harsh discipline. Nor was I surprised by his final letter of goodbye, so patently vengeful in its intent—a letter which, after all, conformed to his life-history mode of nihilistically attacking the ~~sense~~ ~~sins~~ the sincerity of the psychologist who had attempted, against great odds, to support him in his battle against the demons of apathy and death. I could not, however, have predicted, even from that letter, his actual suicide. He had, after all, made suicide threats in the past which he had not carried out.

((Possible title: *Heroism and Heartbreak*. Not bad, but "heroism" might sound like bragging.))

I have described, in an earlier chapter, how, two days after receiving the final note, Tim phoned me for the last time. I will not repeat the details of that agonizing conversation which began with a calm recital on Tim's part of this therapist's virtues. Nor will I repeat my impassioned plea to Tim to return to the therapeutic fold, or my last-ditch offer to fly to his side if he deemed such an unorthodox step necessary to his self-preservation. His response, as the reader will remember, was to reiterate, in a calm, matter of fact tone, the words of that final letter: "What I'll remember best, Wanda, is the ~~beauty~~ ~~sweetness~~ the incredible beauty and sweetness of your smile"—followed by the dreadful blast that I will hear in memory for the rest of my days. Such is the burden of those of us who would attempt to save the unsavable.

((Possible subtitle: *A Young Therapist's Encounter with Apathy and Death*. Well, maybe. Think about it some more.))

227

Another thing I could not have predicted was the devastating impact that Tim's act of ultimate vengeance would have on me personally. As a therapist, I am prepared, am I not, for such continguincies? The answer is yes—I am prepared, by temperament and by years of intensive study and rigorous training, for all manner of unpleasant continguincies. As my colleague and mentor, Dr. Lester Smith, has so aptly put it: "They come with the territory." But—as I have learned from working with Tim and from my close association with Dr. Smith—a therapist is first and foremost a human being, and no one who conjures up the darkest impulses of the human heart can expect to escape unscarred. I have already told about my long period of despair—the "therapeutic despair" so well described by Dr. ((find out who))—a period during which I questioned not only the meaning of my profession but the meaning of life itself. It was a bitter time. I am glad to have passed through it ~~"bloody but unbowed"~~ to have passed through it successfully and to have put it behind me. If Tim Jinks' aim in killing himself was to make me feel bad, he succeeded—but only for a time! The lasting effect has been quite the opposite. ~~I have never, to put it bluntly, felt better in my entire life.~~ As so often happens, it was in losing a patient that I found myself.

((How about a journal article called "The Limits of Therapeutic Intervention"? Great idea! Subtitle could be something like "Decompensation and the Flight to Suicide in a Borderline Adult." Great! Get Lester to help with this but *don't tell him about the book!*))

Although it is not my job as a scientist to point an accusing finger, I think it only fair to remind the reader again that Tim's problems began at the pre-Oedipal stage of development and were the result of deficient early mothering. More specifically, the clinicle picture so well represented in Tim's pathetic letters—the picture of an intelligent adult man giving in to alternate fits of clinging "love" and outraged "hatred"—is strongly suggestive of a mother who was "too good" (i.e., too inviting of love and trust) and "too bad" (i.e., too rejecting) in an agonizingly haphazard fashion. "When she was good," we might say, "she was very, very good, and when she was bad she was horrid."

Perhaps the reader can imagine—as this writer so vividly can—the sight of cuddly Baby Tim innocently playing with his string and his balls under the inscrutable regard of his Janice-faced, schizo-phrenogenic mother. It is little wonder that, at the age of about four months, Baby Tim fell into what Melodie Klein has so movingly called "the depressive posture," a posture from which he would never recover. Nor is it any wonder that, a few years later, the child so crippled could not successfully negotiate the tricky waters of the Oedipus complex.

In the adult Mr. Jinks' case, the borderline disorder—a kind of primitive oral hysteria—was welded to an obsessive-compulsive, es-sentially anal style with strong paranoid, schizoid, narcissistic, and psychopathological elements with a depressive overlay reinforced by philosophical pessimism, nihilism, and other traits of a decidedly "existential" nature. A lifelong masturbator and alcoholic, Mr. Jinks' powerful, unacknowledged homosexual impulses were, to the trained observer, clearly discernible under a thin ~~veneer~~ patina ((that's a good word)) of intense heterosexual fantasy and strivings. The miracle, in this writer's opinion, is not that Tim Jinks killed himself, but that he did not kill himself a long time ago. The fact that such a man—a high suicide risk almost from the day he was born—would work in therapy as long as he did is perhaps the finest tribute that could be paid to those of us who tried so ~~love lone~~ long and so hard to rejuvinate the life-enhancing forces which, however dormant they may become, are present in even the lowliest of living creatures.

In Tim's case, the death-enhancing forces carried the day. I stub-bornly believe, however, that even this death, strongly foreshadowed though it was, was not completely foreordained. Had he been will-ing to work a little bit harder, to put his shoulder to the wheel of life with a smigeon more force, Jim Tinks might well be alove today—not only alive but a successfully functioning man of considerable distinction in the world.

((*Apathy, Eros and Death: A Young Therapist's Encounter with Suicide.* Sounds too intellectual, but keep trying! We need some-thing as good as *Lady of Silences.*))

I like to think that Tim's case might have had a happier outcome if only he had accepted this therapist's offer to continue seeing him after her departure from the hospital in Miami. ((Better change the name of the city.)) This would have entailed his moving to her new place of residence. ~~But no, he would even do that~~ This alternative, however, was not acceptable to Timmy for a number of reasons, some of which were patently flimsy. He became obsessed with weather, for example, and insisted that he could not do therapy in a cold climate!

((*From Tragedy to Triumph: A Young Therapist Conquers Apathy and Death*. Pretty good but still not catchy enough.))

Thus was I forced to treat him by mail and telephone. As the reader has seen, this approach, while not impossible in theory, does present difficult problems of a practical nature, the main one being that the patient, freed from the restraints imposed by the presence of the therapist, may "pad out" his productions with page after page of showy but pointless rumination (for the benefit of the reader, I have carefully edited out most of these tiresome and irrelevant passages). For Tim such freedom of expression turned out to be deadly. His howling insistence ~~that his "love" for this therapist was the "real thing"~~ insistence on the reality-component of his transferential emotions proved to be a massive, indeed fatal, resistance to the fruitful resolution of his infantile conflicts.

My greatest regret is that when I met Mr. Jinks, I had not yet begun my association with Dr. Lester Smith. If Tim could have been persuaded to transfer from the Magnolia Retreat ((better change the name)) to Lost Angels Haven—which, after all, is located in sunny California—he would surely have benefited from the course of joint treatment that Dr. Smith and I have undertaken with Jesse M. and other chronic patients. To dwell on such ifs and mights, however, is, in this writer's opinion, an exercise in futility.

As the Bible ((?)) says, we must ~~marry~~ bury our dead and look forward to a better future. By his final act of vengeance, Tim has put himself beyond the therapeutic pail. Although we can pity him his misery, and although his death is a burden I must ~~bare, his death his death has left deep~~ his death has left permanent scars on the breast of my psyche, I cannot give up the faith

((*Beyond the Therapeutic Pail?* I don't know, it sounds kind of mystical or something. Hey wait a minute! How about *LOSING ONE?* That's short. That's catchy. That's it. *Losing One*—yes yes yes!!! *Losing One: Apathy, Eros, and Death*. I love it! But get "therapist" in there somewhere. Change "death" to suicide.))

the faith that I can alleviate the suffering of some other person who, even as I write these words, may be winding his way to my